# CHRISTOPHER BUSH
# THE CASE OF THE HAPPY MEDIUM

CHRISTOPHER BUSH was born Charlie Christmas Bush in Norfolk in 1885. His father was a farm labourer and his mother a milliner. In the early years of his childhood he lived with his aunt and uncle in London before returning to Norfolk aged seven, later winning a scholarship to Thetford Grammar School.

As an adult, Bush worked as a schoolmaster for 27 years, pausing only to fight in World War One, until retiring aged 46 in 1931 to be a full-time novelist. His first novel featuring the eccentric Ludovic Travers was published in 1926, and was followed by 62 additional Travers mysteries. These are all to be republished by Dean Street Press.

Christopher Bush fought again in World War Two, and was elected a member of the prestigious Detection Club. He died in 1973.

# CHRISTOPHER BUSH

# THE CASE OF THE HAPPY MEDIUM

With an introduction
by Curtis Evans

DEAN STREET PRESS

# INTRODUCTION

## Labouring under Suspicion
## Christopher Bush's Crime Fiction in the Postwar Years, 1946-1952

Seven years after the end of the Second World War, Christopher Bush published, under his "Michael Home" pseudonym, *The Brackenford Story* (1952), a mainstream novel in which a onetime country house boots boy, having risen for some time now to the lofty position of butler, laments the passing of traditional English rural life in the new postwar order, as signified by the years in which the left-wing Labour party held sway in the United Kingdom (1945-51). The jacket description of the American edition of *The Brackenford Story* reads, in part:

> *The Brackenford Story* is the story of a changing England. William saw the political enemies of the Hall gradually successful, whittling away the privilege it stood for. He saw squire begin to sell his land, the taxes increase, the great Hall sold, the beautiful trees along the drive cut down. And then with a Second World War, nationalization, rationing, pre-fabricated houses and queuing. William recalled with gratitude the kindness of his masters and their sense of responsibility for others. He saw that the bad old days of Toryism were not so bad after all. And he never lost his sense of outrage at the loss of something he felt was worthy of preservation.

A few years earlier, in July 1949, Anthony Boucher, the postwar dean of American crime fiction reviewers and a highly socially conscious liberal (small "l"), wrote with genial bemusement of the conservatism of British crime writers like Christopher Bush, in his review of Bush's latest crime opus, *The Case of the Housekeeper's Hair* (1948), making topical mention of a certain anti-Utopian novel penned by a distinguished dying tubercular English writer, which had just been published in June. "However much George Orwell, in *Nineteen Eighty-Four*, may foresee the forcible suppression of 'crimethink' under 'Ingsoc,' English socialism in 1949 takes pleasure in exporting mystery novels which disapprove of the Government and everything about it," Boucher observed with wry irony. "Like most of his colleagues, Christopher Bush is tartly critical of the regime; and an understanding of his unreconstructed Tory attitude is necessary if you're to hope to understand the motivations of this novel."

In both the detective novels and mainstream fiction which Christopher Bush published between 1946 and 1952, Bush, like many other distinguished mystery writers of the Golden Age generation (including Agatha Christie, Dorothy L. Sayers, Georgette Heyer, John Dickson Carr, Edmund Crispin, E.R. Punshon, Henry Wade and John Street), indeed was critical of the Labor government and increasingly nostalgic about a past that grew ever more golden in blissful, if perhaps partially chimerical, remembrance. Yet keeping Bush's distinct anti-left bias in mind, fans of classic crime fiction will find between the covers of the author's crime novels from these years--*The Case of the Second Chance* (1946), *The Case of the Curious Client* (1947), *The Case of the Haven Hotel* (1948), *The Case of the Housekeeper's Hair* (1948), *The Case of the Seven Bells* (1949), *The Case of the Purloined Picture* (1949), *The Case of the Happy Warrior* (1950), *The Case of the Corner Cottage* (1951), *The Case of the Fourth Detective* (1951) and *The Case of the Happy Medium* (1952)--fascinating observation of postwar social malaise in the age of British imperial decay and domestic austerity, as well as details about the rise of rationing, restriction and regulation, the burgeoning black market and, withal, that ubiquitous flashily-dressed criminal figure from Forties and Fifties Britain: the spiv (dealer in illicit goods).

Puzzle-minded mystery readers also will find some corking good no-nonsense "fair play" mysteries. "Few writers can equal Christopher Bush in handling a complicated plot while giving the reader a fair chance to solve the riddle himself," avowed the American blurb to *The Case of the Corner Cottage*, while Anthony Boucher applauded Bush's belated return to the American fiction lists after the Second World War, declaring: "It's good to have Mr. Bush back after too long an absence . . . he presents the simon-pure jigsaw-puzzle detective story with unobtrusive competence." Concurrently in the United Kingdom, author Rupert Croft-Cooke, who himself wrote fine detective fiction as "Leo Bruce," pointedly praised Bush's "urbane and intelligent way of dealing with mystery which makes his work much more attractive than the stampeding sensationalism of some of his rivals."

In the pages which follow this introduction by all means attempt, dear readers, to match your keen wits against those of that ever-percipient gentleman sleuth, Ludovic Travers. Frequently in tandem with his old friend Superintendent George Wharton and with occasional input from his smart and sophisticated wife Bernice Haire, the former classical dancer, Ludo continues to hunt, in his capacity as a sort of special consultant to Scotland Yard (or "unofficial expert," as he puts it), more not-quite-canny-enough crooks. Additionally Ludo, a confirmed fan of American crime films like *The Blue Dahlia* (1946) and *Call Northside 777* (1948), comes to find himself in ownership of the Broad Street Detective Agency, perhaps the finest firm of private inquiry agents in London. In these old and new capacities in the postwar world Ludo confronts his greatest cornucopia of daring and dastardly crimes yet.

Curtis Evans

## NEW SCOTLAND YARD (Cross Section of Organisation)

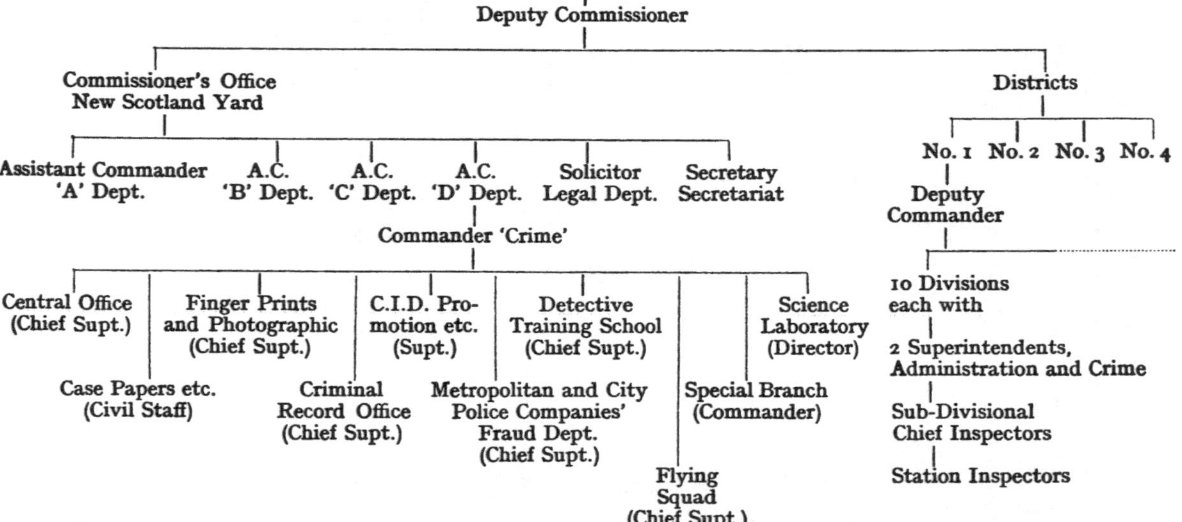



N.B.  With effect from July 1st, 1949, Metropolitan Sub-Divisional Inspectors and Chief Inspectors (including their counterparts in the C.I.D.) became known as Chief Inspectors and Superintendents respectively.  Officers holding the rank of Superintendent were renamed Chief Superintendent.

# I
# THE STORY BEGINS

As soon as I left Chief Inspector Targe, I slipped my car through to Millbank and went along the Embankment. George Wharton was in his room when I got to the Yard.

George was quite polite and even seemed glad to see me. He's different when we're working together on a case, when I'm still very much of an apprentice.

"Up bright and early, weren't you, this morning?" he asked me. "What'd you want to see me about? That job Targe is on?"

I said it was merely to give some information; to act the part of a good citizen. But as he hadn't arrived, I went and saw Targe. I'd only just left him.

"What sort of information?" George asked with a specious mildness. And he actually passed me his tobacco pouch and nodded for me to help myself to what I'd come to regard as my own chair.

"Just the usual," I said. "If a man decides he's going to leave this earth in a hurry, and you happen to have known him—well, it's up to you to say what you know. It might save you a morning at a coroner's court."

George smiled cynically. That means he pursed out his lips and the weeping-willow of a moustache splayed above them like an awning.

"You don't kid me like that. What was fishy about it? You might as well out with it."

"I don't admit there was anything fishy. All the same, I'm prepared to tell you what I told Targe. I'll even expand it a bit."

"Good enough," he said. His pipe was going and he stretched out his legs towards the electric fire. "Plenty of time. I'm not busy."

"That's fine," I said. "I'll make it even longer."

For you, the reader, I'll make it still longer. But before I begin the story there's something else that has to be said. If I, as story-teller, am not to be from the very outset some kind of a laughing-stock, I can't have it thought that I went into that spiritualistic business with unopened eyes. If, on the other hand, I claim that I was inveigled, you'll merely take me for a fool of another kind. I'll let you judge. And we'd better begin with husbands.

Most husbands manage to acquire, or so I imagine, their own particular weapons for use in domestic warfare, or maybe just those slight skirmishes or clashes of will that happen in every home. But most husbands, or so it seems to me, begin with a false estimate of what I might call the armoury of the enemy. They act on the assumption—accept the cosy and casual theory, if you prefer it that way—that in any clash between the sexes man is endowed with some peculiar virility and woman is pitifully, and possibly endearingly, weak. That's more than a fallacy. Act on those assumptions and a battle's already lost. What I claim is that if men are strength, then women are strategy.

Isn't that logical? Bodily strength, so carelessly confused with strength of mind, is obvious enough. From the beginning of time it fell to man to do the heavier jobs. He acquired a monopoly of muscles, and the mere planning of his work, if he were not to arrive at disaster in its execution, made him a fairly logical creature. Strength and logic became largely the perquisites of men. What women developed was what I call strategy. And let me say at once that it was an admirable consummation. It is this control of strategy which is the basis of what we call the eternal feminine—the synthetically mysterious, the bewildering, the maddening and the endearing.

Consider its use as a weapon, and if you are a husband you will know what I mean. In an argument, what you imagine your patience and logic will be met by deft and uncanny shiftings of ground, bland ignorances, introductions of irrelevant matter, quotations from friends, subtle distortions of fact, and analogies so false as to be fantastic. Even before you pin your opponent down, she is away and gone. Instead of being the aggrieved party, you suddenly discover you are the aggressor. If you momentarily lose your temper at such an injustice, you are regarded as incapable of quiet and logical argument. If in despair you mention mastery in your own house and impose your will, then for days you will be met with the patience of a bilious Grisel-da and a mute, martyr-like acceptance more maddening than mutiny. And nine times out of ten, the upshot will be that you will yield for the sake of what you delude yourself is peace and quietness. Your submission will be so abject that you will appear to like it. In plain terms, you will once more have been beaten by sheer strategy.

What weapons have I against all this? Merely the guileful abandonment of man's old armoury and the adoption of the weapons of the enemy. I don't make stands—I shift ground. I don't keep to the point, but worm my way illogically to a point more advantageous. I sow discord among allies and cast doubts about friends. I pretend agreement only to show how disastrous such an agreement can be. And I never impose my will. I admit largely that Bernice, as a human being possessed of an immortal soul, is entitled within legal limits to do as she likes, always provided she is prepared to pay. A good point that, and one that always provokes a wrinkling of the forehead. But the next is even better. It is that it naturally follows that I, too, am free to do as I like. That's the one that can bring a woman back to good old-fashioned logic.

And does it always work? Well, frankly, I wish to heaven it did. Which brings me at last to this story, and the matter of Madame Petriff.

Just a word about ourselves. I was fortunate enough to inherit that small block of high-class flats known as St. Martin's Chambers, and in one of them we live. There is an efficient restaurant which provides such meals as one orders in time, and the services of chambermaids are available. The flats are central and our own is amply commodious. But though Bernice has considerable time on her hands, she has an abundance of interests. There are charities, and she is on the board of one of the larger hospitals. She naturally has plenty of friends and acquaintances and plays a fair amount of bridge. She has money of her own, and what she does with it is usually no concern of mine. But we are what, for want of an apter term, I call a domesticated couple.

On most evenings we are at home, and if we go to a theatre it is almost always together.

I am away a considerable deal at times, but I never have to worry about her being lonely. A year or two back I acquired the Broad Street Detective Agency, and, though I have a first-class managing director in Norris, the business takes quite a lot of my time. I am still—I often wonder why—on the books of Scotland Yard, and if George Wharton is in charge of a case I am brought in as colleague or stooge—what, in fact, is known as an unofficial expert. When Bernice throws bridge parties at the flat, I can find plenty to do elsewhere.

I must say that I know precious little about many of her friends except their names. I may know their husbands or fathers or brothers if they happen to belong to my club, or in the way of business, or through mutual acquaintances. But one or two of the women I know very well indeed: the Hon. Adeline Doxon, for instance. Her father and I—he then very much in the doddery stage—were once on a certain board of directors, and Bernice and I used to dine regularly at 7 Ennison Square. Adeline—she's now in the late sixties—was an only child and always something of a crank. I hazard the guess that her income is still the Crippsian maximum.

In many ways I like her, even if she is a considerable deal of a fool. She has at least a personality and an individuality, and though for Bernice's sake my chuckles or exasperations are kept to the internal, I do find her both refreshingly and exasperatingly amusing. Among her less enslaved intimates she is known as The Boom, and if you hear her on the telephone you will know why.

I never knew anyone more aggressive as a manager, and she is Grand Matriarch of that bloc which constitutes her inner circle of friends. Her interests have been many and bizarre. She used to be the friend of lost causes but now her chief interest is in spiritualism, to use what I believe is an outmoded word. In my connotation that includes séances and that new form of religion or creed or what-have-you which is known as Neo-Quietism, of the Society for which she is President. I know that latter because she once tried to get me financially interested. Not that she isn't generous herself. I regard her as foolishly so. And, as I said, I like her. To Bernice, by the way, she's the nearest thing to an oracle.

And so to that October evening. We had been short-handed at Broad Street and I had been doing the work of an operative on a certain urgent investigation, and Bernice had expected me to be out quite late. She seemed gratified to find me before the fire with a crossword. I told her things had gone much more smoothly than we'd thought. One of our better cases, in fact, and if she cared to celebrate we might have an early dinner and do a show.

"That'd be lovely," she said, and then gave a sigh. "Very nice of you, darling, but somehow tonight I don't feel like it."

She was moving about the room, unbuttoning gloves, taking off her hat and peering in the mirror, and every now and again she would let something emerge.

"I've had a most interesting experience. . . . A friend of Adeline's, really. . . . I don't know what to call her. . . . Acquaintance, perhaps. . . . You'll think it perfectly ridiculous."

I pricked up my ears at that. Whatever this mysterious thing was, I was being a kind of aggressor.

"Uh-huh?" I said, and kept my eyes on my crossword.

Bernice was on the move again. She was bending over my chair and giving a kiss where my hair is slightly thinning. She gave a happy little tinkle of a laugh.

"Adeline does get mixed up in the queerest sort of things!"

She took the chair on the opposite side of the fire and stretched forward to warm her hands.

"Uh-huh?" I said again and laid my paper aside. And I couldn't help telling myself that I'd got myself a fine-looking woman. Almost forty, but one whom most would take for thirty. And always a style and a poise.

She leaned back in the chair and was smiling in a kind of sphinx-like way.

"You'd never guess what I've been doing with myself this afternoon," she threw idly at me.

"I can try," I said. "Perhaps you've been calling on the Aneurin Bevans. Or having tea with Clem Attlee."

"Don't be stupid!"

Then she said she was sorry. She shouldn't have snapped at me like that.

"Of course you *were* just a bit stupid," she told me. Then the enigmatic smile came again. It gave her face an air of sweet yet sorrowful reminiscence. "Not that I don't expect you to think I've been a bit stupid myself."

Instinctively I was giving my horn-rims a polish—a nervous trick of mine when at a mental loss or faced with a dramatic discovery. I wasn't either at that moment. I was merely gaining time. Ancestral voices were prophesying at least an argument.

"Do I ever think you stupid?" I said virtuously. "Far from it. Besides, if you insist on a verdict, why not give me the evidence."

She looked at me. There was a sort of daring, and just a touch of the wary.

"I've been consulting a fortune-teller!"

I wasn't going to be stampeded. I grunted politely and awaited the rest, but that turned out to be a bad move. She said I didn't seem very interested. I said that, on the other hand, I was most interested. I said that once in my younger days I consulted a fortune-teller at a charity affair, and was told, *inter alia*, that I should marry a blonde and have four children. I said it cost me ten shillings and apparently something had gone wrong. (Bernice, I should say, is a brunette and we have no children.) Between ourselves I thought that tactically I was doing well. Bernice was frowning. I don't think she cared a lot for that strategic hint that fortune-tellers weren't always profitable as an investment.

"One has to be silly at times," she conceded me. "If one never succumbed to frivolity life would be merely a groove."

"How true," I observed sententiously, and stirred alertly in my chair. "But tell me about it. Where does Adeline come in, for instance?"

I was so obviously amenable that I heard everything. The fortune-teller was a Madame Petriff, a White Russian or whatever one calls refugees from Communism. She was also a noted medium. She presided—if that's the word—over the séances at Ennison Square.

"One doesn't believe in such things," she said, "but after what happened today I'm beginning to think there may be something in spiritualism as well. This woman was absolutely uncanny. She told me the most amazing things about myself. I felt positively naked."

"Where was all this? At Ennison Square?"

"Of course not," she said, with just a touch of impatience. "The séances are at Ennison Square, but if one consults Madame Petriff it's at her private address. A flat at Hampstead. Very handy for the Underground. Everything has to be by appointment, of course. According to Adeline, she's very strict about her clientele. You can't consult her unless you're recommended."

She left me to digest that much. I could have said a lot of things in my bourgeois way, but I didn't. I might have said, "You bet she's careful, otherwise she might find herself foretelling the future for a copper. Not too good for Madame, or, for that matter, Adeline, to have an appearance before a magistrate reported in the Press."

"You mean she's a superior sort of fortune-teller?" was what I actually said. "Doesn't necessarily depend on it for a living?"

"I don't think she actually does. She works professionally for more circles than Adeline's. But with regard to the private consultations, she's really uncanny."

She was all vivacity as she told me about it. No room with mysterious drapings, and crystals, semi-darkness and the pseudo-magical; just an ordinary, comfortable room and an intimate talk. You let Madame hold something personal that you valued highly, and then she leaned back with closed eyes and after a time began reaching a hand up into the air, as it were, and plucking things down from the dark abysm of time. Rather like a séance for two, but without the mumbo-jumbo.

"My dear, she told me simply everything! Things I'd almost forgotten; about when I was dancing professionally, and Malinoff who behaved so abominably in Rome, and about that gala night in Copenhagen, and about the kind of person I was myself.

All my faults and a few virtues: it made me blush, it was so uncannily true. And she mentioned you. A bit vaguely, of course, but all of it true."

"Most amazing!" I said unblushingly. "And what about the future?"

"Well, nothing too definite," she told me with a frown. "Apparently nothing important's going to happen to me. I was going to be very happy and live to a good old age." Then she gave a little laugh. "There was only one thing I refused absolutely to believe, and that was when she said I'd be a widow."

"Why not?" I said amiably. "Even a Merry Widow. After all, the vital statistics are on her side."

The old strategy seemed to have let me down a bit there, so I hastily shifted ground. I said everything that mattered was that Bernice herself should be satisfied. I might not altogether believe in that sort of thing myself, but people hadn't believed in Galileo. In any case I hoped I was always ready to admit there might be things in both heaven and earth that were well outside the scope of my philosophy. Then I glanced strategically at my watch and made it later than I thought. I was also suddenly very hungry.

As I lay on the borderland of sleep that night I could chuckle to myself with a certain smugness and complacency. One thing I thought I had definitely scotched, and that was any idea of getting me to consult Madame Petriff.

Was I too pious in thinking I had managed things rather well? Consider what some men—even as this publican—might have said. Adeline making an extra penny for her pet medium by advising—or should it be ordering?—her friends to go for private consultations. Adeline, even unwittingly, priming Petriff with details about the past of those friends and giving a shrewd forecast of the future. Or the Petriff woman nosing around and gleaning information for herself. Some men would have got indignantly to their feet and thrust out a finger and been the Victorian husband to the life, especially when Bernice let fall that that afternoon's consultation had cost five guineas!

"You!" I might have said. "You, supposedly a woman of sense and shrewdness, and allowing yourself to be hoodwinked by such duplicity! And paying through the nose for the privilege. My God! And then women expect men to take them seriously."

But no heavy-husband act for me. I'd used merely a little strategy. Besides, life was too short for foolery to matter. And working for years with George Wharton had made me such an expert liar when the cause demanded it that I was sure that Bernice was sleeping with the happy knowledge that in me she had got herself the most understanding and amenable of men.

I didn't know, of course, that I was to be somewhat wrong.

A day or two later I was lunching at my club. I was sitting aimlessly over my coffee in the smoking-room when someone slid into a chair alongside mine. It was a man named Hather.

When someone in the club had introduced us—in 1946, I think—I didn't know much about him, though Hather himself did tell me he'd spent the war years in America doing a rather important job. That day he didn't look a year over thirty-five. He was just under the medium height and slim with it, and after I'd been alone with him for five minutes I was thinking he had the strutting and consequential assurance of a bantam-cock.

Forgive my talking about Hather, but he's someone you've got to know and understand. I didn't like the man, but for some reasons of his own he would often attach himself to me when I was in the club. Let me be honest, if a bit pruriently so. It was the man himself whom I disliked—not the things I heard about him. It was said, for instance, that that talk of his about an important job in America during the war had been proved the most bare-faced of lies, and that he'd bolted over there, after wangling and influence, to dodge both bombs and war. Club chatter also alluded to him as a queer bird, and did it with a droop of the lip rather than a shake of the head. I thought some of that might be put down to jealousy, for Hather was both a celebrity and a monetarily successful man.

I hate to have to prove that I'm unbiased, but when I say that his school was one that had close contacts with mine, and that he, like myself, was a Cambridge man, you may think I had reason to see his virtues rather than his faults. As for his career: after Cambridge he had done a certain amount of writing, but had made no particular name for himself. Then in America he wrote a novel which was a sensation. You may have read it—*Man With Two Souls*. I didn't read it, but I'm told it sold well over here. I heard it described as the first of the latter-day schizophrenics, and that may have set me against it, for the psychic or occult or transcendental—I'm not well up in the jargon—had never appealed to me. Nor did I read the novels that followed that successful first. What I did gather for myself was that soon after his return from America he had become what I would call the chief psychic investigator for the B.B.C. One was always seeing his name down for talks and discussions on the Third Programme, but since I still maintain that the greatest invention of this age is the knob that turns off the radio, his name in that connection was never more than a name.

Why, then, did I dislike him? It was because he was too self-opinionated and cocksure. He never hesitated to give a view, nor would he hesitate to suggest, with more than a touch of patronage, that your views were wrong. Age and experience were merely targets for an inferior kind of wit. He would distort an argument for the sake of a wisecrack, and there seemed nothing he didn't regard with an Olympian irony. You may lift your eyebrows at this, but I thought him mentally unhealthy. Physically he looked healthy enough, if always just a bit dark under the eyes. He was always well-dressed and even slightly scented, but to my mind there was something unhealthy and diseased about him. In fact, to cut the cackle, I just had no use for him. But that afternoon I did try to make use of him.

"Well, how's crime?" he asked me facetiously. He was always very hearty in an approach. "And what about a port? Have one with your coffee?"

I repressed a shudder.

"Thanks, no," I said. "As a matter of fact I have to be off in a minute or so."

"Then there *is* plenty of crime?"

"No more than usual," I told him. "But what about the ghosts?"

"Just a bit shy at the moment."

"But it's still a good racket?"

Somehow I loved being so abominably rude. He only gave a self-satisfied chuckle.

"Heavens, yes! Not that I'm in it for that sort of thing. It's the utter fascination of it all that gets one. In layman's language, it's the stout Cortez stuff. Edging a foot nearer to the unknown. Exhilarating, believe me. Frightening, too, sometimes."

"Ever run up against a woman known as Madame Petriff?"

"But of course!" Then he swivelled a sudden eye on me. "You know her?"

"Oh no. I just happened to hear her name mentioned the other day, that's all. She's a medium or something of that sort, I understood."

"She's a very well-known one," he told me with a slight reproof. "You know Adeline Doxon, don't you?"

"I've known her for years."

"I happened to meet your wife at her place the other day, by the way. A most charming woman, if you'll allow me to say so. But about Madame Petriff. She happens to be Adeline's medium."

"You been to one of this Petriff's do's?"

He winced almost audibly at the crudity.

"My dear fellow, the whole of London—England, too, for that matter—is sticky with groups and circles. One can't possibly investigate them all. But I may say I've been specially asked to a séance at Ennison Square very soon and I shall certainly accept."

I haven't conveyed his tone: the patronage, the condescension, the assumption that he alone could give a cachet. I finished my coffee and was getting to my feet, when a message came for him that the taxi was waiting. He rose, too, and I couldn't shake him off at the cloakroom and we went out of the door and down the steps together. He'd asked if he could give me a lift and I'd said I'd only a few yards to go. Well short of the kerb he waved a farewell hand and moved rather quickly on to the taxi. It looked as if he was suddenly anxious to get rid of me instead of the other way about.

I'm an inquisitive man. I may explain it by claiming to be interested in my fellow men, but that doesn't alter the fact that I'm curious, and at times even rudely so. That's why I took a step or two after Hather, and that's how I came to see the woman in the taxi. Perhaps I should have said *girl*, for she was years younger than Hather.

I saw her clearly. In an exotic sort of way she was uncommonly good-looking, but her face had a whiteness that was extraordinarily dead. Maybe it was the darkness of her eyes and the heavy red of the lips that accentuated and set off that strange pallor of her face. And she seemed listless. In the second or so before the taxi moved off, she didn't turn towards him or speak. It was as if she didn't know he was there or that her thoughts were busy with something incredibly remote.

I walked ruminatively on till I heard a voice behind me. Paul Quint had caught me up. He's literary editor of the *Sunday Report*: a Chestertonian sort of figure, vast and voluminous like a Reynolds' cherub that's arrived at middle age.

"How are you, Travers?" he was saying. "I haven't seen you for quite a time. You been abroad?"

"Only in this England of ours," I said. "Walking up and down in it, so to speak. . . . You're looking remarkably—well, buoyant?"

"I'll have to do something about it," he told me dismally. "But about this going-to-and-fro business. Hast thou considered my servant Hather? Wasn't it he and his wife you were talking to?"

I said I'd been talking to Hather but not to his wife. I didn't even know it *was* his wife. And I was thinking that, since it was his wife, it was curious that he hadn't introduced me. In fact he'd seemed anxious not to introduce me.

"Talking to Hather's a one-sided business," he said. "How'd you get on with him?"

"Well," I said, "since we began this talk with the book of Job, I might add that Satan as usual did the talking and not the sons of God."

"Yes," he said; and: "Hather a friend of yours?"

"God forbid!" I hardly knew I'd said it. I'm usually far less abrupt.

"Can't stand the fellow, either," he told me. "By the way, did you ever read that book of his, the one that all the fuss was about—*Man With Two Souls*?"

"I didn't. I hope that makes me unique."

"Clever book," he said. "Far too clever. But he's a clever devil himself. There's a story to be told about that book some day. I don't know the ins and outs. Good thing for me, perhaps. Libel's a tricky business."

A mystery can gnaw at me like a nagging tooth, but just when I had ready a nice leading question to winkle out some possible disclosures, Quint was halting at the side entrance to a large store.

"See you soon, I hope. My wife's been lunching here. Damnable place to have to meet a woman."

A valedictory wave of an immense hand and he billowed his way through the doors. I smiled at his abhorrence at being seen among the lingerie, but as I went down the steps to the Underground I was thinking about that beginning of a disclosure. It vaguely annoyed me. It was a funny story told, and the denouement admitted. I told myself that the next time I saw Paul Quint—and didn't I owe him a lunch?—I'd bring the talk back to Hather.

That was why I mentioned Hather that evening in the flat. I didn't expect Bernice to make any disclosures. I just threw a stone in a pond and looked for the ripples.

"I remember him very well," Bernice said. "The two of us were at tea at Adeline's. I don't know why I had to be there, but that's how it was. A youngish man, very slim, and rather short. Quite distinguished-looking in a way. Frightfully well-known, of course. Even Adeline was all of a dither."

"Do you know his wife? He *is* married, I believe."

"Oh yes, he's married."

There was an ominous pause. Bernice evidently knew her with a difference. But I couldn't have anticipated what was coming.

"Always looks to me as if she takes far too many sleeping tablets."

I raised my eyebrows.

"The first time I saw her I had a shrewd idea. Since then I've been absolutely certain. She has the look, and occasionally that nervous, slightly unbalanced manner. I ought to know. I saw enough of it during the war."

Bernice had done a considerable deal of nursing and I didn't venture to doubt her diagnosis. I did suggest that it might be dangerous to mention the matter.

"My dear, as if I should!" she told me. "But it's a pity how some of these younger women let themselves go. They live too hectically and sleep too badly."

"You see her much?"

"Not for some weeks now. She used to play bridge of a sort, but she gave it up. She's still a member, I think, of Adeline's psychic circle. And I did hear she was being rather friendly with someone or other. A Greek name like . . . I remember: a name like Maroulis. It *was* Maroulis."

I almost gave a gesture of humorous despair. You warn a woman about libel and she promptly comes out with a thing like that. Then she said something that shook me.

"It's curious, you know, but Adeline hasn't mentioned for ages anything about my joining the circle. But the last time I saw her, this Hather woman did. It was months ago, but she was almost pressing."

"Good God! You're surely not thinking of—"

I just didn't say it. Strategy or something like it rescued me. I said that reminded me that I'd run into Paul Quint at the club, and oughtn't we to ask him and his wife to lunch?

That slid us gently away from the Hathers. I was relieved and maybe the least bit cock-a-hoop. I needn't have been. I didn't know it till later, but Bernice already had something in mind. The only reason she didn't mention it was probably because the moment wasn't too propitious. After all, you can't be strategic till you're sure of your ground.

# AMONG THE SPIRITS

BERNICE PAUSED in her knitting.

"Darling, I wonder if you'd mind if I went to one of Adeline's séances?"

I must have stared.

"I'd have gone when she asked me some time ago if I hadn't thought you regarded such things as ridiculous."

"Now, now, now," I said with what I intended for a humorous exasperation. "You really mustn't put words into my mouth. Wasn't I saying only the other evening that only a fool judges things entirely by his own prejudices? I just don't understand these things—nothing more. I can't understand how all this psychic business works. Which reminds me—"

But Bernice had no intention of being edged away.

"I really ought to go," she said. "Don't you honestly think so yourself? After all, we do owe a lot to Adeline."

That almost took my breath away; in fact, I failed to notice the significance of that word *we*. I could have asked just what we owed her. I could have claimed, and justly, that it was the other way about. I, for instance, had often been ignored for months and had then been arbitrarily and gushingly called in to advise about investments. And hadn't Bernice become little more than an errand-girl or a second-class lady-in-waiting to that dominating old matriarch of Ennison Square?

"If it hadn't been for Adeline I shouldn't have met quite a lot of really charming and interesting people," Bernice was going on. "Besides, one has a duty to one's self to broaden one's mind. Enlarge one's experience, perhaps I should have said."

"Uh-huh," I said. "And what are her séances like? The sort of thing one reads about? I mean things dropping all over the place and tambourines banging from nowhere, and people holding hands in the dark, and so on?"

"You're not taking it seriously," she told me with just a bit of an edge. "Adeline isn't concerned with all that poltergeist side of things. She only tries to contact the relatives of friends who have passed over. I mean it's the *relatives* who've passed over. Or she tries to contact even higher guides. People like Plato or Socrates or ancient Egyptian priests."

I hadn't met Plato since my schooldays, and he and I hadn't been on very good terms. I didn't say so, but I thought there were one or two things I'd like to take up with him.

"I don't quite follow all that," was what I said. "The guide business, for instance."

"Of course I'm not an adept," she told me with a kind of pitying deprecation. "I do know that Madame Petriff makes contact with what's known as a guide, who's the spirit of someone who's passed over. It's the guide who puts someone at the séance in touch with some dead relative, or even with some higher guide. That's really all it is. But I do know—at least Adeline's told me—that methods of getting into touch aren't stereotyped. There're all sorts of different methods just as there're all sorts of circles or groups. That's roughly how it is."

Like Plato, it was still Greek to me. I asked if they didn't sing hymns or something.

"My dear, no. Not necessarily. Adeline usually has something classical played on the gramophone beforehand, but that's only to create an atmosphere. But naturally those present do hold hands so that they're in touch with one another."

She paused in her knitting again to give me a somewhat exploratory look. She said she thought a séance ought to be most interesting.

"Well—yes," I said non-committally, and hoped I'd be allowed to get on with my crossword. "Go by all means. When is it, by the way?"

"Thursday, at Ennison Square. It's something rather special. Martin Hather's going to be there."

"Really?" I tried to concentrate on a clue. Another domestic crisis had been safely passed.

"But, darling, I was expecting you to come with me. Adeline told me to ask you specially."

"What's that?" I sat up in my seat.

"Adeline wants you to come with me. And I'd like you to come."

"Sorry," I said, and with what I intended as a regretful finality. "Absolutely out of the question. After office hours on Thursday night I have some important accounts to go through with Norris. Income-tax stuff. Otherwise I'd certainly have gone."

I was so busy reinforcing that counter-attack that I wasn't watching her face. I added with a pleasant facetiousness that, like Jurgen, one should try every drink once. And that's the kind of fool I was. I ought to have been born dumb and never have learned the signs.

"But it isn't on Thursday night! It's in the afternoon. At three o'clock."

Something was telling me, and with a chill clarity, that I was in the web, and that no amount of wriggling would extricate me. I'm not exactly dull-witted, but I couldn't find a thing to say. And then, of course, it was too late. Bernice was laying the knitting aside.

"I'll let Adeline know at once." I could swear I heard her purr. "I think it's very sweet of you, darling. I'm sure you'll love it once you get there."

From then on I had to pretend that I liked it, even if I hoped to heaven that no one who had for me an iota of respect would ever learn that I had taken part in such damnable mumbo-jumbo. And yet, before I went to bed that night, it struck me that there really was something about trying any drink once, even if one had more than an idea that it might be somewhat nauseating. And, when I came to think of it, it might be interesting to see that bantam-cock Hather doing his crowing on what might be called a chosen dung-hill. It might be interesting—I told myself that as one interested in his fellow men—to study the kind of people who believed in all that hocus-pocus. I wondered vaguely if Ursula Hather would be there, and, somewhat ghoulishly, whether I should open my paper one day and read how she'd taken an overdose. I wondered if Hather were a pipe-dreamer. Rumour said he'd dabbled in most things, and it was something I wouldn't put past him. But Adeline—that grim presiding genius and the one behind Bernice's inveigling—would definitely be there. I told myself with a curl of the lip that sometime I must remind myself to write a book about Adeline.

By that Thursday I knew quite a lot more. Bernice had evidently been picking up information and I gathered that the affair at Ennison Square would have an original and Adeline touch—not that that helped me much since I had no idea of what constituted a recognised pattern. No phenomena, Bernice said; no materialising, but just an attempt to get in touch with the guide, after which he'd take over. I wanted to know more about that guide.

"But, my dear, I've already told you! It's the spirit of someone who's passed on. Generally a Red Indian, because they have some extraordinary magnetism and they can get in touch with the medium."

I let out a breath, even if it was pianissimo. She was adding that people sometimes received the most astounding messages that had convinced them of life beyond the grave.

"What's the usual age in Adeline's circle?"

She didn't exactly answer that. There were far more women than men, she said, and the women were mostly widows or spinsters. She said Adeline's circle was large but select. Attendance had to be by invitation and private. Other circles, so Bernice had heard, were infinitely larger and far less select. I gathered they were what I'd call psychic clubs whose members liked to be titillated by the poltergeist and ectoplasmic stuff. The terms are probably wrong, but you'll guess what I mean.

"And this Madame Petriff is what I'd call good?"

"So they say," Bernice told me. "She works for other groups. Adeline took her up because she's so absolutely genuine and gets such marvellous results. Someone told me that that Greek man—"

"Maroulis?"

"That's the one. The Hather woman's friend. That he recommended her to Adeline."

I had more than an idea that Bernice was just as badly up in the jargon as I was, but I must admit that I changed my attitude towards that séance well before I arrived at it. It seemed mentally snobbish and indeed foolish to approach it with a cynical disbelief, so I told myself I'd attend with an open mind. Both common sense and social courtesy demanded no less. And of all the forms of snobbishness—and heaven knows we're a nation of snobs—intellectual arrogance seems to me to be the worst. And so, though I couldn't delude myself into being a seeker after truth, I could at least rid my mind of a certain amount of prejudice and for one little hour become an alert but courteous listener.

And so to that Thursday afternoon, when everything was so vastly different from what I'd expected. Even Adeline was subdued. She's a tall, scraggy woman with a huge beak of a nose, with a partiality in dress for mauves or pale blues. That afternoon she was in dark grey and round her neck was a black velvet ribbon, a fashion I'd not seen for years. And instead of being festooned with jewellery, she was wearing only a cameo brooch.

An elderly maid—Austrian, I think, and a left-over from the lost causes era—admitted us and took my hat and coat, and then Adeline suddenly shot out of the small drawing-room like a cuckoo from its clock. I didn't even see her till she was on us.

"So good of you to come."

Even her voice was subdued—merely a hoarse whisper that shook the leaves of the palms. Bernice received a maternal kiss, and I, for some unknown reason, a look that was definitely reproachful.

"In the music-room," she told us, and waved vaguely upwards. "I must wait here for Mr. Hather."

We went up heavily carpeted stairs. I whispered that it reminded me of funerals, and ought I to have brought flowers? Bernice hissed warningly. Everything was formal beforehand, she whispered back. Afterwards there'd be tea and everyone would talk.

It certainly was formal. We slid into a couple of chairs just within range of the fire. Ten people were in the room, all seated and all rather lugubrious. It reminded me, in fact, of a doctor's waiting-room, even to the books and pamphlets on a central table. Bernice moved and I saw her nod and smile to a couple of women who'd had the sense to get nearer the fire. They smiled back, then began whispering to each other. I thought they were discussing myself.

Three dowagers were in the far corner and whispering spasmodically in a ruminative sort of way: two in black with a touch of white and the other in dark red; two gentle Friesians, I couldn't help thinking, and a Red-poll, placidly chewing the cud. Not far from them were a youngish couple: the man with an Oxford look about him and the girl stream-lined and alert. A middle-aged woman sat by herself, and Bernice couldn't keep her eyes from the mink. Also by himself was a man of about forty, rather dingily dressed. His eyes just lifted as we entered and then went back to the carpet as if he were interested in its oriental pattern. Lastly was a man of about thirty who didn't seem any too happy about it all. His eyes went nervously about the room, and he was probably in need of a cigarette.

There was a sound—Adeline's whisper, even more penetrative than her bellow—and, as the door opened, a voice which I knew as Hather's before I actually saw him. He looked even more dapper than usual, and he halted just inside the door and looked round with a sort of gratified condescension. Maybe he was waiting for the cheers. With him was another man: almost as tall as my six-foot-three, portly, clean-shaven, and the very spit, in fact, of a Roman consul. I hadn't time for a good look at him. Adeline was addressing us.

"Shall we go on?"

We went through the side door to the dining-room. Extra leaves had been put in the oval table and extra chairs brought in to reinforce the Hepplewhite dozen. Everything went quickly and smoothly. I was seated with the girl on my right and one of the Friesians on my left. Bernice had the consul and the Lady in Mink. Adeline left us, but was back almost at once with a woman who had to be Madame Petriff. There was a polite craning along the table and a decorous stir. Madame Petriff gave a little bow and took the winged armchair at what I'd call the table head.

She was dressed in black. Had she been in, say, mauve, she'd have looked even more plump. She wore no hat, and the jet-black hair was done in a frizzy sort of way round her ears and seemed to give a professional cachet. Either the eyes were darkened underneath or they were naturally large and black, but the effect was highly incongruous in so plump a face. She took her seat and clasped her hands, and looked at nothing in particular.

The curtains had been drawn, but all the chandelier lights were on. Adeline switched half of them off and went across to the radiogram in the corner. The music was audible and no more. I wished it louder, for it was, though somewhat hackneyed these days, an old favourite of mine—an orchestral arrangement of "Jesu Joy of Man's Desiring". We sat there busy with our thoughts, and then Adeline switched off more lights and took her own seat. The room was now a twilight in which we could just see each other and the medium, and little that lay beyond. Then as the music ended, with the mechanism switching it off, everyone began clasping hands. That on my right was cool, and that on my left was warm and slightly damp.

The medium closed her eyes and her head rested against the back of the winged chair. I tried to breathe inaudibly as the moments passed. Five long minutes went, perhaps, and then the medium gave a nervous kind of twitch. The head seemed to shudder and then she was motionless again. Another minute or two and there were quick convulsive movements of the shoulders. Once more she was still, and round the table someone let out a disappointed breath. A couple of minutes and there was a movement of both head and shoulders. As it passed, the head of Madame Petriff slithered gently to the corner of the chair. Two more interminable minutes, and her lips moved.

I nearly shot out of my seat. The sound that came was so sudden, so high-pitched and so incredibly—what shall I say?—vulgar. It was like the piping of a cockney urchin. Though I got more used to it as the séance went on, I couldn't rid myself of those first impressions and the shock of that first sound.

"Good afternoon, everybody. Harebell hope you are all well. Everything is well in the spirit-land. Everyone is happy. . . ."

There was a horrible, precocious heartiness about it that made me wince. The voice had the jerkiness that might accompany a marionette, and there were false intonations that were meant maybe to convey the fact that the guide had only an imperfect English. I wondered—then I stopped wondering and tried to concentrate on the words.

"There is with me now Annabel . . . maybe it is Anna. I do not hear it very well, but she wish to speak. . . . She say now it is Ann and she also have name Bella."

"It is my sister Ann," a voice said, quiet but urgent. "Tell her, please, Harebell, that this is her sister Georgina."

I couldn't see the speaker. To have peered along would have been far too noticeable.

"Ann say she very happy here. All day she do the things she always wish. It is very good. But she say she not so happy now about you. She say you should not move the picture."

I definitely caught a little gasp.

"Harebell, please! Tell her that I was wrong to move it. It reminded me so much of her. I had to move it."

"She say you put it back. She say you unhappy if she unhappy. She happy and you happy."

"Tell her I will put it back."

There was no answer for over a minute.

"She is gone, but I tell her and she say very happy now."

There was a longer silence. Adeline prompted.

"Can you see us quite clearly, Harebell?"

"I see all the time," the voice came quickly back. "I also see great Chinese wise man who will be guide of gentleman who hold hand."

I squinted brazenly round. The reference was to the nervous young man who'd sat in the music-room by himself. Maybe Adeline applied a bit of pressure to his hand. He gave a little nervous clearing of the throat.

"What does he say?"

The answer was unintelligible—a gabble of sounds that presumably were Chinese. Then just when it was getting unbearable, the voice switched to the pidgin kind of English.

"He say he glad you seek truth. He glad some time to be your guide. Many peoples wish speak with you some time. Maybe soon they talk. He was very glad you here today."

You'd never guess what happened next. I shudder when I think of it, but the medium's hand went slowly out and wavered about in my direction.

"I see new friends today. Greeting, friends. Some of you seek the truth, but one man do not believe what I say. He very clever man. He too clever, maybe. He not seek after truth."

I closed my eyes. The hot blush suffused my face and went down to my collar. Then at last I squinted round again, and no one was looking at me or seeming to have experienced anything remarkable. And Harebell was going on talking, though not about me. And on and on the whole thing went for at least another half-hour—pauses, hesitations, questions, and spirits—shall I call them—emerging apparently out of some kind of mist and Harebell passing on snippets of information, which rarely went beyond expressions of content. But there was quite a long conversation about a certain Henry, and difficulty in deciding which Henry it was.

I didn't hear half of it. I was doing a lot of thinking, and principally about the nervous young man. If there hadn't been some trickery in his case, then, as Wharton is wont to say, my name was Robinson. I guessed it was his first séance, and it had been thought necessary to make him a solid member of that circle. Quite possibly, too, that was why Harebell had made a direct attack on myself.

A particularly long silence brought me back to things. I was hoping everything now was going to peter out, and then Adeline spoke again.

"Harebell, have the spirits any other messages?" Harebell had to think about that one.

"There is much news, but there is no time today. There is also news for some who not with you today, but all of it is good. Pierre say tell you number twenty-nine very important. Number twenty-nine."

No one seemed to know Pierre. The head of Madame Petriff moved slightly till it rested in the angle at the back of the chair. Adeline broke the short silence.

"Shall we think now of those who have passed over, with the prayer that they, too, may continue to think of us."

I guessed that that was some sort of ritual, and heads were being bowed, so I bowed mine. Then the silence was heavy, too heavy and almost stertorous. Two minutes must have passed and she gave a little sigh. She stirred. Her eyes opened. Adeline moved quickly towards her. Madame Petriff spoke in her own voice: a tired voice; an almost common voice. One that had never a touch of quality.

"Well, dear, has everything gone off all right?"

"Marvellously!"

"Did you get any nice messages?"

"Quite a lot."

Adeline gave her a little pat, and then gave us all a kind of bow of dismissal. The séance was over. You could hear the breaths let suddenly out and see the beginnings of smiles as we moved decorously towards the door. I looked back and saw Adeline helping Madame Petriff to her feet.

Three minutes later we were at what might have been an intimate little cocktail party, except that the drinks were China or Indian. The firm of caterers had also furnished a couple of waiters, and we stood around in pairs or little groups, and then Adeline would move us about as if we'd get pneumonia if we stood too long in one place. In the middle of a conversation you'd be cut off and find yourself resuming it with perhaps a complete stranger. I put a stop to that as far as I myself was concerned. I took up a position quite near the fire and as good as told Adeline that it would be useless to try budging me.

I asked her, by the way, if we should be seeing Madame Petriff. The question seemed to surprise her. The medium, it appeared—and if the afternoon had been as successful as the one we'd experienced—was always exhausted by her efforts, whatever that might mean. Someone else told me that Madame Petriff would be having tea by herself when she felt like it, and would then be taken home in Adeline's somewhat aged Rolls.

Bernice obviously had friends in the room. It was she who brought along someone I'd heard her mention—a Lady Georgina Dunmow. She was a kindly, simple old soul: rather upset and deeply stirred by that episode of the moved picture.

"My dear sister Ann died when she was only twenty-two," she told me. "This was a portrait by von Herkomer and I had it hung in my bedroom. I was passionately fond of Ann and it distressed me enormously when she died. But we recently had the house decorated and I took a cowardly advantage of it to move the portrait to the landing at the east front. Wonderful, wasn't it? And yet there are still unbelievers."

Hather was the lion of the afternoon, and it was at that moment that he sauntered up and Adeline led Lady Georgina away. Hather looked up at me with an almost insulting amusement.

"Saul also among the prophets?"

"Why not?" I said. "In any case, weren't there also prophets of Baal?"

He gave me a quick look.

"You mean?"

I shrugged my shoulders, then reached out to stop the passing waiter. I took quite a big slice of fruit cake, and when I looked at Hather again he didn't seem too happy about something.

"There're still fools who come to scoff and remain to pray," he told me.

"To scoff would be bad manners," I said. "And haven't we already prayed?"

His bottom lip drooped a bit.

"You're an elusive devil, Travers. But maybe you came merely to pry."

"No need to lose your temper," I told him evenly. "Why I came is nobody's business."

He knew he was going a mite too far.

"Sorry," he said. "I just happen to feel these things a bit deeply."

"And what did you, as an expert, think of this afternoon?"

"Not too bad on the whole. Petriff seems quite good."

"Wonder if you'd tell me something," I said. "What was that number business? Number twenty-nine that was said to be important."

"There's a tremendous occult significance in numbers," he told me. "They're also related to the soul-path, but it's all far too involved to anyone like yourself for me to try even to sketch it out."

Adeline was on us and with her the nervous young man. She told me roguishly that I mustn't monopolise Hather, and might she leave Mr. Brown with me. It was as if I was a baby-sitter.

"This is your first séance, Mr. Brown?" I asked him.

"Well, yes—really." He had quite a pleasant voice, and now he'd hardly a trace of nervousness. "I found it very informative. Rather like a religious service, don't you think?"

"I suppose it was, in a way," I said. "But I wonder if you'd tell me something. Make it between ourselves if you wish, but about that supposed-to-be guide of yours, the great Chinese wise man. Who is he exactly?"

"Well"—he was wondering how I would take it—"Mr. Hather told me that of course it was Confucius."

"Uh-huh," I said. "I'd rather like to have Plato. With a bit of industry and just a few weeks, I ought to be able to talk to him direct."

"That would be rather jolly, wouldn't it?" Then he, too, was giving me a look. I didn't bat an eyelid.

"By the way, sir, I didn't quite catch your name."

"Travers," I said. "For some reason or other, people always prefix the Christian name. Ludovic Travers. Same as George Robey."

He actually gaped. Then I wasn't looking at him. Hather was almost on us, and the Roman consul with him. There wasn't a suspicion of the supercilious about Hather's smile. He had the consul by the arm and it looked like a sleekly trimmed poodle tethered to a Great Dane.

"Oh, Travers, may I present my good friend Maroulis? Loucas, this is Ludovic Travers."

We uttered the how-do-you-do's. Hather took Brown by the arm. I just heard him say he'd like him to meet a Mrs. Somebody, but they were turning away and I didn't catch the name.

"Don't think me too personal," I said to Maroulis, "but are you of Greek extraction? I ask it because I knew some charming people named Maroulis in Alexandria when I was soldiering in Egypt."

"It's quite a common name," he told me. "As a matter of fact, I'm a Cypriot."

"Then you're as British as I am. Curious how misinformed people are. I honestly believe quite a lot of them class Cypriots as foreigners."

He amusedly agreed. I didn't mention that he himself had a faint accent, and maybe because I couldn't tell just what the accent was.

"You're a member of this circle?" he was asking me.

I didn't attach any particular importance to the question. It was true I'd seen Hather make for him as soon as Adeline had led Hather away, and I'd seen the two men talking together, and it was just after that that Hather had brought him along to me. I didn't even see a sequence in those happenings.

"My first experience," I said.

"You think you'll become a member?"

"To be frank, I very much doubt it."

He passed me his handsome cigarette case, snapped his lighter for me, and asked me why.

"I mightn't have the time. But don't think me rude if I also say it's something I'd rather not discuss."

He gave me an amiable shrug of his immense shoulders. Then came something that did make me think. He was putting almost the same question that young Brown had put.

"Did I catch your name rightly, by the way? Was it *Ludovic Travers*?"

"That was it," I said. "But I'm not responsible."

"I thought I'd run up against it somewhere recently." He tapped his skull with a queer, unnatural gesture. "Wait a minute. It wasn't at the Old Bailey?"

"Maybe," I said. "I had to give evidence there recently."

"A murder trial, wasn't it? Some company director or other."

"I expect it was."

He nodded. He said it was quite exciting to meet in the flesh anyone to do with Scotland Yard.

"Would it be in order to ask just what your—well, what your chief work consists of?"

It was so damn silly and obvious. I wondered if Hather had put him up to it. I wondered why.

"The fact of the matter is," I told him, and made it as quizzical as I could, "they get rather bored round there with their own company. That's why they bring in outsiders like myself from time to time, to liven things up a bit. Provide a few murders, and so on."

He tightened up. I had to watch Hather, for Hather seemed surreptitiously to be watching us. Maroulis chuckled.

"You're a diplomat, Mr. Travers."

"Is that a compliment or a reproof?"

He didn't say anything, but he was still smiling as he dropped the cigarette in a handy ash-tray and flicked on the lighter for another. But that discarded cigarette was good for another five minutes. Mind you, it was only later that I remembered that. I do know that no sooner was that lighter flicked on than Hather was moving. He came straight to us. There was someone, he said, whom Maroulis ought to meet, and he gave me a friendly nod as he moved away.

I was turning thoughtfully aside when I heard a movement, and there was the forlorn man who'd been sitting by himself when we'd first arrived and who'd been interested apparently in the pattern of the carpet.

"Excuse me, sir," he said, "but I understand we're all supposed to meet everyone else. My name's Land."

"How are you, Mr. Land? My name's Travers."

"I'm pretty well," he said; "I hope you are."

Land wasn't off the top shelf, there wasn't a doubt of that. Duke or dustman, it makes no difference to me; in fact I think I'd rather talk to the dustman—if he had a modicum of personality. But Land looked definitely dull.

"You a regular member?" I asked him.

"Can't say that I am," he said. "A lady who knows me got Miss Doxon to let me come this afternoon. You see, I'm what you call interested. Lost my wife recently and we were a very devoted couple."

I was wishing I was a schizophrenic, if that's what I meant. It's none too easy to talk with one man and watch another or for another. Hather and Maroulis had whispered together after they left me, then Maroulis had approached Adeline and the two had left the room together. Adeline had come back, but as yet there was no sign of Maroulis. But Land was asking me some question or other.

"I beg your pardon," I said. "I didn't quite catch that."

"I was asking if you knew what that number twenty-nine meant. The guide said it was important and I didn't understand it."

I told him what Hather had told me. Even to me it sounded like gibberish, so no wonder he was shaking his head bemusedly. Then Bernice came up and my forlorn friend edged away. Bernice said Adeline wanted her to stay on for a while and then would send her home in the Rolls, so did I mind going home by myself. We'd ordered no car and had come by bus, so I didn't mind in the least.

"Just speak to Adeline first," she told me, so I did as directed. I couldn't get away for five minutes and then Hather pounced on me again. He said Maroulis had told him about that trial at the Old Bailey and he wanted me to tell him about it. I had hard work shaking him off, but it took another five minutes. Maroulis was now back, but the room had thinned considerably. Only the elderly maid was there when I got to the hall. I'd just tipped her and was leaving when Adeline called to me from the landing. She came majestically down.

"Take these, Ludo, I'm sure you'll be interested."

Tracts and pamphlets by the look of them. I said I was sure I'd be interested, thanked her again for everything, and off I went. It was nearing dusk, and dry, and the least bit chilly. I made up my mind to walk at least to the club. Then I changed my mind. It was the sight of the handy bus-stop that did it.

# 3

# THE FIRST SHOT

A bus had just drawn away so I took the head of any new queue. In less than no time two other people were behind me. A minute later, four or five people were there. It was the rush hour and there was the wonder if all or any of us would get on.

A bus came round the corner. It was what I'd call an open queue which moved instinctively forward as the bus appeared. Three people got off and by that time people seemed to be milling behind me.

"Four only! Three downstairs, one on top!"

I swung on. As I went inside I saw a man craftily beat the queue, and the conductor either didn't notice it or let him get away with it. I had to stand and the gate-crasher was wedged against me. He was puffing a bit as if the final effort had been rather too much. He was shortish, I saw, and fat, and a woollen scarf was wrapped voluminously round his chins.

At Marble Arch I got a seat and the fat man had one opposite me. I make something of a hobby of the study of my fellow men; I like to place them, and identify an accent or dialect. It's the old Sherlock Holmes stuff, maybe, but something, as I've more than once told George, that ought to be in any manual for the use of young detectives. I put my fat friend down as a restaurant proprietor. There was a kind of Soho look about him from the black overcoat and slouch hat and the almost greasy pallor of his face. When he pulled an evening paper from his pocket and began reading it, I could see the pudginess of his hands and the grubbiness of his nails.

I got out at my stop and began walking along Piccadilly towards the club. I passed an antique shop, then something told me there had been a china group that had looked attractive. I turned back and almost collided with my fat friend. The group was Meissen and looked expensive, and I moved on again. There wasn't a sign of him then and I guessed he'd turned up Bond Street. But for that hobby of mine I'd never have bothered my head about him.

I crossed the road at the next lights and at once turned right. I passed a news-stand and then thought I'd buy an evening paper, though one would be waiting for me at the flat. And there was my friend again. He whipped round and was interested in a shop window as he spotted me. I bought my paper and moved on again. That's when I thought things. And yet the whole thing was far too ridiculous. I told myself he couldn't be following me. And then I began to think back. I thought it might be fun to put it to the proof. So I crossed and turned left. I walked leisurely along Jermyn Street. I cut left into a narrow street whose name I'd forgotten and almost as quickly I cut back. And there was my fat friend.

I pretended not to notice him and walked on to Piccadilly. I went down the steps of a large store and into the lavatory of the Underground. When I came out he was a little way along the passage, watching for me over his newspaper. I went on and took a threepenny ticket. I hurried down the moving stairs as if late for a train. At the bottom I went along the corridor and then nipped back into one of those side openings. I saw him go hurrying by and then I went up the stairs again. In Coventry Street I went left and got to the flat by way of Charing Cross Road. I waited for quite a time outside the flat, but there was never a sign of my little fat friend.

I switched on the electric fire, polished my glasses, drew up a chair and did some thinking. Then I decided to take a chance. I rang Ennison Square. Adeline was on the line.

"Bernice has just left," she said, or boomed, and then I thanked her again for the afternoon.

"By the way, I owe you twopence," I said. "You weren't available, so I flagrantly helped myself to a call on your telephone. It wasn't too good, by the way. Anyone else been grumbling about it?"

"As far as I know it's perfectly all right," she told me, and quite indignantly. "Mr. Maroulis used it and *he* didn't grumble."

"Probably something purely temporary," I said. "And while I'm talking . . ."

I went on with some rubbish or other, for I didn't want her to remember Maroulis. But I remembered him. I saw the sequence of things as if they'd been labelled and numbered. Mind you, I did think my deductions were just the least bit melodramatic, but London can be a melodramatic place and this is a melodramatic age. It wasn't too unreasonable to think, for instance, that Hather had told Maroulis that I was connected with Scotland Yard, and that Hather had brought him to me in order that he should worm out of me just why I was at that séance. And if that meant anything at all, it was that something had happened that might conceivably be of interest to the police. And what that was I couldn't imagine. Everything had seemed to me to be remarkably well conducted and the people there far from the kind ever to be held in suspicion by the law. I went back in my mind and saw in my inward eye each happening of that afternoon, and for the life of me I could think of nothing remotely resembling the suspicious.

Yet one fact remained. Maroulis hadn't expected someone like myself at that séance, and my presence there had made him wonder. His telephoning had been done after he had spoken to me—that seemed fairly certain—for he had spoken to Adeline and she had gone with him out of the room, and for the purpose presumably of showing him the whereabouts of the telephone. And the only connection thereafter between me and Maroulis had been that a man had been on my tail.

And what had my fat friend been expecting when he picked me up at the corner of Ennison Square? Presumably that I should go hot-foot to the Yard with the results of an afternoon's snooping. And if I had done so, then as presumably Maroulis would have taken precautions or changed certain arrangements. And that's how vague it all was. And then I remembered that handful of literature that Adeline had given me when I was leaving, so I fetched it from my overcoat pocket with the hope that somewhere in it there might be some sort of a clue.

There was never a one. Most of it was what I might call theosophical stuff, with one four-page extract from a recent lecture by a Belgian lady who apparently spoke with authority and not as the scribes. There were advertisements for new books and, lastly, there was a kind of large visiting card:

BEYOND

THE WEEKLY JOURNAL OF NEO-QUIETISM (price 6*d*)

*President*: THE HON. ADELINE DOXON

*Managing Editor*: A. CORBEL ESQ., M.A., B.D.

You are cordially invited to call at the editorial offices
at RAIMOND HOUSE, W.C.1, where a large and comprehensive selection of literature is always available.

That told me nothing either. There was nowhere even a mention of Maroulis's name. Then I thought I heard the lift, so I put the papers in a pigeonhole of my desk. If Bernice liked to discuss the afternoon—well, that would be that. If those papers were to be an encouragement, then I'd ensure that she never saw them. As far as I was concerned, the sooner that afternoon was forgotten, the better. And since I was feeling snug and comfortable at my own fireside, the forgetfulness could include both Maroulis and my fat friend.

It was Bernice, and the amusing or exasperating thing was that she arrived with a similar packet of information to the one that Adeline had given me. It seemed to have been a custom to provide a newcomer with a post-séance interest, but I was gratified to see that Bernice took her packet out of her bag and stuffed it into a table drawer. She said she had a headache. If we had dinner at once, then she could take a couple of aspirins after it.

She disappeared in the bedroom. I ordered the meal and she didn't appear till it had been brought up. It was more than obvious that she was disinclined to talk about the afternoon, but you can't have a meal together and not talk about something. I thought it an occasion when I might reasonably set the ball rolling myself.

"Sorry about the headache," I said. "It was a rather trying afternoon."

"Yes," she said. "And Adeline can be very exhausting."

"Few people more so. And the séance itself: what did you think of it?"

"It was horrid!" She clicked her tongue in annoyance. "Even to think of it makes me go itchy and sort of dirty all over."

"Yes," I said. "It wasn't too good."

"That horrible Harebell!" she told me. "And everything so illogical. I suppose it was Chinese he was talking and yet he couldn't even speak English!"

"There were worse illogicalities than that," I said. "But what really got me was that business of Lady Georgina and the picture. She simply must have mentioned it to someone."

"Not a word to Adeline," Bernice told me quickly. "I had to pretend to her that it was at least bearable."

"It'll probably be some time before I run across her again," I said. "By the way, did you talk to that chap Maroulis?"

"I didn't like him," she said. "He was so unctuous. I think his manners are largely veneer. And I imagine he flatters himself at being a lady-killer."

I told her he was a Cypriot and wondered if she knew what his actual business was. She didn't know.

"Who were that young couple sitting on our left when we went in?" I said. "I believe the man left immediately after the séance. I saw the girl still there, but I wasn't introduced to her."

"They were the Partings—brother and sister."

"Partings?"

"You know. Sir Algernon Parting's children."

"Oh, the newspaper magnate," I said. "They looked quite a pleasant couple. The girl was quite good-looking."

"Someone told me she's Hather's private secretary. I did notice he didn't do any talking to her. And she left early. I believe her name's Phyllis."

"What about Hather's wife?" I said. "She wasn't there."

"There was just a bit of scandal being talked," Bernice told me, and as if the headache had been temporarily forgotten. "She's in a nursing home. I asked him about her and that's what he told me. He was rather short, as if he didn't want to talk about it. Then Angela Moore-Harborne told me confidentially she'd heard there was talk of a divorce. Who's divorcing whom I didn't gather."

"Ah well," I said, "I don't know the lady well, but I'd feel like congratulating her if she gets a happy release from Hather."

"Let's not talk about it any more," she said. "The whole afternoon is something I'd like to forget."

I wasn't cock-a-hoop that night: if anything, I was relieved and just a bit humble. Deep down in me I'd known that Bernice was of too fine a quality to be lured, even by Adeline, into all that cheap neuroticism. And yet I'd mistrusted her, which was why it was with myself that I was annoyed. By morning I was prepared to forget the whole thing. Strange though it may seem, I even forgot my fat friend, at least till I mounted a bus as usual in the Strand. And even then I was inclined to think that imagination had got the better of me.

I put in the whole morning with Norris, went to my club to lunch and then back to Broad Street. Bertha Munney—secretary and receptionist long before my time—spoke to me as I went in.

"Oh, Mr. Travers, someone rang you up. It was rather funny, really."

"Amusing or strange?"

"I should have said *strange*," she told me. Bertha's a good friend of mine, but she never seems to know how to take me. "It was a man, and he asked if he might speak to Mr. Travers. I asked whether it was private or business, and he said what difference did it make, so I told him you were only the chairman and if it was business I'd put him through to the managing director. If it wasn't business, I said, I could give him your private number. Or he could leave a message. He said he'd ring again. He didn't say where or who to."

"What was the voice like, Bertha?"

"Just a man's voice," she said. "Not very educated. Sounded as if he'd got a sore throat or something."

"Was it a foreign sort of voice?"

"No, it wasn't foreign. What I'd call a middle-aged voice. Very polite and all that, but no class about it."

I said we'd wait for him to ring again. If I was in, she could put him through to me, and if not, she could get his name and address. She said she hadn't got as far as that when he rang off. I said I wasn't blaming her, and we might have been explaining and apologising for minutes if I hadn't given her a pat and moved on.

But the man didn't ring again that day. Bernice didn't go out at all and no message came to the flat. Norris and I spent the next morning at accounts and still the man didn't ring. Then while I was having a drink at a nearby pub where they also give you a good old-fashioned meal, something struck me about a voice that had sounded as if its owner had a sore throat. That scarf which was wrapped round and round the throat of my fat friend—was that to protect a sore throat?

Suddenly I was thinking I'd been a bit of a fool. If I'd been followed home from that séance, and to ascertain whether or not I'd gone straight to Scotland Yard, then surely it wasn't illogical that I should have been picked up the following morning. If so, I'd been followed to a detective agency. But Maroulis didn't know that I *was* the Broad Street Detective Agency. If he were behind things, he must have been considerably alarmed to discover where I'd gone. So as soon as his man had seen me leave the office there had been some telephoning. And he must have been gratified to learn that I was connected with the Agency and hadn't gone there to put a man on someone else's tail.

For a moment I thought I might mention the matter at the Yard: then I decided, and somewhat sheepishly, that I hadn't an atom of honest-to-God evidence which I could quote. Nor had we a spare man at the Agency whom I could put, by way of counter-attack, on Maroulis's tail, nor was I absolutely sure that Maroulis had anything whatsoever to do with the business. But one thing I could do, entirely by myself.

I had to be quick, for it was getting on for midday, and on a Saturday. The man I wanted wasn't in, but his manager was. I described Maroulis to him, said his Christian name was Loucas, and asked if he could tell me anything in confidence. I was asked to wait.

Five minutes later he was telling me that Maroulis was behind the Levant Import Company, whose offices were at Raimond House, Holborn, and that was all he knew. I thanked him and rang off. I was glad to ring off. I wanted to think.

A good memory wasn't needed to recall that the offices of *Beyond* were also at Raimond House. It seemed significant, and then I did some more wondering. If Maroulis was a keen spiritualist, then mightn't he have sub-let one room, say, as editorial offices? Office room was notoriously hard to come by, and it was more than feasible. But that, in a way, left Maroulis in the clear, and I didn't want him left in the clear. Prejudice, maybe, but there it was.

But there was a way to get somewhere near an answer, so I began looking for a taxi. A quarter of an hour later I was getting out at Raimond House. In the passage I consulted the usual list of tenants. The Levant Import Company were on the first floor and so were the offices of *Beyond*.

It was well after noon and I thought I might take a chance. I had a handkerchief ready as a partial covering for my face, but I needn't have worried. No one was going up but myself, and only perfect strangers were coming down the stairs. On the landing was another notice board, and in a couple of minutes I knew that the Levant Import Company occupied the whole of the first floor, except for one room—there'd probably be another leading off it—used as the offices of *Beyond*.

Then I thought I'd risk things. After all, I'd been specifically invited to call there, and I had at least sufficient gifts of the gab to chatter about the kind of publications I was likely to see. So I tapped at the door and listened. Nothing happened.

I tried the knob, but the door was locked. Then I saw a notice below my eye level by the side of the door. It said among other things that the offices closed down at noon on Saturday.

That was that. I'd had my taxi wait and I went straight to the flat. I more or less dismissed the whole thing from my mind till the Monday, and then I rang another man and heard what he had to tell me. He said the Levant Import was a private company, and the manager was an Englishman named Cooden. As far as my informant knew, the firm carried on the usual export business and handled the usual Mediterranean products and exported what the Government allowed them in return. He'd heard Maroulis was behind the business, but he couldn't be sure. He did know he was a comparative newcomer, so to speak. Until three years ago the business was owned by the Greek firm of Gatiopolis, and apparently it had changed hands.

So that again was that. It told me little, but somehow it did serve to dull the edge of appetite. A day or two went by and, as far as I was aware, no one was interested in my movements or in what I did with my time. A week went by and I'd as good as forgotten the whole thing. A month went by and it was something that I rarely recalled.

I saw Hather at the club more than once, but found a way of avoiding him, even if it did involve some discomfort for myself. Then I saw in the *Radio Times* that he was conducting investigations in one or two ghost-ridden houses in the country and that left me free to use the club in a normal way again. We also had Quint and his wife to lunch one day. We didn't talk about the Hathers because Bernice didn't want anything brought up that might recall that dreadful afternoon at Ennison Square, but I managed to nobble Paul quietly. He had to tell me that everything about that *Man With Two Souls* affair had been hushed up, and he never ought to have mentioned the word *plagiarism*. I didn't tell him that he never *had* mentioned it, and that it was news to me.

But as I'm hinting, he was rather shying away from everything, so I didn't press it. He did mention two books of Hather's which were quite good—*The Open Gate* and *The Eighth Veil*—and I said I'd have a shot at them when I had time. And, of course, I promptly forgot all about them.

I virtually forgot about the whole thing. Something of it came back in a different context and after I'd seen that Hather was back in town, and that was when one evening I asked Bernice if she'd heard how Ursula Hather was getting on. She said she had left the nursing home. Adeline had seen her and had reported that she was looking a different person.

"What was the trouble?"

"Probably what I said," she told me enigmatically. "I rather gather it's all hush-hush."

"And that other business—the divorce?"

"That's definite," she said at once. "I still don't know who's divorcing whom, but I do know they aren't living together. They do say that Phyllis Parting is the new girl-friend."

I could have said that some men had all the luck with secretaries, but I didn't. I didn't say anything, and the topic petered out. After that I don't recall more than one or two occasions when I had any recollections of the people who'd been at the séance on that October afternoon. The only person I did ever think about was someone who hadn't been there at all, and that was my fat friend of the numerous chins and the swathed muffler. And when I thought about him it was rather amusedly. Bernice, who's capable of an amusing quip, once said of George Wharton, of whom she's exceedingly fond, that she'd like to have him stuffed. I couldn't quite see George even as a lachrymose kind of hall-stand, but as an expression of fondness, I saw what she meant. And that was how I was beginning to feel about that little fat man who might or might not have been following me.

Well, as I said, time can dull the edge of most things. November came in and went on its way. I was busy enough at the Agency, even if there was no murder case that demanded the attention of Chief Superintendent George Wharton. November almost went, and we came to its last Monday, which was the twenty-eighth.

In another month, I was thinking, we should have had another Christmas—a melancholy thought for a man who occasionally thinks of the past and finds his future growing shorter.

My newspapers arrive early; Boyland, the manager of the flats, always sees to that. And that Monday morning I happened to be up rather earlier than usual. On most mornings I wake just before seven, switch on the electric kettle and make a cup of tea, order breakfast, go to the bathroom first and then have a first look through the papers. After breakfast I have a pipe and read the news more closely, and then I hop a bus in the Strand and get to Broad Street as near to nine o'clock as makes no difference.

But that morning I was up early, and because I hadn't slept with my usual wakelessness. I went to the bathroom before making tea and then I took my cup to the lounge—a horrible word, but what else can one call it?—and lighted a cigarette and began running an eye over the news. I saw the paragraph on the front page of *The Telegraph*:

## FAMOUS SPIRITUALIST DEAD
## GUN FOUND IN FLAT

The body of Mr. Martin Hather, the well-known spiritualist and psychic investigator, was discovered last night in his flat at River View, Millbank, which he also used as offices. It is understood that a gun was found in the room.

Mr. Hather had only recently been engaged on a series of researches. . . .

The rest of it didn't interest me. It was something of a shock. You see a thing like that in cold print, and for a moment it just isn't true. And rather incongruously I thought that his flat wasn't in Millbank. I was certain he lived at a handsome block of flats in Westminster: South Mansions, or something like that. In any case, I could find out.

I was right. The telephone directory quoted South Mansions. Not that it mattered, and once more it was incongruous that I should be mildly amused at my hatred of loose ends. And then

I began to think. I found myself polishing my glasses. I blinked a bit before I put them back, and then I made for the telephone.

Wharton hadn't arrived, they told me at the Yard. I asked about two other people before I got someone who could help me.

"Targe is in charge of things," I was told. "You know Targe."

I knew him well enough. Almost as massive as George Wharton, but with none of George's little tricks. Quiet and careful moving—that was Chief Inspector Targe. Deceptively quiet, perhaps.

"I've got some private information that might be of use," I said. "Is he still round there?"

"He was here a few minutes ago. He's just gone back there. He thinks everything's open and shut."

"All the same, I think I'll see him," I said. "Purely privately, of course."

It was a bit of a job telling Bernice why I wasn't waiting for breakfast, then I didn't bother about the lift but doubled down the stairs. I was in such a hurry that I almost doubled to the garage, and I drove my own car to Millbank. It couldn't have taken me more than five minutes to get there.

4

# NO SHADOW OF DOUBT

WHEN I FIRST saw 31 River View, I couldn't help remembering an April day of far too many years ago. I was a small boy and I'd gone for a walk with my dog. In one of our Suffolk lanes I had been overtaken by a tremendous shower, and I took shelter under a holly tree. When the shower passed and I set off homewards, I came to what seemed to me a miracle, for there was a spot where you could put one foot on wet and the other on dry. I remember I burst into the house, full of this extraordinary phenomenon. My father smiled dryly. He told me the rain had to stop somewhere. All I'd done was to arrive at that spot.

There had been plenty of bombing in Millbank, but it had to stop somewhere, and No. 31 was where it had stopped. That two-storied house rose sheer, as it were, with a bare wall against an acre or two of desolation. To its left stood the remaining seven houses of the road. To its right there was nothing but that cleared space which seemed to have become an unofficial car park. A police car stood just off the road and almost against that sheer side of the house. Other cars were later to be scattered about, and some a good hundred yards back where there was another road. I hope I've made that layout simple. I want you to bear it in mind.

It had been a misty, almost foggy night, and at that hour of the morning it was only just light. I ran my car in alongside Targe's, and I shivered as I got out. There was certainly a view of the river, if only of the cranes that rose in the mist above a wall. There was a sort of muffled quiet, and then the clip-clop of a pony as a milk-float came by. I went the few yards to the road where a uniformed constable was pacing up and down. He stopped me as I came to the gate, for there was a tiny concrete strip where there'd once been garden between house and road. I said I had to see Chief Inspector Targe. He took my name and said he'd see.

I had a quick look at the house itself. It was in a pleasant backwater, and in summer it must have been fine in the upper rooms with a grand view of the river. And Hather, I saw, must have occupied that top floor, for the original windows of the bottom front had been made into one large window of opaque green glass. On it was painted:

*THE ANIMAL DOCTOR*

and on the brickwork at the side was a notice of hours of attendance.

The constable was calling for me to come, so I went up the couple of steps and into a widish passage from which rose a short flight of stairs. Targe stood on the landing waiting for me. He held out his hand.

"Only just heard you were coming, sir. Didn't expect you so soon."

I said it was nice to see him, and it was. And I told him why I'd come. I insisted I was purely a private citizen who knew a little about the dead man, and possibly things that some people either didn't know or wouldn't admit. He said that was good of me. I added that I didn't want to raise any hopes. I'd tell him what I knew and he could estimate its value.

We had moved on to what was evidently Hather's workroom, for there were plenty of books and filing-cabinets, and a desk with an antique corner chair. A table was strewn with papers and literature, and a telephone and a jacketed typewriter stood on another table by the window. The mist was still heavy along the river, and there was only just a dull irregularity that marked the buildings on the far side.

Targe switched on the handsome electric fire, and he took his time over it. That was like him, as I've said, and it wasn't that his mind worked slowly. He could be as quick in the uptake as most. He was a queer bird in some ways: a family man—as Wharton liked to be thought—but with now and again a disturbingly salacious mind.

"Just what sort of information were you thinking about?" he asked me.

"Something else you must judge for yourself," I said, and waved a hand at the chalk outline on the floor. "That where you found him?"

That was where, but with a slight difference. There had been a tiny seeping of blood from his head to a small Turkey rug. The rug had gone to the Yard but ought to be back at any minute. The blood had been Hather's, he said. I asked him to tell me all about it. I said that what he told me might make all the difference to what I knew. He gave a look at that. I added that till I knew the bare facts I couldn't judge what was relevant. He began telling me.

A 999 message had reached the Yard at five minutes past nine on the previous—Sunday—night. It had said that something suspicious was going on at 31 River View, Millbank, and advised immediate investigation. That was all. It was a man's voice and probably disguised, for it had sounded as what had been described as muffled up. Targe didn't add what I knew— that even a message as anonymous as that would have to be investigated. He said a couple of cars had arrived, and that the front door was locked but the back one open.

He himself had been pretty quick on the job and had been at work on it most of the night. A gun had been loosely in Hather's right hand and there'd been a message. Time of death was approximately midday.

"What was the message?"

"The original's at the Yard," he told me. "This is a photostat I've just collected. You needn't worry about handling it."

I had my gloves on in any case. I remember how strange I felt as I took it: Hather so nearly in my mind, and the vague significance of those chalk marks against my feet.

As there are other worlds and this one has become so dull a place, it seems folly to endure boredom. *Vale atque ave.*

I must have been staring at it. I read it again. I read it the third time.

"No signature?"

"No signature," he told me.

"His handwriting?"

"It corresponds with what we've seen," he said. "But we're waiting just to make sure."

"What about the paper?"

He went to the table by the window and opened a drawer. In it were all sorts of papers, but there was also a writing pad. It was a fine quality paper and light grey.

"No envelopes?"

He shook his head.

"Prints?"

"His were on it, and on the sheet he used. All absolutely regular. Just as they'd be when he wrote on it and tore the sheet off. Two sets on the pad, one a lot older than the other. Probably those of the one who wrapped it up for him. The older prints could be when it was handled wherever he bought it."

"Any other writing-paper?"

There were two kinds: one a white parchment, apparently for business, with address and telephone number, and the other a pale blue, headed paper of superb quality. That was in boxes in his desk and there was a faint scent, like violets, when I lifted the lid of a used box.

"Anything important in the other rooms?" I wanted to know.

"Have a look for yourself, sir."

A door on the right opened on a smallish room with typist's table and what I might call all the appurtenances of the stenographer's trade. A woman's beret and raincoat hung from a hook. Part of the room had been cornered off to make a tiny lavatory with wash-basin. I let the hot-water tap run for a minute, but the water was still cold.

"Seen the secretary?" I asked him.

"As a matter of fact I'm waiting for her now," he told me.

We went back and just along the passage. A door to the left opened into Hather's bedroom. It had a lacquered four-poster with silk drapings, and a lacquered suite with a kind of *famille verte motif*. Chinese prints were on the walls and a Chinese carpet on the floor. Another door opened into a bathroom-lavatory that was all in celadon green.

"There must have been a woman to clean the place up," I said as we went back to the bedroom.

"The secretary ought to tell us," he said. "A bit of a sybarite, wasn't he."

He had waved a casual hand at the unmade bed, and the silk pyjamas that had been thrown carelessly on it.

"A gentleman who dabbled in spiritualism a lot, so they tell me."

"Yes," I said. "That's one of the things we might have to talk about."

"You haven't seen anything yet," he told me. "Have a look at this. Just as it was, except the light wasn't on."

The light was fluorescent and what they call cunningly concealed. It was a much larger room that had probably once been a best bedroom. Now its walls were hung dose with black drapery, which was broken all round by a series of pedestals on which stood marble or bronze busts. I spotted Socrates and Confucius and those were all I could identify. On the jet-black carpet close to the draperies and between the pedestals stood a score of things—a glazed pottery Buddha two feet high, a Tibetan praying wheel, a tiny Roman sarcophagus with a broken lid, several devil masks, two Byzantine icons—in fact the devil knows what.

"Queer smell in the room," I said. "What is it? Incense?"

"That's about it," he said. "There's some of it in that table drawer and one of those burner things."

The table was at the far end of the room against the plain black draperies of the back. It was an exotic-looking table in dark lacquer, and on it anything might have been placed. Some few feet in front of it was a praying rug.

"To the Unknown God," I said.

"What's that, sir?"

"Just thinking aloud," I told him. "Any other rooms?"

"Just this," he said and we went back and through a door to a small kitchen with enamelled-top table, sink, a cupboard or two and one of those stoves that heat a room and water. The room was icily cold and in the sink were a dirty cup and saucer and some plates.

"Just the usual water tank up there," he told me and nodded up at a trap door. "Coke bin's outside."

We heard the sound of feet. We went out to the passage.

"There you are, Jack," Targe said. "Everything all right?"

"Probably be along about nine."

"Sergeant Bodney," Targe told me. "Jack, this is Mr. Ludovic Travers."

Bodney said he knew the name, and for some reason he grinned.

"Mr. Travers is going to tell us a thing or two," Targe confided.

"Who's the she who's coming along?" I asked bluntly.

"The secretary," Targe told me.

"How'd you get on to her?"

Targe allowed himself to smile.

"Well, sir, as the Old General would say"—that was Wharton's nickname at the Yard—"ways and means. Found an old envelope with her name on. Made enquiries, and there we are."

"That charwoman's outside," Bodney said. "Want to see her now?"

"Bring her in," Targe told him, and we went back to Hather's room.

She was a respectable-looking woman of about sixty, well wrapped up against the cold. Her name was Straker. What it was all about she had no idea. Targe had put one of the rugs over the chalk outline and he told her Mr. Hather had died rather suddenly. We were just making the usual enquiries. She moistened her lips and kept looking from one of us to another, but she said nothing.

"Just tell us about your work here," Targe said. "Your hours and so on."

Something emerged. Her normal hours were from five in the evening till when she'd finished, which was usually about seven. That included Sundays as well, but on Saturday night Mr. Hather had told her to skip the Sunday and look in on Monday morning for an hour or so. He said he mightn't be in till ten.

"That ever happen before?"

She said it hadn't, not all the two years she'd been working there.

"What time on the Saturday night did he tell you that?"

"When I got here," she said. "Wasn't often he was in on a Saturday. He was sitting there, at that table, and when I come in he was putting something away in that drawer as if he'd been writing or something."

"Was Miss Parting here?"

"Oh, she never come on Saturdays. Only other days."

"And what did Mr. Hather do after he spoke to you?"

"I don't know," she said. "I suppose he went out. I did the bedroom first, and when I come in here he'd gone out. I never saw him again."

"I see. And do you know anything about his meals?"

"Well, he didn't have any breakfast, not worth speaking of. Them con—con—"

"Continental breakfasts?" I suggested.

"That's it," she said. "That's what he once told me himself. Just a bit o' toast what he'd make himself. Sometimes nothing but coffee. He liked strong black coffee."

"What about his other meals?"

"He always went out."

"And Miss Parting? She went out, too?"

"Oh yes. She always went out, too."

I saw another question on Targe's lips, but he didn't ask it. He said that'd be all. If Mrs. Straker would give her address, she could go home, and he doubted if she'd be wanted again. He'd put Miss Parting in touch with her about any future arrangements.

"What was that question you thought of asking her but didn't?" I put to him as soon as she'd gone.

"Well," he said, and rubbed his stubbly chin, "I wondered if this Hather always slept alone in that room of his. Then I thought I'd wait and hear what you had to tell me."

I said it was nothing like that. Then he was picking up that photostat of Hather's last message.

"I'm not much of a Latin scholar, you know, sir, but isn't there something peculiar about this bit of Latin? Oughtn't it to be the other way round? *Ave atque vale* and not *vale atque ave*?"

"Not in this case," I said.

Wharton, by the way, often accuses me of being the world's lightning theoriser. According to him, any one of the world's eternal mysteries could be fired at me—what became, for instance of the *Marie Celeste* or Atlantis—and I could come back with an answer in a flash, and one that was practically always wrong. My contention is that first impressions are always best, and that I'm right far more often than he cares to admit.

"Let's look at it this way," I told Targe and Bodney. "His interests were almost entirely the occult. The sort of stuff we saw in that room. Life beyond the grave, to put it crudely. If he was genuinely bored with this life and wanted personal experience of the next, then first of all he'd say goodbye to this and then greet the next. *Farewell*, as the Latin has it, followed by *hail*."

"Yes," Targe said. "That's a pretty smart deduction, sir. I missed it." He rubbed his chin again. "On the whole, then, and if the writing proves to be his, you'd say everything was in keeping?"

"In the light of what I've said, obviously in keeping."

"And yet it isn't?"

That was a shrewd thrust. I parried it.

"I didn't say so. In any case I'd like to hear what that secretary says. You'll know what I mean as soon as she's questioned."

"Just as you wish, sir. No hurry." He turned to Bodney. "Have a look round in the back there and see if you can make some coffee. Don't know about you, Mr. Travers, but I could do with a cup."

I said I'd had no breakfast and he hollered to Bodney to scrounge something to eat. He offered me his cigarette case, but I didn't feel like smoking.

"Sit down and rest your feet, sir," he told me. "As you're going to be here when this secretary arrives, there's something you ought to know. I had thought of keeping it to myself. I suppose, by the way, you've seen her?"

I said I had. I told him where and when. I described her, and I added that as her father—he was a widower—was wealthy, she was probably one of those sensible women who preferred congenial work to nothing but killing time.

"Good-looking, was she?"

"Not strikingly so, but attractive-looking. Carried herself well. Plenty of what one calls class about her."

"A thoroughbred."

"That's it. A thoroughbred."

"Then it mightn't have been her after all," he told me. "Probably wasn't. Not that we shan't know."

"What *is* all this?" I said, and tried to make it amusedly. "What will you know?"

"Who the woman was who rang up last night just after I got here."

I won't pretend that didn't surprise me.

"I'll tell you what happened," he said. "That telephone went and I picked up the receiver. I've got a technique of my own: learned it years ago when I got into trouble for opening my mouth too wide. So I just sort of grunted. Then a woman's voice said—"

He said he had the exact words. He found the place in his note-book.

"She said, 'Darling, whatever's happened to you! Here I've been ever since lunch driven nearly crazy. Whatever's happened?' Then I gave another little grunt and it didn't work. She said. 'Who's that speaking?' I said, in a voice not my own, that Mr. Hather wasn't there at the moment. 'Who are you?' she said, and then before I could open my mouth she rang off."

"Trace the call?"

"It's being done now," he said. "But that isn't all. It went again about half an hour later. I tried a new kind of grunt, but she rang off straight away."

"But you think it was the secretary?"

"That's right. That *darling* stuff doesn't mean a thing to people like her. I may be wrong, mind you."

Bodney came in with three cups of coffee and some dry biscuits. Targe took a sip of his, said it was hot, and then the telephone went.

"Speaking," Targe said, and then came a yes or two. Then he said he'd hold on. Bodney and I sipped the scalding hot coffee.

"I'll take that down," Targe suddenly said, and lugged out his note-book with his free hand. "Anvil House Hotel, Cockfosters. . . . You don't say! Right. Goodbye."

"Couple of bits of news," he told us. "You read the *Radio Times*, Mr. Travers?"

I said I noted the few things to which I wanted to listen. One could count them on the fingers of a hand for most weeks.

"Happen to notice the Third Programme for last night?"

I said I didn't.

"This Hather was down for a talk at nine o'clock. That's what the *Radio Times* said. But he wasn't, if you get me. It was cancelled and an announcement put out during the week. It was put forward to next Sunday, same time. That's just been checked."

I didn't see it for a moment or two.

"You mean he was set free to meet whoever it was who was anxious about him?"

"That's the point," he told me. "And another thing's just been checked. Those two calls last night came from a quiet little private hotel at Cockfosters. A man telephoned on Friday and made a reservation there for from midday yesterday, just for the night. Gave his name as Harper. The lady arrived all right, and booked as Mrs. Harper and lunched there. Said her husband'd be coming later. She's the one who did the telephoning. She slept alone in a twin-bedded room there last night."

We chewed on that for a bit, but didn't say much. I asked about prints. Targe said the place had been full of prints. The only place there weren't prints was where there should have been, and that was on the open back door. I asked to see it.

The door was in the kitchen and iron steps led to it from ground level. There was a Yale lock and someone had been in and gone out and forgotten to put on the catch.

"But he had sense enough to wipe the knob," I said.

"Yes," he said, "and the one who did it was the one who'd dialled the Yard that something fishy was going on."

"I'm more interested in how he got in than how he got out."

"Must have been a friend of some sort," Targe said. "Must have had his own key. The only prints on Hather's keys were his own." He shrugged his shoulders. "That'll be something else for that secretary."

Bodney was washing the cups. We went back to Hather's room. Targe told me no calls were being put through except those from the Yard.

"Something I've been thinking about," he said. "Something arising out of what that Mrs. Straker told us. Did this Hather know on the Saturday what he was going to do? Had he made up his mind to do himself in, and did he want no one but her to find his body?"

"Looks like it, on the face of it," I said.

"Then something else," he said, and gave me a dry smile. "If that's so, I'm darned if I know what it is you want to tell me."

"You mean, the further we get, everything's the more open and shut?"

"Well, sir, how's it strike you yourself?"

I said I wasn't inclined to disagree. It looked as if I'd made myself very much of a busybody. All the same, I thought I'd like to listen to the secretary. Then the telephone went again.

He gave a yes, then cupped the receiver.

"The wife on the line, via the Yard!"

"Yes," he said, and listened. Then it was not too hard to guess what was said. There were condolences and something about an hour or so's time.

"Hadn't seen the paper till just now," he told me. "A shock and all that. I'm seeing her when we've finished with that secretary. Wish to God she'd come. It's best part of half-past nine."

We'd only a minute or two to wait. He'd begun asking me about séances—to kill time, as I thought—and I'd just begun giving a kind of background, when there were feet on the stairs. Targe slipped out at once.

"Miss Parting?" I heard him say.

"Yes," she said, and it was the first time I'd heard her speak.

"Glad you've come," he said, and was introducing himself as he ushered her into the room.

"Not a nice morning, Miss Parting," he told her cheerfully.

"A wretched morning."

He introduced Bodney and myself, and gave me a nod and a wink. That must have meant that he'd identified the voice.

"Sit here, Miss Parting, will you?" He drew the corner chair out from the desk. "Just make yourself comfortable. We shan't keep you more than a few minutes."

As soon as I'd seen her I'd guessed that she knew. Her face was pale and, though there was no trace of tears, there was a blackness beneath the eyes. She had given me a look as if she vaguely remembered me, then decided apparently that she didn't. Now she was looking at me again. I thought I might as well help to put everything on a friendly basis.

"I think I saw you at a séance one afternoon at Adeline Doxon's," I told her, and gave what I hoped was a friendly smile. "You may have noticed me there."

She gave a little smile, and nodded, then she was waiting for Targe to speak. But for the fingers that toyed nervously with the crystal knob of her handbag, you'd have thought she was utterly at ease.

5

# THE OTHER MAN'S JOB

"You've seen the morning papers?" Targe began.

"Yes," she said, and her eyes for a moment fell. "I bought one on the station while I was waiting for the train."

"You've been away?"

"Yes," she said again. "I was spending the week-end with an old school friend at Sevenoaks. That's where I bought the paper. I didn't read it till I was in the train."

"It must have been an enormous shock."

"Yes," she said. She said it very quietly and her eyes lowered again. "An incredible shock."

"So I imagine," Targe said heavily. "How long have you been working here, Miss Parting?"

"Just under a year."

"Plenty of work?"

"Heaps," she said. The danger of discovery had gone and she ventured on a smile. "Sometimes too much. Dictation and typing and working on manuscripts or research stuff."

"You were trained for the job?"

"Yes," she said. "I'd thought at first of going into one of Daddy's departments, then I saw Mr. Hather's advertisement and I tried this instead."

"You liked it?"

"I loved it."

I like studying another man's technique. Targe was good, I was thinking. But what came next was something worthy of Wharton. He had to assure her that no one in that room had ever heard her voice.

"Well, we're lucky to have someone like you to help us," he told her. "Especially in one little matter that's been puzzling us. I don't want to distress you, but Mr. Hather died at about midday yesterday. Long after that—very late in the evening, in fact—we have an idea that someone was in this room."

The weariness changed to surprise.

"Any idea who it could have been?"

"I couldn't possibly imagine."

"We've all puzzled our wits over it," he said, "and all we know is that he or she must have had a key. Can you tell us who had keys? Naturally you had one yourself."

"I have one here in my bag."

"The bag wasn't out of your possession this week-end?"

"Not for a moment. I mean not more than one's bag usually is."

"So I guessed," he told her. "And we've seen Mrs. Straker. And Mr. Hather's key was on him. Any other keys?"

Her eyes narrowed slightly.

"I couldn't say. It's possible that his—that Mrs. Hather still had a key."

"Of course," he said. "I'd forgotten Mrs. Hather. I'm seeing her this morning and I'll mention it. Any other keys?"

She could think of no more.

"Then it's still a mystery," Targe said. "Not that it matters. But about the actual tragedy. I repeat that we don't want to distress you, but can you think of any reasons why he should decide to take his own life?"

"None," she said. "It was incredible!"

The pale face had flushed. A moment, and she knew she was being too emphatic. The voice was almost inaudible as she added that she still couldn't believe it.

"Let's look at it another way," Targe said. "And while I'm on the subject, may I say that we hope to spare you the ordeal of the inquest. But, as I was saying, let's look at it the other way. Do you know any reasons why he shouldn't have taken his life?"

"He just wasn't that kind of man," she told us quietly. "I ought to know after working with him all these months. I believe his financial affairs were in order. I don't think he had a worry. And he was still young. He had all his life before him."

"Yes," Targe said heavily. "You just can't account for things. But it happened. In our minds there isn't a shadow of a doubt."

He went to his attaché-case and brought out that photostat.

"This is a photograph of the message he left. Will you just look at it and say if it's his writing?"

She was moistening her lips as she took it. You'd have expected her to give no more than a glance, but she read it. There was a quick frown when she came to that Latin tag at the end.

"Yes," she said. "It's his writing."

"No doubt whatever?"

"None," she said. "You couldn't mistake his writing—not when you've seen it as much as I."

The telephone went. One or two monosyllables from Targe and he was in his chair again.

"Well, there's that message," he said. "He wrote it. The gun was in his hand. There's an easy and definite proof whether or not he fired the gun. It's known as the paraffin test. That telephone call was to say the test had been made and he did fire the gun. Which reminds me. Did he have a gun?"

"Never. I think he hated weapons. I've heard him say so."

"This was quite a little gun. What's known as an automatic. A Belgian one. The sort of thing he could have carried in his pocket."

She had nothing to add. He let out a breath and got to his feet again.

"In this drawer is the pad from which he tore the sheet on which he wrote that last message. I wonder if you'd tell us if you've seen the pad before. The cover, or whatever you call it, was taken off by us. It had his prints on it."

"I've never seen it before," she told him. "But why should he need it? There's every kind of paper here."

"Did you ever clear this drawer out?"

"Well, no." She smiled rather lamely. "I never went to any drawer unless he actually asked me. I had practically everything I wanted in my own room."

"That's what I guessed," Targe said. "The pad might have been there long before you came here."

He glanced at his watch.

"I think that's almost all. Except if you can tell us anything about his movements. When'd you actually see him last?"

"On Friday. I left at about five."

"Know what he did at any time after that?"

"I know about Saturday evening. He was at a school dinner. I think it was at Pergoletti's. Mr. Hather was at Felsbury, you know."

"That'd mean a latish night," I said, and she gave me a little smile for suggesting it.

"And the Sunday?"

She had to move warily there. It was a moment or two before she spoke.

"If he was late on the Saturday, then he'd probably want a good rest."

"There wasn't anything on the engagement pad," Targe said. "In fact there was a rather peculiar thing. Just have a look at it. The page, including the Sunday, has been tom off for the whole week!"

She stared at it.

"It *is* extraordinary," she said. "I know there were at least two engagements on it. And look here. There're heaps of engagements ahead."

"Well, there we are," Targe said. "What his reason was we'll never know."

He had another look at his watch.

"Just one last thing. Did quite a lot of people come up here?"

"From time to time, yes. This was his office. He saw people here. He saw other people at their offices, of course, but quite a lot used to come here."

"Well, I think that's about all," Targe said. "Keep your key, Miss Parting, and come here for anything you want. Sergeant Bodney will be here if I'm not. Later on you can hand the key in. And if you can be here again at, say, two o'clock, I'd like to get information about his solicitors, and so on. And I may ask you to make out a list of all the people who've been here. You might think about that perhaps."

She shook hands with Bodney and me, and she was trying to be quite bright and cheerful. Targe went out with her.

"All men are liars," Bodney said to no one in particular. "Must have been a woman who made a crack like that."

Targe might almost have heard it. It was five minutes before he was back and he seemed to resume where Bodney had left off.

"Well, that's that then, sir." He spread his palms in a sort of helplessness. "What could I do? No point in telling her she was a liar."

"I think your handling was first-class," I told him. "I quite agree. It looks a genuine suicide, so why smear that week-end over the pages."

"That's how I saw it," he said relievedly. "I think she co-operated very well. A bit nervous, of course, wondering just how much we knew."

"You think everything's okay, then, sir?" Bodney put in.

"On the whole, yes."

"And what about what you came here to tell us, sir?"

That was Targe again. I said he had me up a gum-tree.

But I told him the precise kind of man I thought Hather was, and I backed it up with instances.

"There you are, then," he said. "He was one of those neurotics. Nerves all strung up. That's the way these cocksure people always are. They get to the state where one last brain-storm means the end."

"I was thinking about that engagement pad and trying to work it out," Bodney said. "I think that's another proof. He knew this week wouldn't matter, so he ripped the page off."

"You found it in the waste-paper basket?"

"Mrs. Straker emptied it on the Friday," he said. "That's when he must have torn it off."

I merely nodded.

"And that writing-pad," Targe said, and got quite worked up. "I can see him, sir, waiting for pluck enough to fire the shot. He sort of walks round, opening drawers and so on, just as nervous people do. He sees that old pad and that turns the trick. Then he writes that message."

"Any impression on the page underneath?"

"Just a slight one. You can see it for yourself. It was written with a pen, not a pencil. They've checked the ink with what was in his pen."

"Good enough," I said. "The only other thing I ought to tell you is about his divorce. Or do you know about that?"

He didn't, so I told him what I knew. We agreed it made no particular difference, except that it might have contributed to the general brain-storm.

"Where does Miss Parting live?" I asked him.

She lived at Lancaster Gate. Sir Algernon was an invalid—crippled with arthritis—and she had her own rooms in the house. That's where Targe had enquired, and he'd been told that she was spending the week-end with friends but was expected back early that morning.

"Well, I'll be jogging along," I said. "Sorry I wasn't any help."

"Not at all, sir," Targe was good enough to tell me. "You didn't know all that we knew. There *might* have been something fishy. And that divorce tip might come in handy. Which reminds me. I ought to be getting along myself."

I shook hands, said I could find my own way down, and then I got into my car as I said. When I reached the Yard I didn't get out at once. I sat on for a good five minutes, thinking and jotting down notes.

* * * * *

As I've told you, I gave Wharton a much more detailed version of what I knew about Hather. I even told him about that séance in some detail, but with never a word of what came after. If I'd told him about my fat friend it would have set a different key. He wouldn't have taken it seriously, and that would have coloured what was to come. As it was, he seemed interested, and his nod was quite judicial when he asked how it all tied up with the suicide.

"This has to be, of course, between our two selves," I said. "I saw Targe as a private citizen. It's his job, not mine—or, for that matter, yours. So let's imagine we're sitting in my place over a bottle of beer and we've nothing to do with the Yard. We might be discussing a film we've just seen."

"Why not?"

"Right," I said, and went carefully over everything that had happened at River View. I gave facts and made no comments, but I must have been talking for half an hour.

"Well, Targe seems on top of the job," he said. "But speaking in a private capacity, wasn't there something wrong about that writing-pad?"

I knew what he meant. But George loves climaxes and effective curtains, so I raised my eyebrows enquiringly.

"Don't tell me you didn't spot a thing like that," he said. "He wrote that last message on the pad. Then he tore off the sheet. Why?"

"Lord knows," I said. "He could have left the whole pad."

"And who put it back in the drawer?"

That was his climax.

"Targe obviously imagines Hather did," I said. "Who else could have put it there? Though why a man who's balanced on the deep end and is just about to take a dive into eternity should bother to be tidy is something I find a bit queer."

Strangely enough he didn't comment on that.

"Perhaps he was still making up his mind even after he'd written the message," was what he said.

I thought he was shifting course a bit, but I had to agree.

"One other thing strikes me," he said. "Not that it's important. Someone went in the house at about nine o'clock last night and saw the body. Why they went then was because they relied on the information in the *Radio Times*. They knew Hather'd be at Broadcasting House."

I asked him to sum up.

"Well," he said, "from what you've told me, this Hather wasn't a very nice specimen. And from what I've picked up in the course of a good few years, I think this psychic stuff is nothing but a dirty racket. Mind you, I'm not saying your friend Miss Doxon's anything but genuine. She's just the sort the wise boys in the racket like to get hold of."

"And from the evidence you think Targe is right in taking everything as open and shut?"

"From the evidence—yes. Message in his handwriting, gun in his hand and prints right, and he fired the gun. What more do you want?"

I hardly knew what to say. I think I must have smiled a little wanly.

"I think I'd like to be left with not one single possible doubt. I'm not cleverer than the next man, George. I don't see things that other people miss. I just see what I see and hear what I hear."

"Oh?" he said, and gave me a bit of a glare. "Then why not get it off your chest."

I took out the envelope on which I'd scribbled those notes.

"First Hather himself," I said. "I agree with Phyllis Parting that he wasn't the suicidal type. He loved himself far too much. He had his own little world and he was on top of that world."

George grunted. As an opening it wasn't too good.

"Now the message he left," I went on. "It consisted of one rather cheaply cynical statement, and a Latin tag. I'll be highbrow and call it a miniature of one of Hather's possible poses. I think most people would say it's just the thing that Hather would have written, and I can't help thinking such an opinion very superficial. May I put a question or two?"

"Carry on," he told me largely, and there was a definite smirk as he said it.

"This first," I said. "He didn't give a damn for his wife. He was divorcing her or she him. But I gather he did think a considerable deal of Phyllis Parting. But when I read that last message of his I could find nothing in it for her."

George shrugged his shoulders. He didn't think much of that either.

"Let's take the position as it was at midday yesterday, when Hather committed suicide," I said. "He'd arranged to spend from that midday till the next morning with her. He knew she'd be waiting for him at that hotel. Surely only a sadist would have shot himself and left never a word. No mention of circumstances. No mention of forgiveness."

I checked him as he went to speak.

"Let me add something else," I said. "Bodney's theory that he knew well beforehand what he was going to do, and fixed things so that Mrs. Straker would find his body on the Monday morning, is excellent on the face of it. I don't say it's what he and Targe *want* to believe. I merely see it in a different way. I say that Hather changed Mrs. Straker's times because, as he told her, he wasn't getting in this morning till ten. He wanted the water warm and the place nice and tidy when he and Phyllis Parting got back. He thought that if he gave her the Sunday evening off, she wouldn't notice anything unusual about being asked instead to come in for an hour on the Monday morning."

"I agree," George said. "I'm on your side. But Targe is still right. A lot of things might have happened after he saw that charwoman on the Saturday evening."

It might have been instinctively but I'm damned if he didn't bring out those antiquated spectacles of his: the ones with the plain glass lenses that he hooks on when questioning a witness or suspect: the ones that he imagines give him a deceptively innocent air.

"You're missing the wood for the trees," he told me. "Targe thinks or knows it's a genuine case of suicide. He has what satisfies him as conclusive evidence, so why should he go chasing his own tail?" He snorted at me, then the look was suddenly crafty. "But nothing's been said about the really important thing, and that's *why*. Call Hather neurotic, overstrung—call him what you like. I ask *why* did he do it. He had that girl—an attractive girl, so you've said—waiting for him at that hotel. Yet he committed suicide. And why?" He almost spattered the word at me. Maybe he took the protective gesture for an interruption.

"You let me finish," he said. "Let's look at him. On the Saturday night he goes to an Old Boy's Reunion or whatever you call it. He's merry and bright. He comes home—easy to find out when—and sleeps at his flat. There it is," he said, and waved an ironical hand. "He wakes up and may have stayed on fairly late in bed. And then at midday he kills himself! He's no longer merry and bright. And why? Because something happened between the time when he got up and the time when he shot himself. He didn't get a letter because it was a Sunday. If one had come by the late post on Saturday night he'd have seen it. If he went out, where'd he go? If someone came to see him, who was it? That's the crux of things. *If* it was murder—and it isn't—and I was handling the case, that's what I'd concentrate on. But Targe is no fool. He doesn't need to. He knows it's a plain case of suicide."

He waved a hand of dismissal and leaned back.

"Fine!" I said, and I'd have liked to clap. "I'm with you all the way. But one other little matter. It may sound trivial after that effort of yours. But I've spent a lot of time trying to show you the exact sort of man that Hather was—a showman, a poseur, incredibly self-satisfied, conceited, self-opinionated and cocksure. A strutting little bantam-cock—"

"I got all that."

"Then tell me this," I said. "He wrote that last message—not to anyone in particular but to the world. His little world. But oughtn't he to have signed it? Signed it with a flourish? Oughtn't there to have been that last panache?"

He said it was a point. He mumbled something about people not being normal in brain-storms.

"And one last thing," I said. "I think Targe's idea of Hather prowling round the room, opening drawers and shutting them and so on, was a bit far-fetched. I don't see why such a restlessness should culminate in Hather's ripping off the top sheet from that engagement pad. Telling himself that the future didn't matter. And—mark this, George—that sheet, unless Hather burnt it, was ripped off on the Saturday. There was nothing whatever in the waste-paper basket. So the ripping off of that sheet didn't depend on what happened to Hather on the Sunday morning."

"That," he said, and pursed his lips. "Where're your brains? Hather didn't rip off that sheet. That was ripped off by whoever came in on the Sunday night. That person came in to see Hather but found him dead. Probably he was the one who'd seen Hather that morning. He saw his name on that engagement sheet, so he ripped it off and took it with him."

"Yes," I said, and I admit it was dismally. George knew about things only at second-hand and he'd seen them far more clearly than I.

"You leave everything to Targe," he told me and got to his feet. "He knows what he's up to. Always did."

I said I'd no other intention.

"And what's it all boil down to?" he asked me as he put his spectacles back in the battered case. "That Targe is certain and you're not so certain. In plain terms, you'd like to make a murder case of it. You think just because this Hather had enemies—"

"Enough to pack the Albert Hall."

"Exactly. You think that's enough to constitute murder."

"I know," I said. "Live and learn."

"What's wrong with that?" he fired at me.

"It's a good tag," I said. "So's the one about smoke and fire."

"And about fools rushing in." He chuckled at that. It sounded to him like a good one. It even sounded a bit apt to me.

"Not bad, George," I said. "I think I'll let you have the last word. Hope I haven't been boring you too much."

He gave me a look which was intended to mark concern.

"Now don't take it like that. All of us make mistakes. You're not the first by a long chalk."

We fixed up a lunch for the end of the week and parted like sworn brothers. But as I went out to my car it was that word *chalk* that came curiously to my mind: the chalk on the carpet to mark where a body had been. And somehow I was all at once possessed of a stupid obstinacy. Maybe I hadn't been quite so much of a fool. But what I could do about it all was a vastly different thing.

# 6

# STRANGE CLIMAX

QUITE A LOT of my thinking is done at night when my head hits the pillow, and it may be an ironic comment when I admit that it rarely fails to send me to sleep. That night I thought about Hather and his end and I decided to take Wharton's complacent advice. As far as Ludovic Travers was concerned, Hather could rest quiet in whatever grave he was soon to be put. I even had a blush or two for myself. I thought of Logan Pearsall Smith and that bursting of a man's ego that he mentions in *Trivia*—the man who so far unbent as to be the life and soul of the hilarious party and then, at home, away from the cocktails, and after maybe a glance into the mirror, felt the onrush of shame, and tore his hair in horror and uttered a plaintive, "Oh my God!" Maybe it was that that sent me to sleep.

I didn't go to the inquest on the Tuesday, but I read about it in the evening papers. And when I read one thing, I wished I'd been there.

You've heard Targe's evidence already and the medical evidence at second-hand, but after that there seemed to me a something queerly significant in the fact that no one appeared who saw Hather at that Old Boys' Dinner: no one, in short, who could state his mood on leaving. I don't say that what evidence there was was rigged. I just give facts and—you already know I'm biased—show that the evidence was on suicide from the word go. Mrs. Straker was there, for instance, and question and answer made it clear that Hather hadn't wanted his body found till the Monday morning. It was hinted that he didn't want to distress a very efficient and sensitive secretary, but that secretary wasn't called.

*But Maroulis was.* That was why I wished I'd been there. Not that the paper account didn't tell what there was to tell: Loucas Maroulis, described as an importer and a friend of Hather, and, like him, deeply and altruistically interested in the occult. And my dear old friend Targe! He'd thought it apt for Maroulis to tell the court that the loss of a wife had first interested him in life beyond the grave. (Snivels in court.)

Undoubtedly, Maroulis admitted, Hather had been depressed. He had spoken more than once of suicide. But Hather, he also admitted, was a man who could hide depression. And then Maroulis had the effrontery to quote in that none too perfect English of his some lines of Lionel Johnson's—that last verse of his *Precept of Silence*:

> Some players upon plaintive strings
> Publish their wistfulness abroad:
> I have not spoken of these things
> Save to one man, and unto God.

I could imagine the coroner pricking his ears at that. "You mean?"

And then Maroulis diffidently explaining. Hather didn't wear his heart on his sleeve. The deep things, the real things, the tears at the heart of things: those could be spoken of only to God—and perhaps Loucas Maroulis.

And then I could tell myself I was a fool to work myself up into such a passion. Hather was dead. The verdict was the usual one with its mention of unsound mind. And what did it matter to me in any case? I hadn't liked Hather. I ought to be glad he was dead. But I wasn't. I was indifferent to whether he was dead or alive. But there were things to which I was far from indifferent. You can't stop a nagging tooth except by a visit to a dentist. And for the doubts that still persisted in gnawing at me I had no dentist but myself.

*       *       *       *       *

On the Wednesday morning I managed to get Targe on the telephone. I congratulated him on finishing the case and said I had something purely personal to ask him about, though in the same connection. We made a rendezvous for coffee at a little place near Westminster Bridge.

I was prepared to lie unblushingly, and I certainly was off to a good start. As soon as the coffee and cakes had come, I mentioned Ursula Hather.

"You're going to despise me for this," I said. "Or being a married man, will you know what I'm getting at? It's like this. Mrs. Hather's a sort of friend of my wife and you know what women are."

"Should do, sir," he told me. "I've had enough experience."

"You'll not be betraying confidences," I said. "You tell me what I want to know and I'll twist the facts round so that no one knows where they came from. About Mrs. Hather, then. Where's she living now?"

He made no bones whatever about telling me everything: far more, in fact, than I'd have dared even circuitously to ask. The house at River View had always had a bedroom, it appeared, in case Hather was working late and found it convenient to stay there instead of going to the South Mansions flat. Targe said that was a posh place. And he added salaciously that Mrs. Hather must have been several kinds of a fool.

"Look, sir: it's only ten minutes' walk from River View to South Mansions. Do you tell me a man's so exhausted he couldn't walk that far home? That didn't kid me."

"Something behind it?"

"Of course," he told me largely. "He'd kidded *her*. Nice little place to put in a night with a lady-friend."

"Uh-huh," I said. "And where's the widow living now?"

"At that posh flat," he said, and seemed highly amused. "You see, they hadn't actually begun the divorce proceedings and he'd put off making a new will, so she comes in for everything. Between ourselves he left quite a bit. I'll bet anyone she's married again inside six months and doing herself proud on his money."

"What'd you think of her?"

"What they call a real nice piece of homework." He remembered in time that I'd said she was a friend of my wife. "Well, you know what I mean. Smart. Got up to the nines. Nice pleasant way with her, though."

"Upset at all when you saw her?"

"I think she'd been shedding a few tears," he told me. "As a matter of fact I didn't stay very long. She hadn't anything particular to tell me, and, to tell the truth, I didn't feel so comfortable. Women crying always upset me."

"Well, that's that," I said, and passed him the last slice of sandwich cake. "But leaving the gossip and getting to business. Just between ourselves, did you ever have any ideas about who it was in Hather's flat that night?"

"Well, no," he said. "There wasn't any particular point in enquiring. But I don't mind telling you we changed our minds. We think Hather left that back door open—well, not open; just off the catch. He probably opened it every morning. He did that morning, so we think, and then he didn't slip the catch on. I think that one who dialled the Yard saw someone messing about at the back. Didn't want to give his name for fear he'd be called in as a witness."

"And that was the someone who wiped off the back-door prints?"

"It had to be. Mr. Hather didn't need to wipe off any prints. Besides, he opened the door from the inside. If anyone was making an entry, it'd be from the outside."

"Hather might have gone out," I said. "But I didn't see his shoes."

"Quite clean," he said. "Well, not clean, if you know what I mean. Just as they'd be if he wore them the previous night. Which he did."

"He hasn't a car of his own?"

"Didn't like driving in London traffic, so his lady told me. Can't say I blame him."

That was all. But when we stood for the usual moment or two outside, he said the funeral was the following morning.

"Your lady going, sir?"

"I doubt it," I said. "She doesn't like funerals. She may send flowers."

"It's not a funeral, it's a cremation. Same thing in the end."

"That secretary," I said. "How's she getting along?"

"Oh, she's away and gone," he told me. "Sort of cleared up and took her belongings." He gave another salacious little chuckle. "You and I could tell a few things, sir, if ever we wrote our reminiscences."

"You bet we could," I said. Then we solemnly shook hands and I watched him move ponderously off.

No will, I was telling myself as I turned back to Whitehall. Hather didn't make a new will. He'd contemplated suicide and he'd finally fired the shot, and yet he hadn't made a new will. Nothing whatever left to Phyllis Parting. Everything going to a wife of whom he was trying to get rid.

I gave a Whartonian grunt. A man gave me a look as if he'd thought I'd given a belch. Wharton, I said to myself. What'd he say if I told him there hadn't been a new will. Then I guessed what he'd say. He'd say it was only one more bit of evidence of the distracted state of Hather's mind. And then it struck me that there was just a faint possibility that he might be right. In any case what could Wharton do about it? Unless he cared to stir up a whole lot of trouble and find himself a fool for his pains, he could do no more than I—and that was exactly nothing.

But the few minutes I'd spent with Targe had made me curiously unsettled and I didn't feel like going back to Broad Street, not that there was anything to demand my attention now that Norris and I had finished temporarily with accounts. Then I remembered something I wanted from the Army and Navy Stores, so I crossed the road and made for Victoria Street. That was how I came to meet Land.

I suppose we'd each be twenty yards or so short of the main entrance to the Army and Navy when I caught sight of him. First there was the usual don't-I-know-that-person sort of feeling, and as we drew nearer I spotted him for Land. Land, that forlorn sort of soul I'd met at the séance. But it was Land with a difference. Forlorn? Not a bit of it. His head was up and he was swinging along like a guardsman. We drew still nearer and I saw that that moustache of his was no longer droopy. Its ends had been waxed and drawn out to points like needles, and the effect was something rather rakish.

You must imagine all this in a very few seconds. It's a wide pavement there and he was on the outside and I hugging the other side ready to go in at the main entrance, and that was why he hadn't noticed me. Then a woman got in my way and I made a violent swerve, and at that moment Land and I met face to face. I saw a look of surprise, and then my momentum carried us apart.

Then I looked back, thinking that he might want to speak to me, and there he was, looking round over his shoulder. I turned and expected him to wait for me or come back the few yards to meet me. But he didn't. Suddenly he was hurrying on and nipping into the store through another door.

I told myself that was extraordinarily queer. It almost looked as if he were definitely avoiding me. Or perhaps he hadn't really remembered me. But that was absurd. I'm the sort who's once seen and never forgotten. Six-foot-three of me, and lean at that, and a hatchet face—a newspaper reporter once called it patrician—and huge horn-rims. My hair refuses to lie flat at the back, and Wharton once told me I reminded him of a secretary-bird.

Nor, when I came to think of it, did Land act like a man who had business that he'd suddenly remembered. A look at myself coming back towards him and he'd fairly bolted into the store. But I have an imp of mischief and perversity who occasionally possesses me, and this was one of his moments, so I hurried forward and went through the same door.

That huge floor is a mass of departments and I had few hopes of spotting him. But my height gives me an advantage, and as I looked across towards the perfumery counter I caught sight of him. And he caught sight of me. It was as if he was on the lookout for me just as I was for him. But at the sight of me he moved hurriedly away. People hid him and display counters hid him, and though I moved pretty quickly myself, I lost touch with him.

A minute or two and I came back towards the stairs, and then I saw him again. He was just nipping into a lift that seemed already full. The doors closed and the lift went up.

I made for the stairs with people getting in my way, and all at once it struck me that my behaviour was irresponsible, or far from dignified to say the least. So I slowed down. I made my way to the book department and I don't say that I didn't keep my eyes about me. But I saw no other sign of Land. And when I had finished my business I still kept an eye around as I went downstairs, but devil a sign of him did I see.

I was lunching at the club, so I crossed the street and waited for a bus, and all the time I was wondering what could be the meaning of that extraordinary behaviour on the part of Land. I wondered, too, which was the real Land. Was it that forlorn sort of soul who'd spoken to me after the séance in a monstrous little voice and had alluded rather pathetically to the recent death of a wife? Or was it the Land of that morning—jaunty, care-free and on top of the world? I didn't know. I did smile to myself as I found a ready theory: that it was weeks since I had seen the man and meanwhile he might have found himself another mate. And then as I sat on the bus I wondered something else. Had Land been at that séance under false pretences? Had that forlornness and the diffidence of manner and voice been nothing but a pose and disguise? And if so, what was his purpose in it all?

I didn't know. When I got to the club I didn't know, and then for a time I forgot about him. In the cloakroom I saw Paul Quint, and we arranged to sit together at lunch. And over the meal we naturally talked about Hather.

"Well, he's gone," Quint said with no assumption of grief. "The cremation at twelve o'clock tomorrow morning, I believe."

We discussed the man and we even tried to find his good points. Quint, as a critic, could find quite a few in his novels.

"Let me see," I said, and wrinkled up my brow. "Weren't you telling me confidentially some time or other about that first book of his—the one that made him? Did I gather there was a hint of plagiarism, and everything had been hushed up?"

There was no need for reticence. The laws of libel become much less fearful when one talks too freely of the dead.

"I never did get the ins and outs," Quint told me. "I had it from an American publisher who was over here, and he had it from someone else. I think there was a lot of truth in it."

"But isn't plagiarism something of a racket?" I asked him. "Aren't charges brought out of notoriety or hoping something can be made indirectly? A sort of blackmail?"

"That's fairly frequent," he said. "A best-seller is always liable to be very much of an Aunt Sally. But about Hather—I don't really know. I do remember now that everything was settled out of court. It's a devil of a time ago, mind you."

Then his brow was suddenly wrinkling.

"There was something else. It's just come back to me. I understood—maybe I was wrong—that the person who claimed a theft of ideas was a prisoner-of-war." He waved an impatient hand. "I've forgotten. Something of the sort. The whole thing might have been sheer gossip. You never know."

I didn't learn any more. It was true that he had been tremendously surprised to learn that Hather had committed suicide. According to him it was club and literary opinion generally that Hather should have been the last man in the world to choose that way out. He was far too much in love with life to wish to leave it.

"I'd have liked to see that statement he left," he said. "That might have thrown a light on things. Pity it wasn't published."

That evening I had a word with Bernice about the extraordinary conduct of Land. I recalled the man to her and she remembered him. She said she remembered him rather vividly for two reasons: one because he looked as if he needed someone to mother him, and the other because he was a fish out of water. But when I told her about that encounter outside the Army and Navy, she smiled as if she knew I must be exaggerating.

"It couldn't have been the same man," was her final explanation. "People do look very much alike, you know."

I said doggedly that I hadn't been mistaken. And she still hadn't accounted for the reactions of Land at the sight of myself.

"I thought him a fish out of water," I said. "I even mentioned him to Adeline and I believe she said a friend had asked to have him included that afternoon. I'd like to know who it was."

"That should be easy," she said. "Why don't you ring Adeline again?"

I had various reasons which I wasn't prepared to instance, but I did manage to get hold of Adeline after dinner.

"Land?" she boomed at me. "Who's Land? Never heard of the man."

I laboriously explained. I said it was that afternoon when Hather had first come to one of her séances. My first experience, too, if it came to that.

"Too dreadful about Mr. Hather," she said. "It's done a great deal of harm to the cause, you know. There was a suggestion that he should join the directorate of *Beyond*. We were going to make a really big thing of it, and now . . ."

It took me some time to get her back to what was for her very dry Land. She said she faintly remembered, but so much had happened since then. And did I realise that there were over sixty members of her circle if one included country members. I said I did realise all that, but this man Land had been specially admitted, so to speak, at the request of one of those members. She said she'd forgotten. That kind of thing was always happening. Only the other day . . .

That dreadful voice boomed on and on till in utter desperation I gently replaced my receiver. Then I fixed things so that she couldn't ring back.

"I suppose you heard every word?" I said to Bernice.

She laughed. And she must have heard, for she asked no questions.

"That woman ought to have a silencer," I said. "I'd like to rig up her dentures with a set of baffle-plates."

"Why get all hot and bothered?" she asked me sweetly. "It isn't as if this man Land really mattered. Besides, you may have scared him that afternoon. You do say the queerest things, you know, at times."

So there I was, once more the aggressor. I had a quip ready, but it wasn't uttered. I switched instead.

"By the way, what do your friends think about the *affaire* Hather?"

"I don't know that they think anything," she said. "Not people who play bridge. One or two of Adeline's friends seem to have been rather cut up."

I left it at that. But that night when waiting for sleep I thought about that séance and the men who'd been there. Hather, accompanied by Maroulis, and now Hather dead and Maroulis had given—volunteered was the better word—evidence at his inquest. Land had been there, and now he was very much of a mystery, too. Then there'd be Phyllis Parting's brother, and he'd disappeared as soon as we'd left the séance room.

"You asleep, Bernice?"

"Not yet," she told me grumpily.

"What is Phyllis Parting's brother's name? The man who was with her at that séance?"

"Ralph . . . Why did you want to know?"

"Just wondering about him. Why he didn't come in for tea after that séance."

"He had to get back to Cambridge."

"Not Oxford?"

"Cambridge," she said firmly. "He's at Trinity."

I grunted a thanks. And apparently Ralph Parting wasn't at the Home of Lost Causes, and I almost owed him an apology. But I did rather wish that there had been some mystery about him as well, for there'd been something mightily peculiar about that last of the men—the nervous young fellow who'd looked even more of a fish out of water than Land the forlorn. And I remembered how he'd given almost an Oh! and his eyes had popped when I'd given my name as Ludovic Travers. Maybe he, too, read the murder trials. And if so, he hadn't been unctuously gratified at meeting me—which had been the pose of Maroulis. Brown—I remembered the name—had been almost scared.

Then, of course, I went on from there to what had happened after I left Ennison Square that late afternoon, and it was while I was reviewing what had happened between myself and my almost forgotten fat friend that I fell asleep.

Things couldn't go on happening. That Thursday was prosaic enough, even if I did go in search of adventure. I went, in fact, to Victoria Street at a time just before that when I'd seen Land the previous day, and I hung about and did some lurking, but I saw never a sign of him.

After that I pottered about, had lunch in Coventry Street, put in the afternoon with Norris and then rang Bernice that I'd be in for tea. I bought an evening paper just before I hopped a bus, and I found what I was looking for—the funeral rites of Martin Hather.

I learned nothing new and read nothing beyond the trite and expected. It hadn't even made the front page, and there wasn't even the smallest picture. Thanks to spread headlines and large print it had been stretched to almost a column, and, as I remarked, the reporter might have taken the whole thing by guesswork, even the list of representatives of this and that society in which Hather had been interested. Most of the account was taken up by a literary obituary, little of which was news to me. I'm afraid I smiled rather ironically at the last sentence which, as a kind of after-thought, said that the dead man left a widow but no children.

Bernice had tea waiting for me and I'd just settled down to it when the telephone went. Bernice was nearer and she took it. Almost at once she was beckoning to me, and her hand was cupping the receiver.

"George Wharton!" she told me in a hoarse whisper that wouldn't have shamed Adeline Doxon.

"Hallo there, George," I said cheerily.

There wasn't a cheery answer back. I guessed he was wanting to break, for some reason or other, the next day's date for lunch, but as soon as he spoke I recognised the official voice.

"You busy?"

"No," I said equally tersely. "Why?"

"Can you be outside the National Portrait Gallery in ten minutes' time?"

"I think so. Why?"

But he'd already rung off. I shrugged my shoulders as I replaced the receiver. George was like that, and I was wishing to heaven he'd be a little less reticent.

"And I got these muffins specially for you," Bernice said reproachfully.

I said it couldn't be helped. I just grabbed a couple of muffins and chewed on them greasily in the bedroom, changed my waistcoat and pullover, washed my hands, grabbed my heavy overcoat, gave Bernice a hasty kiss, and shot out and down the stairs. Even then I made it only just in time.

George reached over and opened the door and I got in alongside him at the back.

"What is it this time?" I wanted to know.

"Something a bit fishy," he told me. "It set me thinking."

There was an answer to that, but I just waited.

"Following on that Hather business it's a bit peculiar. Remember telling me about a séance where you saw Hather? And telling me about a woman medium, a Madame Petriff?"

"What about her?"

He gave a snort. I'd cut in too far ahead.

"A bit too much about her," he said. "We're going to her place now. She's just been found strangled."

7

# THE HAPPY MEDIUM

HAMPSTEAD ITSELF is a kind of oasis in the middle suburbs, and Maple Grove can strike one, too, with something of surprise. It is not like Church Street, a flash-back, as it were, into the eighteenth century, but more of a Victorian survival. As Bernice had told me, it was handy for the Underground. After our car passed the station we went on for a couple of hundred yards, maybe, and then one turn and a second turn brought us into the quiet little road.

Its trees were planes, not maples: a kind of poetic licence perhaps. The houses had originally been smallish and detached, but now a good few of them had been converted into double flats. Number 20a was a bottom flat. It had a front door and a side door, whereas the top flat was entered by an iron staircase from the back. The small front garden belonged to the bottom flat and the slightly larger back garden to the top flat. There were also two entrance gates, plainly numbered. That on the right was Madame Petriff's as you come in from Hampstead High Street.

Our car drew in behind the other two, and Wharton and I got out. It was a clear but cold night. George's shoulders were hunched and his hands were deep in the pockets of his overcoat—the same old coat with the velvet collar. I think it was an old friend. If it had been mine I'd have used it as bait for moths.

He went between the two parked cars, gave a nod at the constable's salute, and quickened his pace along the short concrete path. At the open, lighted door he gave a holler. A man came out.

"Evening, sir. Chief Inspector Valley."

"Where is she?"

"In here, sir. This way, sir."

We went just along a passage and through a door to the left. I looked round at the room where Bernice had sat with Madame Petriff. I looked down with Wharton at Madame herself.

She lay, cheek on the carpet, slightly curled up as if she were asleep. One leg was thrust back from the black skirt and showed a black lisle stocking. Trailing behind her neck was a short length of white cord that looked like picture cord.

The door just beyond her head was open. Anders, the police-surgeon, came through. He gave Wharton a cheery nod.

"Well, what happened to her?" Wharton said.

"Blow on the back of the skull and then strangled," Anders said. "Nice clean job. Nothing messy about it."

Corpses, to Wharton and Anders, are five a penny. I don't like them. I like to know how they got to places, and then I like them out of the way. I don't even like Anders's nice clean ones. There's something grimly final about death. And corpses are rarely the problem. It's what happened to make them corpses. That's why I didn't watch while Wharton squatted by what was left of Madame Petriff. I was more interested in the room.

It was an unexpected room. I'd seen Madame and heard her speak. For all that blether about White Russians, I'd placed her as Cockney. I'd expected a snug, cluttered-up, very low-middle-class living-room, but that room was nothing of the sort. There wasn't a piece of furniture in it to which I'd have given storage room as period antique, but the chairs and chesterfield were good, the carpet good quality, the two tables not too blatantly reproduction. On the table under the bay window stood a large glass vase of expensive-looking chrysanthemums. A low book-case, filled largely with books in their jackets, stood to the left of the fireplace. The mantelshelf wasn't chock-a-block with rubbish, and the pictures were all colour reproductions of masterpieces. The one that hung over the fireplace was of one in the National Gallery—"Fortune-telling" by le Prince. At that moment it seemed an ironic comment.

"That's as near as you can get?" Wharton was asking.

"Just a bit later than this time last night," Anders told him. "Between six and eight."

"That's a devil of a gap."

"It's up to you," Anders said. "You tell me when she had her last meal and I'll pin it down all right."

"Excuse me, sir," Valley said, "but we may be able to get a bit nearer. We know she had one visitor last night."

The top flat was occupied by a Mrs. Hooby, a widow with a girl of seven. The girl, Doris, had been to tea with a school-friend and as she came home she saw someone going into Madame's side door. It was half-past six and dark, and all she saw was a figure entering the dimly lighted door and she just heard Madame's voice as the door was shut.

"Looks as if it might fit in," Wharton said.

"Like to see the little girl, sir?"

"Plenty of time," Wharton told him. "Better get your men to work. Anything found so far?"

Valley hadn't had time, and he'd waited for Wharton. He'd only looked through her handbag. Nothing unusual in it.

Wharton stepped over the body and through the door. Anders gave me a cheery nod as I followed. He frowned questioningly. He was wanting to know the particular mood that Wharton was in. I shrugged my shoulders.

"Nice clean kitchen," Wharton was saying. "A dam' sight too clean. Everything washed-up and put away."

"What'd you expect?" Anders asked him amusedly. "A couple of dirty cups? Lip-stick and finger-prints?"

"Might have been handy," George said. Anders was an old friend, but I wondered what the reactions would have been if I'd made that quip.

We looked round at nothing in particular. There were flashes as the photographs were being taken in that other room, and then George shrugged his huge shoulders and said it was cold.

"Pretty expensive, a flat in a spot like this?" he asked me.

I guessed it was. I said that Madame must have been making more out of spirits than the pubs did.

"Where's her bedroom, Anders?"

"There're a couple," Anders said. "We go through here."

We went back to the living-room. The finger-print men were at work and Valley was watching. Wharton beckoned him through to the bedroom. Anders stayed behind.

The bedroom was commonplace. A roll-top desk of some yellow wood stood to the left of the one window. The furniture was fumed oak. On the white bedspread lay a coat and hat.

"Looks as if she'd been out," Wharton said. "Hadn't time to put things away before the visitor turned up. That desk open?"

Valley said it was locked. The keys were in the handbag, but he hadn't tried them.

"How'd you get on to it all?"

Through Mrs. Hooby, Anders said. There was a good insulating layer between the flats, but she could often hear Madame Petriff moving about, and could just catch occasionally the sound of voices when she had company. But Mrs. Hooby hadn't noticed anything peculiar till that Friday morning, and at first even that wasn't too peculiar. It was that the newspaper still protruded from the letter-box and the bottle of milk was still by the door, and that was at ten o'clock. She noticed that when she came back from doing some quick shopping and all she could think was that Madame had been called away somewhere the previous night.

Valley asked leave to elaborate a bit. He wanted us to have the exact lie of the land. Mrs. Hooby's workroom, for instance. She was the widow of a warrant officer and had built up a quite flourishing dressmaking business operating in her flat. Her workroom was above the bedroom where we were.

"That's why she could hear the telephone going," Valley said, and pointed to where it stood on the desk. "Not that she paid a lot of attention to that, but then her own bell went at about eleven that morning and there was a youngish lady enquiring about Petriff. She seemed quite agitated to hear she was away. Then about three o'clock a very superior elderly lady came in a taxi. She said she had an appointment and she couldn't understand why Petriff hadn't let her know. She actually hung about in the taxi for a bit and then went away. She wouldn't leave any message with Mrs. Hooby. Then the telephone rang at regular intervals and Mrs. Hooby began to think there might be something wrong. Her little girl was out, so she slipped on a hat and coat and came and reported at the station. I happened to be there, sir, and that's all."

Wharton grunted.

"And when you first looked in here, were the curtains drawn?"

"Like they are now, sir. You can't see even a glimmer from outside. The light wasn't on, of course."

Anders's head came round the doorway.

"She can go now?"

"You ought to know," Wharton told him. "Don't forget about the clothes. Soon as—"

The telephone went. I was standing by the desk. "Uh-huh?" I said softly.

"That you, Madame Petriff?"

I cleared my throat gently.

"She isn't here at the moment. I'm a friend of hers."

"But she's back?"

"Yes, she's back."

There had been a frantic urgency in the voice. Now I thought I heard a sigh of relief.

"Can I give a message?" I said. "Who are you, for instance?"

I thought for a moment she was off the line. A second or two and the voice came again. It had changed. It held suspicion.

"Who are *you*?"

"Just a friend. But won't you come along? Madame will be here by then."

"Not till you tell me who you are."

"A friend. Just a friend."

The line went dead. I replaced the receiver. Anders was in the room and the three of them hadn't stirred while they watched me and listened. I told them what I'd heard.

"It might have been that agitated young woman who called this morning?" Wharton asked.

"Might have been," I said. "A youngish voice. More than re-lieved to hear Petriff was home."

Anders backed to the door.

"Soon as we pick up where she spent the afternoon, we'll let you know," Wharton told him. "We'll get busy on that right away."

Anders said he'd keep her on ice.


Wharton stood looking round. Then he sent Valley for the keys. There were four keys: a Yale for the doors, a key for the desk, a key for a drawer in the window table of the living-room and a smaller key that looked as if it might open a smallish box. Wharton opened the desk and pulled up the top.

Either Madame was an untidy person or someone had been there before us. A small drawer was partly open and another had been carelessly shut with a paper of some sort protruding. Wharton had a look at the powder dusting on the keys.

"No prints?"

"The faintest blur," Valley told him. "The last time they were used was with gloves on."

"Right," Wharton said and glanced at his watch. "Tell that neighbour we'd like to see her in about half an hour's time. In her flat. Ask her to keep the little girl up."

The bottom drawers of that desk were crammed with oddments of what I'd call clothing. Madame had been loth to part with anything that might reasonably be expected to come in handy. There were feathers and ribbons, pieces of material, various garments, a couple of hat shapes. There was also a really fine shawl. And in the bottom drawer of all we found something in a box—a turban. Wharton gave a pleased little grunt.

"In the old crystal-gazing line once—eh? That might give us a line on her. And damned if here isn't the crystal!"

He'd been rummaging at the drawer back and he brought it out. He balanced its weight on a palm, then he put it back.

"A photograph and description ought to bring some news," he told me. "I had an idea that that's what she might have started off as."

The urgent thing was to discover if Petriff had spent that last afternoon at home or out, so we got to work on the small drawers at the top, with George taking one side of the central partition and I the other. It was he who found the engagement book.

It was a cheap little diary book with perforated leaves. The used ones had been tom off, but on the current week was only one entry, and apparently for the woman who turned up in a taxi. She was noted in pencil as "T.G. 3.0."

"Someone named T.G. and due at three o'clock," George said. "That fits all right."

The Tuesday of the following week had an entry for a C.M. at three o'clock. George flipped over the pages, but there were no more entries. He gave me a reproachful look.

"Thought you were telling me in the car that she used to do jobs for a whole lot of circles, or what the devil you call 'em?"

"Why not?" I said. "They were regular jobs. She didn't need to write them down to remind herself. But look, George. We've got Adeline Doxon as a starting point. You ring her up, a bit pontifical, and hear if she knows of any other groups."

I told him the number and I warned him he'd have to keep her pinned down. I waited for his start when the booming voice first belaboured his ear-drums, then I left him to it and had a quick look in the other room. Valley was watching the finger-print men at work.

"Any luck so far?"

"Lousy with her prints," he told me. "One new one in the kitchen and a beautiful set on a bottle of whisky."

He led the way to the kitchen and there it was. There were two bottles on the middle shelf of a cupboard: one with just a little gin and the other a good brand of whisky that had been lowered by about a couple of tots. He showed me the prints.

"Looks as if she tippled the gin and the whisky was for a boy-friend," he said. "And he didn't come very often either."

I told him to hold those prints as if they were diamonds, and he'd better rush a photograph to the Yard, just on the off-chance. Then I went back to George. He was still at it, but in a couple of minutes the roar of argument died away.

"God, what a woman! Like talking to a ruddy hurricane."

But he'd learned something. Adeline had the vague idea that one of the Petriff woman's groups was at Camberford. She also said that her own affairs were every other Thursday.

"Let's try to find a bank statement," I said. "There may be an entry or two."

Everything was nice and handy. She didn't use a local bank but one at Golders Green. Her paying-in book showed useful deposits in cash: one, for only the previous week, was of thirty-five pounds. Then we found the bank statements for over a year, and then we struck oil. Cheques had been paid by the honorary secretaries or treasurers of three groups. I noted with interest that Adeline had given private cheques and at ten guineas a time. The others were three guineas, three guineas, and five pounds.

We couldn't help noticing that she had had over a thousand pounds of the new savings certificates, and that her balance at the bank looked as if it might be five hundred.

"And fools like me work for a living," George said bitterly. "Wonder what else she's got salted away."

That was something he'd look into later. He'd do some telephoning at once, he said, and I might as well do the needful questioning in the top flat. I told him about the prints on the whisky bottle. I said I hoped they were Hather's.

"Got him on the brain, haven't you?"

"Didn't we more or less agree on the way here that everything might be tied up?" I reminded him. "If they don't belong to Hather, then I wish it's Maroulis."

He clicked his tongue and was lifting the receiver.

One or two sightseers were standing on the far pavement when I came out. I went through the other gate and round to the back. Before I reached the landing an outside light was switched on and the door opened. I showed my warrant card.

Mrs. Hooby was tall and slim; a pleasant-looking woman of about thirty-five. We went through the spotless kitchen to a little sitting-room. A girl was sitting on a low stool, reading a book by the fire. I guessed she went to some little private school, for her tunic was green with a monogram in yellow on the left breast. The white blouse was really white and her hair was done in a pig-tail tied with a ribbon.

"This is Doris."

Doris was tall for her age. She gave me a look and ventured a smile.

"A good girl?" I asked her mother quizzically.

"Well—at times."

"That's the kind of boy I was," I said. "A sharp girl, so they tell me. Keeps her eyes open and notices things."

"Tell the gentleman about it, darling. About seeing someone going into next door."

Doris was a slow starter, but I heard it all, and it didn't vary from what had been told to Valley. At half-past six Madame had admitted a someone at her side door. Doris had seen a kind of blackness move in the faint light that came through that door. She had as faintly heard Madame's voice and then the door had closed.

"There's a light that can be switched on over that door," I said. "Was it on, Doris?"

She said it wasn't, or she'd have seen.

"Did you see anything at all of Madame Petriff?"

She'd only heard her voice.

"What sort of shoes were you wearing, Doris?"

Her mother cut in there. There had been a lot of rain that morning, as I knew, and Doris had taken her overshoes. That was all I wanted to know. The feet had made no sound on the pavement, but, even so, Madame had been cautious in admitting the caller.

"I think that's all," I told Mrs. Hooby. "Later on you'll both be asked to write everything down, so to speak, but that needn't alarm you."

I found a half-crown among my small change.

"Oh, thank you!" Doris said. "Mother, may I buy that book I wanted to buy. You know—"

"Time for that in the morning," her mother told her. "You run off to bed now, darling. It's after your time. Say good night to the gentleman."

"A charming daughter you've got," I said when the door closed on Doris.

"She's a good girl," she told me pridefully. "She's all I have since her father died."

We sat down again. It was only a quiet, friendly talk, I said. Anything she could tell us that might help to find out who'd done a pretty horrible thing.

"It *was* horrible," she said. "It was a dreadful shock. All the same, I'm glad I went to the police."

I said we were grateful. And I supposed she knew quite a lot about the dead woman.

"Well"—she smiled diffidently—"we were neighbours."

"Good neighbours?"

"I don't know about myself," she said, and gave that diffident smile again, "but she was a good neighbour to me. I didn't have too easy a time after Fred was killed in Malaya. I know the house is mine—"

"Just a moment," I said. "Let me get this clear. You own this flat. And hers?"

She explained. Her father-in-law had been a jobbing builder. Forty years ago he'd built Maple Grove and he'd retained one house for himself. When his son had got married he, then a widower, had converted the house into two flats, and he had retained the lower one. He had died two years ago and Madame had been taken as tenant.

"What rent did she pay?"

"Three pounds and rates," she said. "I'm told I could have had ever so much more."

"But you were satisfied because she was a good neighbour?"

"A very good neighbour. I can't tell you all she did for me. Recommended no end of people. Really high-class people. What you'd call society people, some of them. I've more work than I can properly handle."

"That was good of her," I said. "And how did you find her? Secretive at all about herself?"

"Oh no—not really. I know her husband was a Polish gentleman who came to England years ago and was naturalised. He was an artist of some sort, and he must have died quite a long time ago. She always said she'd been a widow for some years."

"She was a Londoner, wasn't she?"

"Yes. Born in Lewisham, so she told me."

"Do you know where she was living just before she first came here?"

She frowned. It took some remembering, but she thought she'd been in rooms, at Catford. But she'd been all over England in her time, owing to her husband's work, whatever that had been.

"You're going to miss her," I said.

"I am. She was always so cheerful and happy. She said that being in touch with things beyond the grave couldn't help making anyone happy. She wanted me to join a circle, but, of course, I hadn't the time. And there was Doris. But she was certainly a one to cheer you up if you felt a bit depressed about something."

"She used to have a lot of callers?"

"Well, not a lot. She mentioned that soon after she came, and, as I told her, I had plenty of callers myself."

"Did you ever see any of them?" I hurriedly added that I wasn't hinting at snooping. Had she ever happened to see any by chance.

"I generally work at the other window," she told me, "but I did occasionally see someone if I happened to hear a taxi or something and think it was for me. Ladies they were, generally."

"Ever see a dapper kind of gentleman? Thin and about five-foot six?"

She slowly shook her head.

"Or a tall man with a Roman nose? Six foot and broad?" She hadn't seen him either. And though at times she might hear voices very faintly in the room beneath, she never recalled hearing a man's voice.

"Well, that seems everything," I said. "You'll be asked, as I mentioned, to make some kind of a formal statement. Nothing very alarming. But one other thing. Did Madame ever tell your fortune?"

She smiled.

"More than once—only for fun. That wasn't her real work. She was a medium, you know. Very much in demand. She *could* tell fortunes, she told me, but she only did it to oblige friends."

That seemed to be all. She'd heard no noises or strange sounds after Doris had reported that half-past six caller. When I asked if Madame drank at all, she said she didn't. But she'd suffered from indigestion and occasionally took a little gin as medicine. She'd said it did her good.

I shook hands with Mrs. Hooby and thanked her. I used the Whartonian commendations, and she was blushing with gratification when she switched on the landing light. She called another good night when I turned at the bottom of the steps.

When I got back George was still rummaging in drawers. He said there'd been nothing much in the table drawer in the living-room, and now he couldn't make out what the fourth key was for. His idea was that it was the key of a cash box, and that the unknown caller had taken it away. I gave him a resume of what I'd just learned.

I'd happened to give a chuckle. He wanted to know, and peevishly, what was amusing me.

"Something just footling," I said. "Something that just occurred to me about Madame. Mrs. Hooby's describing her as always merry and bright. The happy medium, in fact. See the joke?"

If he did he didn't go into convulsions.

"What's wrong with it?" he said. "You saw her yourself, didn't you? Wasn't she that type?"

I thought quickly back. Madame Petriff emerging from the trance. Adeline hurrying to her. The smile—a wan smile, but a smile for all that. The question to Adeline.

"Well, dear, has everything gone off all right?"

"Yes," I said. "She probably *was* a cheerful sort of soul."

"So I'd be if I'd been milking a lot of suckers to the tune that she had," he told me. "And I'd take good care to make myself pleasant to my landlady if I was getting a place like this in Hampstead for three quid a week."

I asked what he'd been doing and he said he'd got things moving at each of those three places where we'd found her groups. With any luck we might have news in an hour.

"Thought I might have found a cheque she hadn't paid in," he said. "One that might have been given her that afternoon, if she was out on a job. Thought I had something when I rumbled the secret drawer."

He'd noticed that one of the small drawers was shorter than the others and had found a smaller drawer at its back. That was where she kept her cash. Sixteen pounds had been packed into it in notes. He had them in an envelope and was hoping to do something about prints.

Valley came in with a plain-clothes man. I gathered that he was to be on duty at the telephone from then on.

"You can get cracking in here now," Wharton told Valley. "We'll clear out for ten minutes or so."

He added for the benefit of the man at the telephone that a press message had gone out. It might catch a very late edition and it might not. Every caller's name and address was, if possible, to be taken. Any conversation was to be noted in full.

We went out. Stars were shining and it was a cold dry night after the morning's heavy rain.

"That Doxon woman's probably been gabbing to half London," George told me. "I had to tell her Petriff was dead."

"How'd she take it?"

"Nearly broke my ear-drums. Blethered something about being a great loss to the cause."

We were moving along the pavement towards the High Street. I asked where we were going. Where we went was to a pub. All they could give us with our beer was biscuits, but it was better than nothing, and heaven knew when we'd get a meal. A quarter of an hour later we were back.


# 8

# PLAN OF CAMPAIGN

As we went through the living-room I noticed the handbag.

I asked George if he'd looked through it. He said he'd found what Valley had called the usual—a compact, a comb, a handkerchief, her keys and some loose change. And a ration book in the name of Lotte Petriff.

"Not Lottie?"

"Lotte," he said. "Looked phony to me. Made to match up with the Petriff, I shouldn't wonder."

Valley wasn't in the bedroom. He'd had a brainwave about a couple of prints: the one in the kitchen and another on the vase that held the chrysanthemums, and had gone to the upper flat.

There was a spare bedroom used as a kind of lumber room and the print men moved into it. George and I got to work on the desk again. Then Valley came in.

His hunch had been right. Doris Hooby had been in the kitchen on the Wednesday and Madame had given her an apple. Mrs. Hooby had admired the flowers and had put a hand round the neck of the vase to steady it while she smelt them. She'd told Valley that Madame was very clean and tidy, and the living-room always had to be kept just so-so. On account of visitors, Valley added.

He went through to the spare room. The man at the telephone sat phlegmatically on. George and I began emptying drawers. He found the letters: seven of them and no envelopes. Each was from a woman member of some circle or other, and six of them urgently asked Madame to try to get into touch with a dead relative. The other letter was from Lady Georgina, and referred to that séance I'd attended, and the portrait that had been moved. It was short and beautifully written, and somehow it made me furiously angry.

"All written in the last six weeks," George said. "Looks as if she never kept her letters. These probably slipped her memory."

We found old notices of talks and lectures, but never another letter. Either Madame hadn't a close friend or relative or she burnt things as they came. And there wasn't a single photograph or snap-shot. But we did find the red note-book.

It was about eight by five and had a stiff cover. Its paper was ruled and a margin had been drawn on the left-hand side of the pages. In the margin were numbers: one to three hundred and twenty-three. Opposite the numbers were initials, and, occasionally, notes. Some numbers and initials were scored through. Some were marked with a tick. This is an example from page 5:

    79   JF.
    80   C.P. (Father, Fred. Car acc.)
    81   R.G.L.
    82   C.F. ✓
    83   A.C.D.

84   T.H.
85   W.A. (Eva 10. Sc. fever)
86   K.F.
87   G.P.T. ✗

"What the devil is it?" George said testily. "A list of members of the people she worked for?"

I said that seemed to be it. Number 83 was almost certainly Adeline Clarice Doxon. Then I remembered something.

"Have a look at this letter, George. It's signed by a Winifred Arne or Aine. She asks Madame to keep on trying to make contact with a daughter Eva who died of scarlet fever at the age of ten. The address is Halliwick Road, Edmonton."

"I get it," George said. "The notes are what you might call ammunition. Reminders. And what's a tick for?"

I didn't know, unless it was that that particular person was a satisfied customer. And I didn't know the meaning of the cross against G.P.T. George counted the ticks and made them forty-seven. There were only eighteen crosses. Then I looked for Lady Georgina Dunmow. She was 279, and G.D. She had no tick against her initials and yet she might be considered as satisfied.

"We'll have to get in touch with some official or other," George said. "He may give us a clue." His knuckles rapped the book. "Might have to interview the whole three hundred. Half the Yard'll be on it."

He threw the book exasperatedly at the open drawer. It missed. He changed his mind and put it into his breast pocket. Then the telephone went.

"For you, sir."

"Speaking," George said. He gave a grunt or two. The grunts became purrs. He said to wait while he got something down. He wrote it down. He said, "Good!" and "Good!" again. He thanked the caller and said he'd be seeing him.

"Got it!" he told me. "She was at Edmonton. Usual fortnightly do of the Tannery Lane Spiritualism Society. Three to four. She had tea there at half-past four and left at a quarter to five. Said she had to get away early. One of the believers drove her by the Cambridge Arterial to the Piccadilly Tube at Bounds Green. She could have been home here nicely before half-past six."

He was ringing Anders at once.

"That you, Anders? Got what you want. Two cups of tea, a muffin and a sticky cake at half-past four. . . . No, I don't think there'd be anything after. . . . Right, and about that contusion. . . . You don't say! . . . I see. Be hearing from you."

That latter part was translated, and elaborated. George's idea was that the caller came through to the living-room. Maybe Petriff asked him if he'd like a cup of tea or a drink, and when she turned he struck her a blow on the back of the skull and then strangled her with the cord. According to Anders, the weapon used might well have been the butt end of a heavy revolver. The skin had been broken and there had been some bleeding, but that hadn't been the cause of death. Anders thought it had definitely been a man. A woman wouldn't have used that sort of weapon.

I looked at my watch and the time was after half-past ten. I rang Bernice and told her not to wait up. She said Adeline had rung her, and did I think that she—Bernice—would have to give evidence. I reassured her. With the immunity of distance I could have said a whole lot of things. Some of them, or so I guessed, she'd be thinking for herself.

Wharton pulled out his pipe, and put it back again. The print men reported no prints but Madame's in the spare room. Then the telephone went again. This time it was information about the prints on the whisky bottle. The Yard had no record. Wharton said they'd taken their time about finding it out.

I was feeling a bit peevish myself, for I didn't know when I'd been in so cold a house. When Valley told us it was freezing outside George asked him what he thought it was doing in that room. There was a scuttle of coal in the living-room and he'd better get a fire going. And one in the bedroom as well. And what about some tea.

We both felt better when the tea came and the living-room fire was nicely ablaze. You can't think when you're trying to thaw out fingers and feet. All I'd been thinking of was a hot meal and then a warm bed. Now I wouldn't have minded making a night of it.

"Let's see how we stand," George said. His pipe was going and he had a chair by the fire. Valley and I had the chesterfield. Our two pipes were going and the room would soon have a pleasant fug.

"What about you?" he asked me. "Got any ideas?"

I said we were probably all in the same boat. There were things we didn't know, things we suspected, and things we definitely knew. We might put in the last class Anders's opinion that the strangler was a man and that the blow that had stunned Madame had been from the butt end of a heavy revolver. She had apparently hurried away from Edmonton because she'd had an appointment with that man: also she'd admitted him surreptitiously at the side door, and therefore he was someone who wasn't anxious to be seen.

George agreed; at least he said we had to begin somewhere and we might as well start with that. He thought the caller and the strangler were the same, though we'd know about that when Anders had examined the stomach content. He added that it was possible that the strangler was the one who'd left his prints on that whisky bottle.

"Hers were on it, too," Valley said. "She handled it when she unwrapped it and she brought it in here. He handled it and then she took it back later."

That was so obvious that George should have snorted. All he said was that the interesting thing would have been if her prints *hadn't* been on the bottle.

We went over the things we knew: that she had kept no letters or papers that she didn't need and that what she did need was locked up; that apparently she had no personal friends or relatives, and no solicitor, and had made no will; that as a medium she had been in regular demand, and that she'd made some useful extras by fortune-telling, and that latter in such a way as to avoid collision with the law. But all those earnings didn't account for the money she'd saved. Even if she lived cheaply, her outgoings still had to be at least five pounds a week.

"There's something to which I'd like to call attention," I said. "Valley doesn't know this, but I saw her once and heard her speak and Mrs. Hooby confirms the impressions I gathered then. This Madame Petriff was lower-middle-class Cockney. She had no particular schooling and no refinements as we might say. If you'd seen her in a shop and heard her talking, you'd have taken her for a housewife getting on towards middle age. She wasn't common, and she wasn't vulgar; she was just what I've said. But isn't that out of keeping with this room?"

George didn't quite get me.

"The bedroom and the kitchen are in keeping," I said. "This room isn't. Think of the room we might reasonably have expected to see—the kind of furniture, the ornaments, the pictures. Then look at this room. There isn't even an aspidistra. No bamboo, no rubbish. It's a room that isn't altogether in my line, but it's one I wouldn't be ashamed to have. I shouldn't blush for it. Feel the springing of that chair you're in. Feel the linen of the loose cover. And the carpet, and the curtains—they're all fine quality. Above all, look at the pictures. They're modern colour prints on the lines of the old Medici prints. They're framed in keeping, and I'd say they cost a tenner a-piece."

"Mightn't she have once been in better circumstances?" Valley asked.

I ought to have snorted. I merely said that that didn't change her schooling and background. In her time, from what we'd found, she'd depended for a living on pure fortune-telling. That kind of person, even if given four hundred pounds to furnish a room, would have packed it with atrocities.

"And look at the choice of these prints," I said, and got to my feet. "Each has a kind of bearing on spiritualism or prophecy or foretelling the future. This is Pieter Breughel's 'Belshazzar's Feast'; this is Gozzoli's 'Resurrection'; this is Michelangelo's 'Christ at Emmaus' and this Rembrandt's 'Saul and the Witch of Endor'. This one over the mantelpiece is 'Fortune-telling' by le Prince, and it's the one that would hit any caller clean in the eye. A kind of subtle hint, if you like, that fortune-telling was reasonably old, definitely fashionable and still in good taste. But do you tell me that Madame Petriff chose these prints? Not on your life. You see her in the bedroom and the kitchen. Here you see someone else. The someone, I suggest, who furnished this room for her. Who set her up here, and for some reason of his or her own. The one who could also afford to pay her moneys far in excess of what she actually earned."

"You should know," George said. "All the same, that doesn't sound like our whisky-bottle friend."

I said I wouldn't be so sure. Whisky wasn't a drink you could limit by class. Madame might have thought it the only drink for the man concerned. It was a good brand, and what was left in the bottle proved at least that he hadn't been a guzzler.

"All I'd add is this," I said. "I can't see this man investing in Madame Petriff and getting no return on his money. That, so it seems to me, is one of the vital things we have to find out. This wasn't a robbery with violence. There wasn't any sex side to it. What I feel is that her murder arose out of what I've just been saying."

"In other words, sir, she was killed because she'd double-crossed somebody or was asking too much money or because she knew a bit too much."

"That's how I see it, Valley."

"There's a lot in it," Wharton said, and there must have been something if only because he hadn't begun picking holes. "But that gets us to what it was that she and this man were mixed up in."

"There we have a dead certain start," I said. "It simply must have been connected with what she principally was—a professional medium who also did a little fortune-telling as a side line. I think one should concentrate on the former. I have private reasons—nothing to do with the case—for thinking that the fortune-telling was as open and above-board as it ever is. Everything was mixed up with the spiritualism side."

We heard the telephone. Wharton was called into the bedroom and he wasn't there a couple of minutes.

"That was Anders," he told us. "Everything ties up. Death at about half-past six. That means it was the caller who did it."

He added a grim something else. According to my theories, it was all tied up with spiritualism. Three or four hundred people to be interviewed and their alibis tested. A nice little job for a wet afternoon.

I said it might come to that. It might, in fact, be some days before we picked up any kind of a lead. On the other hand, I thought I saw the possibility of a short cut. It wouldn't cost us anything. George could, if he thought so fit, go on working outwards from Madame Petriff while I spent a couple of days on the short cut.

"And what *is* this short cut?" he wanted to know. "Not the Hather suicide?"

"That's what it is," I said, "only I prefer to call it simply the Hather Case."

I had to enlighten Valley a bit before I could get into my swing, and then I gave George a complete account of that afternoon at Ennison Square. I'd already enlarged on it in the car that evening and it was George's own fault that he hadn't heard the whole thing then. I even told him about the man who'd been on my tail. If I'd told him that in the car, he'd have treated it as a joke. Now he listened. He even listened to the strange conduct at the Army and Navy Stores of my friend Land. But he was crafty enough to make a reservation.

"According to this"—that was the reservation—"Hather and Maroulis were interested in your presence at that séance only because you were connected with the Yard. And yet you assure me that nothing fishy went on that afternoon."

I said that was so. I said that I had no doubts that Maroulis, with Hather's connivance, had put a man on my tail because he wanted to be sure I didn't go straight from that séance to the Yard with anything I'd found out. The next morning I'd been followed to the Agency, and steps had been taken to find out what my connection was with the Agency. When it was discovered that I hadn't gone there as a client, the man had been taken off my tail.

"Let's get down to brass tacks," George said. "What money is there in this spiritualism business?"

I said I didn't know. Maroulis and/or Hather might take a rake-off from subscriptions and sale of literature. Adeline Doxon had spoken of the loss to the cause by Hather's death and how she had hoped to get him on the directorate of that journal—*Beyond*. If the sales of that could be made nation-wide and there was a big advertisement revenue, there might be money in it.

"But you don't think so yourself," he told me shrewdly.

"I don't know what I think," I said. "That's why I'd like to look into things. I do guess that people—generous people—like Adeline Doxon were almost certainly handsome contributors to the cause."

He had another objection. He'd looked into Hather himself, though he hadn't told me so, and he doubted if he'd have lent himself to graft and roguery. Hather had assured sources of income and a reputation. He was primarily an investigator.

"That doesn't say he didn't get his nose dirty," I said. "You can't always stay completely on the outside. He might have discovered something in the course of his investigations and then succumbed to flattery or bribery. There're few things I'd have put by him where his nasty little ego was concerned."

George said it was all very vague. There wasn't anything into which we could get our teeth.

"I'm standing up to be shot at," I said, "but I see the hand of Hather in this room. There's a perfect touch about it. Everything is exactly right. The right people would have felt at home in it, and yet it isn't so sumptuous or modern as to call attention to itself. No one needed to be ashamed of coming to this road or this room."

"That's largely surmise."

"It's what I feel in my bones," I told him. "Look at other things. Hather came back to England just over two years ago. Maroulis acquired a business in London about two years ago.

Madame Petriff has been here two years. Both Hather and Maroulis had an interest in spiritualism. Maroulis gave evidence at the Hather inquest to prove what no one else had suspected—that Hather had been suicidally minded. Wherever I touch on things I find a connection."

"Keep this strictly under your hat, Valley," Wharton said, "but Mr. Travers wasn't satisfied about Hather's suicide."

"As a private individual," I said.

"Exactly. But doesn't one thing arise if Hather was killed by someone else? If he and this man Maroulis and Petriff were all tied up in something illegal, then wouldn't Hather have been wiped out for the same reasons that Petriff was?"

"Just what I've been getting at this last half-hour," I said. "Give me a couple of days and let me nose round. Targe needn't be brought in at all."

"Who're you going to see?"

I still had to say that I didn't know. Thoughts weren't so clear as they'd been an hour ago, but after a sleep I ought to know. And naturally I'd keep in touch and rush along anything I happened to pick up.

"A couple of days aren't going to make all that difference," he told me, but still as if it wasn't wholly without risk to let me off the leash. "Let's leave it as read. Keep me informed and I'll do the same with you. One little thing has been bothering me, though. It's this fourth key. Have a good look at it."

I'd seen it before. Valley had a look at it and thought what we'd thought—that it was the key of a small cash or deed box.

"Plenty of room for it in that desk of hers," Wharton said. "It's one of those patent desks with a key that locks the drawers the same time it locks the front. What I'm saying is she wouldn't have carried a key that opened nothing. If there was a box, then it's gone. And if it went, then you bet your life it had something mighty important in it."

"Not letters or papers," I said. "They could have been taken and the box left. And that would have looked less suspicious. It looks as if the box held something that made it more convenient for it to be taken away box and all."

"Well, there it is," George said, and got to his feet. "The place has been gone through with a small-toothed comb and there's nothing the key fits."

As far as I was concerned, that was all for that night. George and Valley were staying on for yet another examination of Madame's belongings, but a car took me home. Bernice had left a Thermos of soup and some bread, and it was nearly one o'clock when I got into bed. I'd thought I was mentally tired, but my brain was active enough to keep me planning the next day's work. And I'd been foolish enough to stir it to activity by doing a couple of things before I'd turned in, for I'd looked in the telephone directory and found that Maroulis's private address was Flat 7, Gainsborough House, Kensington, and I'd rung the Yard and arranged that Sergeant Matthews should pick me up in the morning at half-past eight. Even when I went to sleep I had no precise idea where we'd be going, but at least we'd be on our way. For days I'd been nagged at by Hather's death and things which no logic could satisfactorily explain. I'd wished a dozen times that I had the authority to question and probe, and now I had that authority. And I had a couple of days in which to prove not that Targe had been wrong, but that I had been right. From that angle I didn't like it as much, but there it was. From the moment when I woke in the morning it would be entirely up to me.

I set the alarm clock for half-past six, and when it went off I lay on for a time and tried to plan my day. Lancaster Gate and Kensington ought to follow one on the other and I thought I'd try to see Maroulis first and then circle round to Phyllis Parting. After that I'd have a word with Ursula Hather, and I could make an appointment from Lancaster Gate. But from then on I didn't know, unless I went along to the office of *Beyond* and had a look inside.

I had breakfast early and read what my two papers had to say about the death of Lotte Petriff. Each had no more than the bare paragraph that George had sent out. Then I rang Maroulis's flat and got through to him. I said I was speaking as from

Scotland Yard and I'd like his help in the matter of the murder of Madame Petriff. I never heard a voice more astonished than his.

"Murder of Madame Petriff?" he said. "My dear fellow, you must be joking."

"Then you haven't seen a newspaper?"

"I haven't. I actually came out of the bathroom to answer your call."

"Well, it's true enough," I told him. "She was strangled yesterday evening."

"At her home?"

"Yes," I said. "You ever been there?"

"Why should I?" he said. "I was merely assuming she had a home. Now I come to think, I believe she lived out Hampstead way."

"Yes," I said. "I spent most of last night there. But about a short talk with you. Nine o'clock suit you? Only a matter of a few moments."

He told me to come by all means, though he didn't know how on earth he could help. I thanked him, hung up, waited a minute and then tried Phyllis Parting. It was the butler who answered me. He said she was in but not available. I said it was urgent and if there was an extension he was to put me through. He said he'd see what could be done, so I waited. A minute or so and I heard a drowsy voice.

"I'm Travers," I told her. "The man you saw with Chief Inspector Targe on that Monday morning at Martin Hather's flat. I'd rather like to see you officially at about half-past nine at Lancaster Gate. A matter arising out of the death of Madame Petriff."

"I'm sorry," she said. "I didn't quite catch all that."

I went over it again. There was no drowsiness when I'd finished.

"Not that medium?" she said, and, "You *are* the man who was at that séance of Adeline Doxon's?"

I assured her I was. I said she'd see Madame Petriff's death mentioned in a paragraph in *The Times*. And might I slip in and see her at half-past nine as I'd said.

"I think so." Then a queer question: "What day is it?"

"My calendar makes it Saturday."

"Saturday," she said, and there was something different in the voice. I had to wait quite a few moments before she said she would see me.

A Saturday, I thought. A Saturday exactly one week ago she'd been at Sevenoaks, establishing a sort of alibi for the rest of the week-end. From Sevenoaks she'd gone to town and on to that Anvil House Hotel to wait for Martin Hather. No wonder her voice had changed when I told her it was Saturday.

Matthews was well before time, but I had only one other thing to do. Note-books are never obtrusive when George and I and no-matter-who-else have a conference. A note-book is merely somewhere to hand, and one just jots down this or that which happens to strike one. At Maple Grove I'd jotted down, the names of the three circles in which Madame Petriff had been interested, and now I copied them on a sheet of clean paper and put the paper in my wallet. Two minutes later we were off.

9

# MERRY MEETING

IT WAS a cold, dry, frosty morning with a keen north wind and a clear sky. That somehow made for optimisms. Days before the strangling of Madame Petriff I'd hinted things to George Wharton and cast a cloud of dubiety over the way that Targe was handling the death of Martin Hather. Then I had tried to show that the Petriff killing proved me right, and there I was with forty-eight hours in which to demonstrate that I hadn't been merely a know-all and busybody. I wasn't exactly on a spot, but I hadn't a doubt that I was faced with something that might be called tough. In fact to call it tough was an optimism in itself.

We had a driver, and Matthews and I sat at the back. We'd worked together before and he was the kind I like to work with. He reminded me, for one thing, of my own early days with George Wharton: he was youngish, he listened and watched and kept his own counsel till he was asked for it. There was an aura of the cheerful and cheering about him, and his mistakes, like my own, had at least an originality.

I'd told the driver to take things slowly, but when we got to Kensington I'd managed to give Matthews a fairly well-filled-in outline of the case. I didn't minimise what we were up against, and I couldn't do more than sketch out roughly our plan of attack.

"Don't you worry, sir," he told me. "Something'll turn up. It always does."

I said I hoped to heaven he was right. Maybe it wouldn't do any harm, though, if we sang a verse or two of the Old Hundredth.

We were slightly early so we circled round and waited for best part of ten minutes, and it was just on nine o'clock when we rang the bell of Maroulis's flat. The block had looked solid rather than showy, but I'd kept an eye about me as we went in and up, and I'd put those flats in the six-hundred-a-year class, which meant that Maroulis's income had to be pretty big. I didn't change my mind when we stepped inside.

I introduced Matthews. Maroulis asked us if we'd had breakfast. I said we had but we wouldn't keep him long from his. He said he rarely worked on Saturdays and his time was his own.

"Sit down, gentlemen," he told us, and waved a hand at a chesterfield. "Cigarettes are on the table."

He looked immense in a suit of light-brown plus-fours. But he didn't look worried. It was true that he'd given me a shrewd look when he'd admitted us, and I'd thought him surprised to see there were two of us. But I hadn't explained Matthews. It wasn't bad policy to make him ask the questions or leave him with something that might faintly disturb.

"An extraordinary thing this Petriff business," he told us. "When you told me this morning you could literally have knocked me down with a feather."

"I know," I said. "It wasn't a robbery. Nothing was taken as far as we can judge. Just a cold-blooded calculated murder. It's inexplicable. That's why we've got to cast round for anyone who might give us even a hint."

"I doubt if I can help," he said. "I've known of her for a few months or so. Purely as a medium, of course. Our late friend Hather got me interested in that sort of thing and I'm afraid I've become a bit of a fanatic."

I took out that sheet of paper. I said there was one thing he could perhaps do. Could he add any more to those three circles for which we knew that Petriff had worked? He took the paper, wrinkled his forehead as he read it, then shrugged his shoulders.

"I know these by name," he told us. "As a matter of fact I've attended more than one meeting at Camberford, but any others—I just don't know."

I put the paper back in my wallet and looked suitably depressed.

"That's one hope gone," I said. "And you've no idea whatever who might have killed her?"

"My dear fellow, how could I? Till you just mentioned it I thought it was one of those robberies. But you say there's nothing missing."

"Not as far as we can trace."

"There we are then," he told us. "That sort of woman wouldn't have a private life of any sort. Or would she?"

He was too interested. I almost mentioned the missing box, then kept it to myself. What I said was that a private life, so to speak, was one of the things we were working on: the fact that in the last two years she seemed to have accumulated quite a lot of money. I added that we'd probably have a goodish bit of auditing to do—to ascertain her working income, as it were, and then try to discover where the balance came from.

"You think there was a balance?"

"We're sure of it. There's some undisclosed source of income. We haven't a doubt about that."

"But what could it be?" He shrugged his massive shoulders. "A simple sort of woman like that. But wait a minute. What about her late husband? Did he leave her anything?"

"Possibly," I said. "But that doesn't explain the fact that two years ago she apparently had nothing and since then she's been living up to her suspected income and has nevertheless managed to save the best part of a couple of thousand pounds. That's in strict confidence, by the way."

"Naturally. But it's amazing. And this money wasn't missing from her house?"

"Safe in Savings Certificates and at the bank."

"Extraordinary!" He shrugged his shoulders again. "It just shows you never can tell."

"Well, that seems to be all," I said, and shuffled gently as if about to get to my feet. He was on his at once, none too sorry to see us go. I sat pat.

"You mentioned Hather just now," I said, and he slowly sat down on the arm of his chair. "I was most interested in what you said at the inquest about his being depressed."

"I know," he said. "It seems to have caused surprise." The smile was a sad reminiscence. Hather, in his opinion, had gone too far. He had identified himself too much with what Maroulis was calling the unknown. Vistas that terrified him had been disclosed.

"To anyone who didn't know him as well as myself he was just the same alert and cheerful person he always was—at least outwardly. This is in confidence, of course"—he leaned forward and his voice sank appreciably—"but I'm sure the verdict was a right one. His mental processes were definitely disturbed. Believe me when I say I could have said far more than I did. But one had a man's reputation to consider, if nothing else."

"That was generous of you," I said, and I did get to my feet. "Sorry to have kept you from your breakfast."

"I shall have the better appetite," he told me. "Or I should have done if I didn't feel so upset about that unfortunate woman. That, and thinking about poor Hather again."

He shook hands with me first and then Matthews. He asked as a favour if he might be informed of any developments. And if he remembered anything that looked like being of use, then he'd let us know. I said that was good of him, and I almost held out my hand again and as we went along the corridor I was thinking that my last look at him had shown more of a Roman consul than ever. His look had been somehow judicial and only faintly grave. Put him in a toga and he might have heard disturbing news from some far-flung frontier.

"What'd you make of him?" I asked Matthews.

Matthews said he'd been a bit too interested in that question of robbery. He ventured on a question of his own. Why hadn't I buttoned him up and then broached the matter of an alibi. I said I didn't want to rush things. I preferred to leave him with everything in the air, so to speak; to make him worried and force him to take action.

"What sort of action?" he wanted to know.

"That's what we've got to be on the look-out for," I told him, and took out that sheet of paper. "When we get to Lancaster Gate, you go on to the Yard and get his prints checked with those we found on that whisky bottle. Then come back. I have an idea Miss Parting might do more talking if she saw me alone."

I saw her in what was evidently her own room, for it was full of her own possessions. Electric fires may be convenient, but I like the kind of fire that was burning cheerfully in the grate. It made for comfort and intimacy, and I was going to be uncomfortably intimate.

I thought she was looking unwell. She was thinner than when I'd seen her only a few days before and there was still a tell-tale blackness beneath the eyes. But she was quite assured. There was never a false note when she mentioned the horror of Petriff's murder and nothing false or maudlin in the brief sympathy.

But there was still no friendliness in the room, so I mentioned Adeline Doxon and soon we were instancing vagaries and managing to smile. We talked about Roedean and Newnham, and what things had been like in my Cambridge days. And those, I added regretfully, had been before she was born.

"No!" she said. "I'm not a child. I'm twenty-six."

"Unfortunately it's still true," I said. "I'm just about old enough to be your father."

That amused her. I leaned forward. I hoped the smile was fatherly.

"I wonder if you'd let me talk to you like a father: tell you something in very strict confidence."

"I don't see why you shouldn't."

There'd been something slightly uneasy in the smile. It went when I told her what I knew. I hope I did it gently. I think I made it clear that it was something between her and myself alone.

"So you knew," she said, and moistened her lips.

"Yes," I said. "There're things we have to find out. Martin Hather was dead and you were pretty close to him and we had to be sure. But we're not moralists. All I wanted was that you and I shouldn't be talking on false pretences."

I feared she might cry, but there was never a sign of tears. Maybe she'd had a week in which to cry. All she did was to justify herself and him. His wife was a horrible creature: just how horrible she couldn't begin to say. She'd been virtually blackmailing him about the divorce, and Hather and herself were entitled to some little happiness.

"Don't answer this unless you feel like it," I told her. "Was that twenty-four hours a week ago to be the first you'd ever spent in what I might call intimacy with Martin Hather?"

It was quite a time before the clamped lips opened.

"Yes," she said. "There'd have been something beastly about staying at the flat."

"That's all I wanted to know," I said. "Now I can tell you something else. You'll give me your solemn word that you'll never breathe a thing to a soul?"

"If you think it's necessary."

"Believe me, it is," I said. "It's this. I don't believe Martin Hather committed suicide. I believe he was killed."

Her eyes opened wide. Her face lighted. The lips parted. Then all at once her face was buried in her hands. It was wretched to hear her sobs. It was a minute or two before she could speak again.

"I'm sorry," she said, and was giving a last dab at her eyes. "I shouldn't have been so stupid. I hate a woman who bursts into tears."

"Don't reproach yourself," I said. "Just tell me this. You were glad or sorry?"

"Glad," she said, and the eyes were lighting again. "I knew it! I tried to make that man Targe believe it, but he persisted in treating me like a child."

"And you didn't want to insist on giving evidence because of—well, what he didn't know?"

"Yes," she said. "I ought to have done it, whatever happened. I owe it to Martin."

I told her more. I wasn't there to hear the little she might know about Madame Petriff. I was there to enquire into the death of Martin Hather. It was all desperately secret, of course, but I was relying on her to help me.

"I *will*," she said. "I'll do anything. Anything you like."

I said that ostensibly everything was over and done with. If Hather had been killed, then the killer knew himself in no danger. He might get careless and that would be our chance. What she could do to help I couldn't at the moment say. It might mean a spell of patient waiting till something definite emerged, but meanwhile I'd like her to tell me things that maybe she hadn't told Targe.

"About visitors, for instance. Who actually was in the flat during that last week?"

She had to think. She mentioned a producer from the B.B.C. who was making a first rough draft of a radio presentation of some spiritualistic material. He had been twice, on the Monday and the Thursday, and just to discuss the script and the general handling.

"Maroulis," I said. "The man who said at the inquest that Martin Hather had suicidal tendencies—"

"He was a liar!"

Her face was pure venom. The fingers were clenching till the knuckles were white.

"That's something we're keeping strictly to ourselves," I said. "Knowing's no good. We've got to prove. But was Maroulis in the flat that week?"

"I don't think I've known him there more than twice," she said. "He certainly wasn't there last week, at least while I was there. I know that Martin used to see a lot of him, but it was always elsewhere." She shook her head. "I didn't tell Martin so, but I never really trusted him. Now I hate him."

"And no one else was in the flat?"

"Not that I can think of. . . . But wait a minute."

Her lips moved while she thought back. Then she had it.

"Hugh Winster came. On the Wednesday it was. In the afternoon."

"Winster? Who's he?"

"An author friend of Martin's. They were at Clare together."

"A good friend?"

"Well, I think so. Martin was awfully haphazard and casual with his friends. He had so many. But he always seemed pleased to see Hugh Winster. I don't mean he often came to the flat, but I do think Martin used to see him outside. Lunch and that kind of thing, you know." She smiled. "I rather like Hugh Winster. A bit of a bear, but quite charming."

"Any harm in my seeing him? I mean, he might let something drop."

"I think it would be a good idea. But he doesn't live in town, you know. He lives at—where is it now? I remember. At Humbledown. That's near Epping."

I jotted that down, then got to my feet. I said so far so good. But everything had to be frightfully conspiratorial. If she remembered anything she thought I ought to know, then she should ring me at my private number at between seven and eight in the morning. That was the only time I could guarantee to be in.

"But you'll keep me informed?" she asked me at the door.

I said I would. But she mustn't get impatient. It might be days before what we called a lead turned up.

"Just one other thing," she said, and blushed faintly. "I hardly like to mention it, but if there's any question of money I'd like to—"

"Good of you," I said, "but the taxpayer pays."

She actually laughed and I laughed. It wasn't even a joke. It was just a sign of how things stood.

She must have pressed a bell, for the same old butler who'd admitted me was waiting at the foot of the stairs with my hat and coat.

"A cold day, sir."

"A *very* cold day."

"But fine."

"Yes," I said. "For the time of year it's uncommonly fine."

I didn't know how fine it was till I got into the car. Three minutes later we were drawing up at a police-box and I was dialling the Hampstead number. George Wharton was out but expected back at any moment.

"Tell him this," I said to Valley, "and watch his face. Those prints on the whisky bottle. They're Maroulis's. We've just checked."

"You don't say!"

"And tell him this. Maroulis assured me before I saw him this morning that he'd never been inside the place. He pretended he didn't even know where she lived."

"Right, sir. I'll let him know the minute he comes in."

I went back to the car. The driver asked where to. I told him to wait while I thought it out.

Maroulis had been to Petriff's flat. After I'd left he'd probably see through that little trick of obtaining his fingerprints. So what would he do? I didn't know and Matthews didn't know.

"Depends on who else is mixed up in it," he said. "Can't you think of anyone, sir, he'd want to warn?"

I said I couldn't. Then I remembered *Beyond*. I told him about it and how the offices were almost a part of Maroulis's own.

"Might do worse than have a dekko then, sir?"

Then I remembered something else and had a quick look at my watch. It was a Saturday and that office would close at midday. But it was still well short of eleven o'clock. The car moved off towards an ultimate Holborn.

*　*　*　*　*

I was definitely taken with the idea of seeing that Hugh Winster whom Phyllis Parting had mentioned. If he and Hather had been at Clare together it was not unlikely that they had been at the same school, and maybe at that dinner on the night before Hather's death. They had certainly seen each other during the week.

We had come the Piccadilly way and I asked the driver to draw in at a bookshop. I hadn't time to look at shelves, but asked at a counter if they had anything by Hugh Winster. I was offered two novels—*Panting Time* and *The Lowing Herd*. What they were about the girl didn't know, but she said she'd heard they were good. I took them both and wondered about putting the seventeen shillings on the expense account.

I gave Matthews one and asked him to have a look through it and get an idea of what it was about. I tackled the other myself and I had more time than I'd thought, for a couple of traffic jams held us up and we had bad luck with the lights. So I did quite a fair job on *The Lowing Herd*—published, by the way, in 1947. The actual herd seemed to be the officers in a German prisoner-of-war camp, and the book dealt with the effect of that life on men's nerves—their squabbling, their open hatreds, plans of escape that ended in futility, one private escape and its reverberations, and finally the settling of a vendetta or two when the camp broke loose en masse as the Americans neared. The actual writing was distinctly good.

We were turning into Holborn and Matthews passed his book back. It was about a man trying to make good after the war, he said. A prisoner of war who'd come back after five years to find he'd lost his wife to another man. He hadn't got so far as to know what happened, and before he could tell me any more we were drawing up just beyond Raimond House. I said I'd better scout round alone, so I gave Matthews the book again. I said it would pass the time. He grinned and said he certainly got some tough assignments. Why couldn't it have been a detective novel or a western.

Raimond House seemed no busier than when I had seen it before. Outside the office of *Beyond* I listened for a moment and there wasn't a sound of talking, so I gave a polite little tap and walked in. I got the shock of all shocks. At a table to my right and away back from the counter, a man was cutting slips of paper from a stencilled sheet, and he turned his head and gave me a formal look as I walked in. Then he seemed to go limp. His mouth gaped a bit, and the hand let the scissors fall. As for me, I had to look quickly away or maybe I'd have had some limpness, too. For the man with the scissors was no other than my fat friend!

I was looking through the pamphlets on the counter when he came up to me. I glanced at him casually, as if I'd never seen him in my life.

"Good morning," he said in that wheezy voice of his. "Anything you were looking for particularly?"

"As a matter of fact," I said, "my wife asked me to call in and get her a copy of that official publication of yours. Is this it?"

He gave me the copy of *Beyond*, and I paid him. I noticed that on the table where he'd been working was quite a stack of copies, and I'd seen him inset in one a slip that he'd cut from the stencilled sheet.

"Would you like to leave me your wife's name and address, sir?" he was asking me. "She may like to become a subscriber. We welcome new subscribers."

"I'm afraid that's up to her," I said, and smiled at him pleasantly. "If you're a married man you'll know what I mean."

"I know what you mean," he said, and he forced a chuckle that made his chins wobble.

"You're welcome to try," I said, and gave him the name and address. He must have summoned a considerable deal of cunning while he wrote the information down. His look had just the right touch of the puzzled.

"Haven't I seen you somewhere before, sir?"

"I don't know," I said. "I don't seem to have seen you."

"It just occurred to me," he said. "You know how it is. You think you've seen someone and then it turns out you haven't—or you have."

"That's how it goes," I said, and let my eyes lift beyond him to the room. "Is one allowed to have a look round? There might be something I'd like to buy."

"By all means," he told me, and waved his pudgy hand at the packed shelves. "The prices are all marked on the covers or inside."

I went round the open end of the counter. It was a largish room and rather like a subscription library of some country town. All the books were strictly what I'd call business—spiritualistic, theosophical, and psychic stuff. Most were English, a few were translations and a very few foreign. I was looking at one of the foreign ones—*Mehr Licht* by someone named Halst— when I noticed two things. The first was that my friend had not continued his clipping, and the second that he had thrown a newspaper to cover the small pile of clippings and stencilled sheets. I gathered that he was preferring to keep his attention wholly on myself—and then the door suddenly opened.

A youngish woman came bursting in. She was a handsome brunette and the first thing I noticed about her face was the flash, as it were, of scarlet lips. She practically flew to the counter, had her bag as quickly on it and whipped it open. Perhaps I haven't given you an impression of her haste, but from the time she opened the door till the time she opened her bag and spoke couldn't have been more than three seconds.

"Oh, Mr. Corbel! I'm so glad I made it." She let out a breath. "I just *had* to get here in time."

I'd caught a quick alarm on Corbel's face. I couldn't have believed he'd be at the counter so quickly. His hands were raised and fluttering agitatedly.

"Would you come back in ten minutes? I have this gentleman to attend to."

That was sheer rubbish. I was in no one's way. I was so far at the back of the room and so motionless that in her hurry she hadn't even noticed me. But I moved quickly in that indecisive moment before she turned. I lifted the end of that newspaper and one of those clippings went into my pocket. The lady turned and went out. I sauntered back towards the counter.

"Don't see anything—"

"Some people can be very annoying," he told me. "That lady you just saw is the kind we don't encourage here. We keep choking her off, but she won't stay away."

"Takes all sorts to make a world," I said. "But, as I was saying, I don't see anything I happen to want just now. And I'm in rather a hurry. I'll drop in some time next week."

"Always glad to see you," he told me as I moved casually towards the door.

In that open space that formed a kind of landing, I saw something out of the corner of my eye. The lady hadn't gone far; in fact she was waiting within a few feet of the door, ready to slip in the moment that I left. I moved on to the top of the stairs before I looked back. There was no sign of her. She'd already gone in.

I went quickly down the stairs and into the car. I told Matthews there was a change of plans. I described the woman and told him to follow her in the car. If she went into the Underground, he was to leave the car and the driver would go back to the Yard and wait. If Matthews had the woman's name and address in time, he could rejoin the car and they could pick me up at the National Gallery at two o'clock. If he didn't have it by then, afternoon arrangements were cancelled. Matthews would report to me at my flat at any time after six o'clock.

It was a bit muddled, but they seemed to understand. But there just wasn't time if they didn't. I nipped out of the car and walked towards Chancery Lane. When I was well covered by pedestrians I had a look at that slip that I'd taken from under the newspaper.

> Owing to unforeseen circumstances, the usual weekly supplement cannot be issued. Other arrangements will be made immediately.

To me that was little more than gibberish. If it meant anything, it was what it said—that *Beyond* had a weekly supplement that couldn't be sent out that particular week. But what I did wonder about was *unforeseen circumstances*. What unforeseen circumstances did I know about myself? Only the sudden death of Madame Petriff, and surely her death—even her murder—couldn't influence the issue or otherwise of a supplement to the official publication of spiritualism groups. Then something else struck me. I stopped at a kiosk and dialled the Yard.

I was lucky. George was there and not at Maple Grove. I told him about my fat friend and how he turned out to be the managing editor of *Beyond*. I mentioned the stencil outfit. I read him what was on my slip.

"This is the curious thing," I said. "Cyclostyling is a rush job. It'd have been cheap enough and reasonably quick to get slips printed, but apparently this Corbel couldn't wait. And I think he was in a hurry because Maroulis had reported my visit. Where it all ties up I don't know. I thought I'd just report it so that you could see what you made of it."

He said it was interesting. And what was I doing next? I didn't mention the Lady in a Hurry for fear she should turn out to be a dud. I said I might be seeing Mrs. Hather, but not before three o'clock. I asked if there were any developments at his end, and he said he had an idea or two but he hadn't made up his mind about seeing Maroulis.

I walked on to the Strand and turned into Simpsons for lunch. Matthews still had one book, but mine was open beside me while I ate.

10

# STRAIGHT FROM COWARD

AT TWO O'CLOCK I was outside the National Gallery, but there was no sign of the car. I waited for twenty minutes, then rang the Yard and said I shouldn't need the driver and I'd ring later about the next day's arrangements.

I'd hoped to get to Epping that afternoon for a word with Winster, but I wasn't without another string to the bow. The trouble was, of course, that Ursula Hather mightn't be at home, but Westminster wasn't far and I decided to risk it. So I took a bus and got off at the Abbey. I cut through to the left and into Great Smith Street and was almost as far as the Tate before I discovered I was wrong. When I got to South Mansions I knew I should have cut through by the Houses of Parliament—not that it mattered, for it was only just after three o'clock.

It was a showy block of flats. The reception hall was a bit garish and a smell of meals came from the restaurant. The deep-piled carpet of the stairs had an ornate pattern, and the numbers on the doors were polished chromium and rather too decorative. Flat 12 was on the first floor and as I came up to its door I could hear the sound of jazz music from inside. I pushed the bell and nothing happened. I gave a loud rap at the door. A moment or two and the door opened. It was Ursula Hather, but I'd never have recognised her. She had a drink in the free hand and a cigarette drooped from her mouth. I thought she'd had plenty to drink, for she seemed to sway slightly as she looked up at me. And there she stood with the door open. I stepped inside.

"I'm Travers," I said. "You remember me? Mind if I come in?"

I'd stepped into something straight from Noel Coward. I'll go beyond that first flash of it as I saw it, and add a moment or two to that first quick view. In the left corner beyond the big window was a cocktail cabinet, its top crowded with glasses and bottles. Ahead of me, to the right of the handsome electric fire, was a radio gramophone and it was from there that the music was blaring. With his back to me a man was conducting the music with a walking-stick for baton, and his hips kept twisting like a hula-hula girl's. Along the wall to his right was a long chesterfield with a low table before it, and on it were two ash-trays and a tumbler with a drink. By the table in a corner of the chesterfield sat a very large man who looked about thirty-five. His shoulders were hunched and his hands were on his knees. One hand had a grey glove. The other held a cigarette. Our eyes met and his eyebrows lifted enquiringly. Then he let out a bellow.

"Julian! . . . Julian, damn you! Turn that bloody thing off!"

Once more things happened quickly. Ursula Hather closed the door, and I thought I heard a slight belch. I thought I'd better do some explaining. And I had to think fast. It looked remarkably as though my visit could no longer be official.

I began extemporising. I doubted if in any case she'd question my word.

"You do remember me, Mrs. Hather, don't you? Your late husband introduced us some time ago outside the club. You were in a taxi. You said you'd met my wife."

"Of course," she said, and I was sure she hadn't an idea who I was. "Do come in. And let me get you a drink."

We advanced to the centre of that handsome room. The big man was now on his feet.

"This is Hugh Winster," she said, and there was a hesitation as if she'd already forgotten my name.

"My name's Travers," I told Winster, and he smiled, and I smiled. Phyllis Parting had called him a likeable bear, and somehow he looked like one. And certainly I liked his smile.

"Julian, come here!"

That was Ursula. Julian didn't want to play. He was tinkering with something in the inside of the gramophone.

"Come here, Julian!"

The tone was definitely angry. Julian stretched himself and began coming. Ursula said something about it being Julian Blange.

"Good God!" I said as I looked at him.

Blange was looking a bit sheepish.

"Well, well," I said roguishly. "The last time I saw you, your name was Brown."

"Oh, that," he said. "That was just a rag."

Two voices came at once. Winster was asking what it was all about, and Ursula wanted me to name my drink. I said I'd have a whisky with plenty of soda.

Blange took my hat and coat and dumped them on a chair. Winster was still wanting to know what it was all about.

I'd heard the squirt of the soda. Ursula came shuffling across the carpet with my drink. It looked pretty strong to me.

"Hugh?"

"No more for me," he told her emphatically.

"Julian?"

"Not for me, either."

She shrugged her shoulders and turned back towards the bar. Winster hoisted himself up and followed her. I noticed that he was slightly lame.

"No, darling. No more for you. Come and sit down."

"Blast you! Can't I drink on my own birthday?"

Blange was unconcernedly lighting a cigarette. Winster said something that I didn't catch.

"I *don't* talk too much," she told him, which was as good as telling me what he had said. But it had steadied her. She pettishly shook off his arm, but she came back. She stubbed out the cigarette and held out her hand to Blange for another. Winster got there first and it was he who held the lighter. She sank into a chair alongside mine. She crossed her legs and didn't worry about pulling down a skirt.

"No real necessity to explain all this," Winster told me with a dry smile, "but the fact is it's Ursula's birthday and I was asked to make one at lunch. We've not long been back, but I'm afraid we've all drunk quite a lot."

"Sounds like a lawful occasion," I said, and lifted my tumbler. "Here's happy returns."

Blange grinned fatuously. Winster took a sip of his drink to keep me company.

"Oughtn't I to make a speech or something?" Ursula asked poutingly.

"No!" Winster told her loudly and firmly. "We've all made enough speeches. Besides, Mr. Travers is a guest. Let's do some listening. What was that about Brown?"

"I can explain that," Blange said. "It's all very asinine, really, but it was quite a time ago—almost pre-war—when Ursula was mad about all that spiritualism stuff, I thought I'd see what it was like, so I wangled a show through the Boomer. Mr. Travers happened to be there."

"Darling, you might have told me."

"It was just a rag."

"But something's been puzzling me about it," I said. "We were having quite a nice chat till you discovered I was connected with Scotland Yard, and then you shied. You just faded away, and I wondered why." I smiled urbanely around. "I wasn't doing a job of work. I was in mufti, so to speak, as I am now."

There was quite an awkward silence. Ursula was frowning. Blange was hunting for an explanation.

"I don't really think so," he said. "I think you must have imagined it. No offence, old boy, and all that."

"Maybe I did," I said. I added, almost belligerently, that I didn't like the Scotland Yard tag on me when I was about my private occasions. Maybe I'd been a bit too sensitive.

"Forget it," Winster told me. "Have another drink."

I indicated I still had some. I was wondering where the next topic was coming from. Winster himself supplied it, or led up to it.

"What's your precise function at the Yard, if one calls it that?"

I told him I was an unofficial expert, called in occasionally on murder cases.

"That's funny," he said. "There was one in the paper this morning."

"That Madame Petriff affair?" I said. "Not quite in my line. Not that I wasn't interested. I'd seen her in action at that séance Brown—I beg his pardon: Blange—and I were at. A curious creature."

"A horrible woman!"

"Shut up, Ursula," Winster told her sharply. "You keep your mind off such things. Ursula had a bit of a nervous breakdown not so long ago," he told me. "That's why I have to be so rude when I'm here, and that's not often. She drinks too much and talks too much and thinks about the wrong things."

"Don't we all?" I said. And I think it was then that I realised that the room was uncomfortably warm. Not only was the central heating full on—I could feel it just behind me—but that electric stove was going full blast. I felt a stickiness under my collar, but no one else seemed to be worrying.

"Funny thing about talking and all that," Blange said. "People think fools say the wrong thing at the wrong time. That's wrong, you know, when you come to think it out. What they say is the wrong thing at the right time or the other way round. If they didn't they wouldn't be fools."

Then he was asking what I thought—had the idea been his own or had he read it somewhere.

"We'll credit you with an epigram," Winster told him, and turned to me. "Tell me about this What's-her-name woman, the one who was killed. You say you saw her once?"

I was glad to talk about anything, so I told him about the séance. He seemed remarkably interested. He said there was a novel somewhere in what I'd said: that Petriff woman, for example, and her origins and marriage and rise in her profession, and perhaps her end. Blange said it would take a lot of research. Then he switched to Harebell and did an imitation including a bit of pseudo-Chinese. He was pretty good at it, too.

"The whole thing was a fake, of course," he told Winster. "Feeble, on the whole, and quite innocuous."

I wasn't inclined to agree, and as my arguments might have brought in Ursula Hather I glanced round at her, for while we'd been talking our heads had got closer together and there'd been a definite trio. But Ursula was asleep. Her head was sideways in the angle of the chair and her mouth was just a bit open. Her cheeks were flushed with the heat and a wisp or two of hair was over the damp forehead. She wasn't too pretty a sight.

Winster hoisted himself to his feet. He frowned at me and grimaced.

"Better get her to bed, Julian. I've got to get away. You coming too, Travers?"

We could have jumped on the pile of that carpet and not have wakened her, but we tiptoed across to our hats and coats. Blange quietly opened the door.

"Be seeing you," he whispered to Winster.

"Don't know when," Winster told him. "I'm up to the ears in that book."

Blange gave me a nod and a grin; the door closed and Winster and I moved off along the corridor.

"A queer ménage?" I said reflectively.

Winster shot me a look.

"You're not one of those highly moral blokes?"

"God forbid!" I said. "The world would be a dull spot if we couldn't let our hair down."

He didn't comment, and all at once I was feeling at a disadvantage. It wasn't the bulk of him and it wasn't because of some moral ascendency. Maybe it was because my very first sight of him had made him a kind of sane oasis in the childish insanity of that room. He had been sitting there like a cynical observer. And with no obtrusion he had dominated the room. Talk had been turned *his* way. People did things the way *he* wanted them.

"Where are you bound for?" I asked him when we were outside.

"Liverpool Street," he said. "I live out in the long grass, near Epping. It's a damnable train service, but my basic just won't run to it."

"I'd like to drop in for a chat some time," I said. "I'm that way fairly often."

"Do," he said. "You know Humbledown?"

I said unblushingly that I knew it slightly.

"My guvnor used to be vicar there," he told me. "A hell of a place now. Absolutely ruined between the wars. I've a sort of cottage as you come in. A damn' great wistaria all over it. You can't miss it."

"I'll drop in some time."

"Fine!" he said, and gave me a quick smile as he moved off. Then he turned practically at once, and I noticed how he had to give a kind of swivel with the game leg.

"Something I wanted to ask you." Was the look cynical or merely amused. "Don't think me rude, but just *why* did you turn up this afternoon? I mean, you never seemed to tell anyone why."

I laughed.

"To tell the truth I forgot all about it. And I don't think there was a moment you could really call propitious."

"You're right there," he told me.

"Also my hostess seemed to take me for granted. But between ourselves, I knew Hather pretty well and to a less degree so did my wife. It was her idea I should call with condolences."

He gave a little grunt and nodded.

"And very good of you, too. Sorry everything was how it was, but it wasn't my show. If it hadn't been for the death and all that there'd probably have been fifty people there. Ursula likes parties."

"It's understandable," I said. "It's been nice seeing you, in any case. I've just read a book of yours, by the way, but I'll tell you about it when I drop in."

"Good," he said, and gave that friendly smile again.

We went our different ways. After a yard or two I looked back and he seemed to be walking quite quickly with hardly a sign of a limp. A few yards on I looked back again and he had gone.

A queer afternoon, I thought. Blange far less of a fool than he'd made himself out to be. And then I realised something else. All that luring me into talk about Madame Petriff had been with the expectation that Ursula Hather would do what she did—fall asleep. They'd had her in full view all the time, and when I'd slightly moved my chair that had made her just out of my view.

So I'd been the puppet and the other two had manipulated the strings. And I thought of something else. Just why had Winster kept Ursula Hather from talking? What was it he was afraid she might say? And why—charmingly put though it was—had he been so anxious at that last moment to know just why I had called that afternoon at South Mansions? I didn't know. All I could do was guess. And the guess was that he knew something about Ursula Hather which he didn't want me to know. He was being the watch-dog. And if so, he'd now have to go on being the watch-dog. Unless he thought me an utter fool, he'd have a guess of his own—that I'd be going back to South Mansions and choosing a time when he wasn't there.

*    *    *    *    *

I knew that Bernice would be out. When I'm busy on a case she uses my absences to pay overdue calls and look up neglected friends. But she'd left me a note to say she hoped to be in by ten o'clock.

I didn't feel hungry, but I made myself some tea, and over it I had a look at *Beyond*. My fat friend, as I'd expected to read, was Arthur Corbel, still given as M.A., B.D. The journal was printed and published by a firm just off Ludgate Hill, and I gathered that unless there was a room that I hadn't seen, Corbel did the compiling and editing at home. I wondered what he was paid and I wished I could have a look at his banking account.

But things fitted in. His Raimond House office closed at 5 p.m. Maroulis had wanted me followed that night and apparently Corbel had been the handiest one to put on my tail. It must have been just about five o'clock when Maroulis had rung him, and what with one thing and another—Hather, for instance, keeping me in talk—Corbel had just made Ennison Square in time for my departure. Not that that particularly mattered now that Corbel had been identified.

As for the contents of *Beyond*, they were what I'd expected—accounts of circle meetings, résumés of talks and lectures by people considered important, and trailers of forthcoming events. As for the advertisements, they were incredible. There we were half-way through the twentieth century and I was reading advertisements for yogis, mediums, planchette boards, hypnotism, palmistry, astrology and the devil knows what else. The whole was of the size of a children's newspaper, and ran to eight pages. Printing and paper were both quite good. And then I thought of something. And I hoped that Adeline would be at home.

She was. I said that, talking of Hather, what had she meant by that remark about hoping to have had him on the directorate of *Beyond*.

Adeline's far from a bad business woman, even if she's deplorably unsafe about her investments. She told me straight away that they were going ahead with the scheme and that Maroulis would probably come in instead of Hather. The idea was that every circle or group in the country should be circularised or interviewed with the hope of making *Beyond* the official publication for at least all England. Provincial groups would naturally have representatives on the new board. I said it seemed quite a good idea.

"Perhaps I'm confusing it with some other publication," I said. "But does *Beyond* publish a weekly supplement?"

"Supplement?" She bellowed the word. "Never heard anything so ridiculous! Why on earth should one need a supplement?"

"That's what I thought," I said. "And as you've never heard of one—"

I was careful to pause.

"Of course I haven't heard of one. There *isn't* one."

"I know," I told her. "I'm saying there isn't one. I'm admitting I got it confused with some other publication."

"Probably *The Times*," she snapped at me, and after a few reverberations we rang off.

That was curiouser and curiouser, but I wasn't going to let it worry me. I got my pipe going again and began skimming through the pages of that novel of Hugh Winster's. I thought that since I'd seen the actual man, the book itself might have some new significance—and I was right. All at once it struck me that it might well be autobiographical, so I turned to the beginning and began reading it much less quickly. I was at it when Matthews arrived.

"A bit early," he said, "but I think I've got all you want." I told him to start from where he picked her up.

"First of all she went along to a ladies' lavatory," he said. "Couldn't very well follow her down there, so we waited till she came up again. Then she looked about for a taxi and couldn't get one, but she hopped a bus and got off at Piccadilly Circus. She went underground at Swan and Edgar's Corner, so I went after her, thinking she was going somewhere by train, but she went on and out at Regent Street and into the Café Royal. I slipped a waiter a tip and had lunch in the same room—stood me back just over fifteen bob. Just about a quarter to two when we came out and she walked Shaftesbury Avenue way and into the stage door of the Colodium. I hung around and had a cosy chat there when the show started. Matinée at two-thirty. The play's a comedy—*Little Girl Blue*. Her name's Minden Hope. Stage name probably."

"I seem to remember the name," I said. "I've seen her in something or other, some time or other. Anything else?"

"Yes," he said. "I picked her up at just about five o'clock. She must have been in a bit of a hurry because she took a taxi at the traffic lights. If it hadn't been for that I couldn't have got one myself. Bit of luck as it was. We went on to Waymore Street, just off the Bayswater Road as you come in. Number twelve. Looked like a little flat; at any rate she let herself in. Then I came straight back here."

"Pretty good work," I said. "Everything apparently open and above-board."

"Yes," he said, "except why she went home. There's an evening show at seven-forty-five. Anyone'd have thought she'd have stayed on. Got herself some tea or something and spun it out, then gone back to the theatre."

"She may be married for all we know," 1 said. "But there's something I'd just like to know."

I got the Yard and asked for Wharton. He was there but in conference. I asked to have word rushed to him to ring me as soon as he was free.

I brought in a couple of bottles of beer and began telling Matthews about my afternoon. He seemed tickled at my account of what he called high life below stairs, and somehow gratified that I'd actually met the man who'd written those two novels. That made him remember the one in his coat pocket, and he handed it over. He said he hadn't had time to read any more.

But he agreed with me that we might be on to something. Ursula Hather might have been mixed up in her husband's death and Winster had somehow found it out. As for Blange, why shouldn't he have been the man who rang about something suspicious going on at River View.

"I think you're right," I said. "But we've got to move carefully. I'd put her down as a first-class liar and absolutely unscrupulous. The one I'd like to investigate is Blange. I have an idea we can do that through Winster."

Then the telephone went. George was on the line.

"It's half-time, George," I said, "but I think I'm on to something else. You got that red note-book on you? The one from the Maple Grove desk?"

He told me to wait a minute.

"Hallo?" he said. "What is it you want?"

"See if there's anyone with the initials M.H.—M. for Mary and H. for Holly."

I could hear him grunting to himself as he turned the pages.

"M.H.," he said. "It's number 93. What's the idea?"

"Is there a tick against her name?"

"Yes. Why?"

"Don't quite know yet," I said. "It's just a lead I'd like to follow up. Anything from your end?"

"Yes," he said. "I had our friend come to Hampstead. Kidded him I thought he could help, then shot those fingerprints of his at him. And what do you think?"

I let him have his curtain.

"He was just tickled to death. Said Petriff had a fainting-fit at some do or other and he advised whisky in her bedtime milk. Said he gave her the bottle from a case of his own."

"Pretty smart that," I said. "Did he show familiarity with the house?"

"Devil a bit. I was on the look-out for him. You never saw such an act as he put on. Walked right past, then came back. Sort of peered round, then risked it. Came right to the front door. Didn't even seem aware there was one at the side as well."

"Anything else?"

"Nothing that won't keep," he told me.

He added that from then on I'd get him at the Yard, and then rang off.

"He's a clever devil, that Maroulis," Matthews said when I told him. "Is there such a thing as an Italian Cypriot? Now and again I thought I caught a bit of Eye-tie. Just the way a chap I knew there used to talk English. Good at it, he was. Practically perfect, like this Maroulis, only every now and again you'd catch something. I spent most of my time there in the war, once we'd landed."

I said Maroulis might have had an Italian mother. But one thing I was betting—that Wharton was already setting the wheels in motion. By the time he'd finished he'd know almost as much about Maroulis as that gentleman did about himself.

He asked about the Sunday arrangements and I said I thought I might call on Winster. I said we'd take my car so as not to make things too obvious, and I might work Matthews in as my brother-in-law. I got out a road map and together we concocted a story that ought to fit.

"I'd better posh myself up," he said.

I said he hadn't better be too posh. Rich but not gaudy, I said, and he got the idea even if the quotation went over his head. But you don't need to know *Hamlet* to hold down a job at the Yard.

11

# IN THE LONG GRASS

BY THE MORNING everything had to be changed, for overnight I'd made what seemed to me a dramatic discovery. After dinner I'd gone pretty thoroughly through *The Lowing Herd* and I was more than ever convinced that the book was largely autobiographical, for it seemed to me that in those scenes in that German Oflag, no author could achieve so vivid a verisimilitude unless they had been part of himself. Then there were the characters which also seemed almost certainly to have been drawn at first hand, and in one of those camp vendettas there was such a fierceness and intensity that Winster himself must have been the man with the grievance.

There was no mention of a character that even remotely resembled Hather, and yet it was straight to Hather that the first discovery brought me. There was nothing of brain work in it, or even luck, for it stared me clean in the face. Paul Quint had mentioned plagiarism in connection with Hather's *Man With Two Souls*. He had known little about it except that the charge had been brought by a prisoner of war, by which I gathered that he meant a man who was a prisoner of war at the time of the charge.

But if Winster had been a prisoner of war, then mightn't he be the one who'd accused Hather of plagiarism? The two had been contemporaries at Clare, and Winster was obviously an old friend of Ursula Hather. The only snag was that if he'd once had a grievance against Hather, the causes had been removed, for Phyllis Parting had definitely put him among Hather's friends. But I certainly thought the whole thing worth exploring, not that I was quite so precipitate as to think I had a fine new suspect. And, of course, the original object of the visit to Humbledown remained—to try to get from Winster all the news I could about Ursula Hather and Blange.

But plans had to be altered. I couldn't sit in Winster's house and ask an indefinite series of questions without some little authority behind me. I could trap him into things, maybe, but that seemed a poor policy, and one that might make him a clam if I should happen to need him again. Whether he had once been a bitter enemy of Hather or not, I wanted him very much on my side.

So I took a police car and drove it myself, and explained the changes to Matthews on the way. I wasn't—or so he thought— the secretive type like Wharton, who always likes to spring surprises, and he wasn't worrying about hearing things only at second hand. And he'd have at any rate a chance of running his eye over Winster and I hoped to be able to wangle an adjournment to the local pub.

When we were coming into Humbledown we changed seats. We'd asked the whereabouts of Wistaria Cottage a goodish way out, and it took us by surprise when we came on it when the village was still not in sight except for a church steeple away to the left and just visible above the tops of the winter trees. We overshot the cottage, in fact, and had to come back, and that gave me a good look at it.

I wouldn't have called it a cottage, but a small Georgian house. I learned later that in the eighteenth century it had been the home of the then curate, and a path led from the opposite side of the road across the fields to the church. A wistaria wholly covered the front as Winster had told me, and tall hedges of lilac and laurel shielded it at the sides and front. There was no front gate, but only a side one which led to a far too modern garage built into the side of the house like a lean-to. A path forked from that longish driveway to the front porch.

The gate was open and Matthews drove in. He stayed in the car and I knocked. Inside I could hear a typewriter going, but Winster heard my knock.

"Well, well," he said. "You're a pretty prompt caller."

I said I'd explain, but he didn't seem disconcerted as he drew back to let me in.

"Not too tidy," he told me. "A woman comes in but not on Sundays. A hot meal on Saturdays and cold meat Sundays. I often have a snack at the pub."

He drew in a chair to the wood fire. I said it was a nice room and a cosy one—and it was. It was a man's room and the fire was a good one. It was colourful with book jackets and the chintz of chairs. There was a gem of a Sheraton sideboard, and on the mantelshelf a couple of good bits of early Staffordshire. There was incongruity, of course, and the kind that makes for variety. It was an ordinary baize-covered card table, for instance, on which his typewriter stood, but the chair in which he had been working was a corner one, and almost certainly Chippendale. Winster was colourful, too. He had no jacket but only a turtle-necked yellow pullover and greenish corduroy slacks.

"Too bad of me interrupting your work," I said.

"Not a bit," he told me. "To tell you the truth I'm dam' glad of a rest. It's something I've no particular heart in. Has to be finished for a contract. What'll you drink? A short one or some beer?"

"You're making it awkward," I said, and smiled diffidently. "To be perfectly frank, I'm here on false pretences. After I left you yesterday I was shoved on to that Petriff enquiry. At this moment I'm a copper engaged on a job."

His head went sideways as if he didn't quite get it.

"Not supposed to drink when on duty," I said and not too seriously. He laughed.

"The hell with it. What shall it be? A short one, or beer?"

"Beer."

"Fine," he said. "You're a man after my own heart. And what about your man? Wouldn't he like a bottle?"

I said his name was Matthews and he was only my driver, but I thought there'd be no harm trying him with a beer if only by way of incrimination. He went through to another room and came back with glass tankards and bottles. He insisted on taking Matthews's drink out himself.

We settled in our chairs, long legs stretched to the fire.

"Didn't someone tell me you were at Cambridge?" I asked him.

He said he was. We talked about that for a minute or two, and he was questioning me about what things had been like in my day.

"You'd have made a devil of a Rugger forward," I told him.

"As a matter of fact I was—of sorts," he said. "I went down with flu just before the Varsity match or I'd have been playing. Always preferred cricket though. My old guvnor was frightfully keen on it. If I'd had a lot of luck I might have got a blue. But there we are. The war came and that was that."

"Tough luck," I said. "And you didn't think of going back after the war?"

"Out of touch," he said, and shrugged his shoulders. "No more fun and games for me in any case."

"You got knocked about a bit?"

"Yes," he said. "I was one of the gang that was trapped behind the Maginot Line. A captain, attached to the Seaforths." He smiled with some grim amusement. "I must say the old Hun did a pretty good job on me before they dumped me in the Oflag."

"The hand badly smashed?"

"Not too badly," he said. "It's a bit unsightly, so I usually wear a glove. The trouble is I still sometimes forget and go and hurt the dam' thing. Not a lot to worry about. Still a finger to use on the old machine."

"That reminds me," I said. I'd removed the jacket from that novel and tried to make the book look less new, and now I fetched it from my overcoat pocket. "I've just read this a second time and I must say I enjoyed it immensely. I wondered if you'd autograph it for me."

He scored out the printed name and signed his own, and he was saying what vain creatures authors were. One word of praise and they couldn't help a thrill.

"But what about this 'on duty' stuff you were trying to put across me," he wanted to know. "You weren't serious?"

I said I was. I told him in strict confidence that the higher-ups had the far-fetched idea that the deaths of Petriff and Hather were somehow connected. I was only a paid employee but had to carry out instructions, and my instructions had been to interview as many people as possible who'd been close to Hather. Other people were doing the same thing about Petriff.

"Why Martin Hather committed suicide I can't imagine," he said, and shook his head at the half-filled glass. "He was a queer devil, though. Went in for esoteric stuff and all that. Damned unhealthy, I call it. Very high-strung, too. Always was."

"You knew him at Clare?"

"He was a third-year man when I first ran into him," he said. "And three years older at that. I don't know why we cottoned on to each other. Probably the attraction of opposites. I had literary yearnings in a vague way and he was already doing quite a bit of work. Perhaps that was why he took me up."

I made myself suddenly pregnant with an idea. I wrestled with it. I mentioned some dim chatter of a literary critic whose very name I'd forgotten and out of the inchoate I managed to make some sort of form and sequence. I hoped I did it artistically.

"That's extraordinarily clever of you," he told me admiringly. "As a matter of fact you're right. I was the one who accused him of using my ideas. My mother—she's dead now—sent me that book of his, and I wrote to him care of his American publishers and didn't get an answer, so I wrote to the publishers themselves."

"How amazing!" I said and shook what was intended to be a sheepish head. "It always flummoxes me when I try to work something out and I find I'm right. But tell me what happened."

"Well, when I got home I saw him. He was always a casual sort of cove and he swore blind he'd never heard a word. But we settled it quite amicably."

He smiled to himself.

"Rather funny in a way. He owned up about using my idea and wanted to know what I'd have made out of it if I'd used it myself. I said probably nothing because it wasn't up my alley, but possibly a couple of hundred pounds if I'd had a crack at it and found a publisher. He gave me a cheque on the spot!"

"He did!" I said, and then I thought that something was somewhere wrong. A hefty great chap like Winster and a shrimp like Hather: the Winster who'd tamely taken a cheque and the Winster who'd dominated that room at South Mansions.

"It was a dirty theft," I said. "I don't know why you didn't land him one under the jaw."

"Life's too short," he said. "Besides, I wasn't in an Oflag. You may breathe out threatenings and slaughter then, but things aren't the same when you're home and out of it all." He chuckled. "And I'll tell you a couple of other things. I couldn't possibly have written that book. I put up a bluff. And what did I get for it? Two hundred pounds! And something else. I've made as much more from ideas I've sold him since. The idea at the back of *The Eighth Veil* was mine." He chuckled again. "Oh no. If I'd have kicked the little skinny arse off him, what'd I have got? Nothing."

"Maybe you were right," I told him. "All the same, two hundred pounds wasn't too much considering what that book really made him. But what *was* the idea? Something on the Jekyll and Hyde lines?"

"Lord no!" he said. "It was a dam' clever idea, though I say it myself. Imagine a man with two souls. Two spirits, if you like, though what it boils down to is two lives. The hero—if you like to call him that—has two lives. It comes to him in a persistent series of vivid dreams, then he gets mixed up in all that spiritualism stuff and a medium tells him the same thing. He actually believes it. He knows it. He knows he can afford to die once and still be alive. You get the idea? He ought to be a happy man, but he isn't. He gradually gets terrified, quite paradoxically, by the fact that as soon as he loses one life he's on the same footing as other men and liable to die wholly at any subsequent second of time. That was the sort of psychological stuff Hather just revelled in. I'd never have done it myself."

"And what was the ending?"

"Well, I had the idea in 1939. I knew like you, perhaps, we were in for a war. I imagined that war and our hero joining up. He's still terrified of losing that first life of his and he manages to keep behind the front line. Then he has to go up, and it sort of comes to him that he can be a real hero at no cost. He can get a V.C. and even get killed, and still be alive to collect the cross and the glory. And he actually gets the chance to do so. But here's the queer ending as I imagined it and as Hather used it. He attempts to rescue a man under fire. He's seen to be hit, he staggers, then he picks up the body and goes on. Then he falls again. His dead body is later brought in and what is discovered is one bullet in his head and another in his heart."

"What an ending!" I said. "He lost one life and before he could get back with his man a second bullet killed him."

"That's it," he said. "A good idea and Hather made a good book out of it. Probably the best idea I ever had. I wish to God I could have written it myself."

"Yes," I said. "It's the kind of thing I get myself to sleep with. I like to get into bed and fasten my thoughts on a fine film I've just seen, and drop into sleep with it. Not only a film. It may be a book that has appealed to me. Tonight it may be that outline you've just told me."

"Thanks," he said, and rather shyly. "That's a pretty fine compliment."

"So let's leave it," I said. "Tell me about Ursula Hather. What's she really like when she's cold sober?"

"A mixture," he said, and smiled to himself as he looked vaguely up at the ceiling. "I've known her all my life. Her father—you'd never believe it—was old Canon Maze of Cledfold, about six miles from here, and a pal of my guvnor's, so we saw a lot of each other. They had money, though, and we didn't. We weren't exactly paupers, but you know what I mean. She went the usual round and finishing school in Switzerland and tried the stage for a bit and then the old boy died and she came in for the money." His lip drooped slightly with the smile. "Once we were almost engaged. Then the war came and she ran across Hather and married him and that was that. She still regards me as a kind of brother—when she thinks I can be useful."

"And what's she like in herself?"

"Good-hearted. Generous. Very haphazard. Too fond of the bright lights. Which reminds me."

He swivelled round in his chair and the gloved hand pushed aside the empty bottle. His face had suddenly a queer earnestness.

"I wonder if I might ask you to do something for me?"

"If it's possible," I said.

"It's this. Go easy if you have to question her about Hather. He was an awful swine where she was concerned. He drove her into a nervous breakdown and she hasn't been long out of a nursing home. Then there was his death and altogether she's shot full of nerves. You heard me trying to shy her away from Hather yesterday. You mayn't have known what I was doing, but that's what it was."

"I know now," I told him soberly, "and I'll do what I can. I most certainly shall have to see her, but I'll let her down very lightly. So long as I get something to please the higher-ups."

"That's fine," he said. "And you'll want to see Blange?"

"You tell me about him."

"Well, don't think him a fool," he said. "You caught him yesterday on the wrong leg. Julian is no man's fool. He got an M.C., with bar, in the war, by the way, and as a commando. And he's got brains. His father was old Wilfred Blange of Blange and Cotman—you know, the big estate agents. He's a Cambridge man, by the way. A Trinity man. Used to be a dramatic wallah. He did some dabbling with the stage, too. That's how he ran across Ursula."

"He's marrying her?"

"Most decidedly. They're simply mad about each other, though you mightn't think it. Be dam' good for her, too. He's a much more sober-minded cove than you'd think. He'll cut out all that high-light stuff. Do her the world of good."

I glanced at my watch. I remembered something.

"You weren't at Felsbury, by any chance?"

"No," he said. "At Repfield. So was my old guvnor."

I got to my feet. I asked where the local pub was and if they could give my man and me a snack.

"Afraid you have to order it," he told me. "You know how things are. But I always go along myself. Just for a breather. What about us all going? Just give me a couple of shakes to slip on a collar and tie."

He wasn't gone more than five minutes and when he came back he told me with a grin that there'd be panic at the Haymakers. They set their watches by him on a Sunday morning. He always rolled up at a quarter-past twelve every day. Maybe the police had been notified and they'd be dragging the local ponds.

"It's only half-past," I said. "But again, that reminds me. What about my higher-ups?"

He looked surprised.

"I've got to show something to justify the expense account," I said. "They'll ask me if I got your alibi."

"Alibi?" His eyes narrowed. "Alibi for what?"

I shrugged my shoulders.

"Not my fault, my dear fellow. You ought to know what red tape is by now. My instructions are to interview anyone I can who knew and was friendly with Hather. Believe me, that includes getting an alibi."

"But that's sheer lunacy!"

I shrugged my shoulders again. Maybe it was. But there was a something I could tell him in the strictest confidence. The higher-ups suspected that someone had been with Hather on the Sunday morning just before he killed himself. They also knew that someone had been in the River View flat at about nine o'clock that same night. Those were the times for which I had to find alibis, and I didn't like it better than he.

"That won't trouble us," he told me. "Wait till we get to the pub."

He and I sat in the back and Matthews drove. And he'd been right about that desecration of his village, for before we'd gone a couple of hundred yards we could see the pink tetter of bungalows.

"Slowly now!" he suddenly said, and tapped Matthews on the back. "Draw in at that cottage. Where the man is working."

He drew in alongside the fence. An elderly man looked round at us, then grinned and flicked a finger to his forelock as he caught sight of Winster.

"Come here a minute, Jim."

Jim came as far as the fence.

"Jim does my garden for me," Winster explained. "He's a bit of a scoundrel, but you can sometimes believe what he says. This gentleman and I've been having an argument, Jim, and there's a small bet on it. He says he saw me in London last Sunday morning and I say he didn't. You tell him."

Jim snorted.

"If he see you, sir, then he seed your ghost. You was here."

"How do you know?"

"How do I know? 'Cause I happened to call in at the cottage about half-after eleven and you was there. You'd hurt your hand—"

"Never mind about that." He said in a loud sotto voce that Jim was a long-winded old devil. "You'll swear I was at the cottage at half-past eleven?"

"Swear it? I'd swear it on Judgment Day."

"Give him half a crown," Winster told me, so I found one and handed it over. Jim grinned. He spat on it for luck.

"So far, so good," Winster told me, and he was grinning, too. The car moved on and another couple of hundred yards brought us to what had once been a village green. The pub was on the far side. Winster said the car would be safe.

The three of us went into the saloon bar. Only one elderly man was there, but the sound of voices was coming from the adjacent room. The landlord came through at the sound of the door.

"Hallo, sir," he said to Winster. "What's been happening to you? Caused a regular commotion, you have."

"Oh?" said Winster innocently. "Why's that, Harry?"

"Look at the clock!"

"What *about* the clock?"

The landlord gave me a look as if he couldn't believe his ears.

"Why, look at it! Aren't you always as regular as clockwork at a quarter-past?"

"You seem to think so," Winster told him, and gave me a nudge to let the landlord see it was all a joke. "What time was I in last Sunday morning?"

"What time was you in?" He clicked his tongue. "A quarter-past twelve, same as you always are."

"Was I?" Winster asked innocently, and shrugged his huge shoulders. "If you say so I suppose I was. But the next thing you'll be saying is I was here Sunday night, too."

"Course you was here Sunday night! After church, same as you always say. You and Fred here was talking politics till best part o' nine. Ain't that right, Fred?"

Fred finished his drink and wiped his mouth with the back of his hand.

"Trying to make out he was a Socialist. Then he played darts."

"You may be right, but I don't think so," Winster said. Then his good hand shot across the bar and into the landlord's belly. "Can't help pulling your leg sometimes, Harry."

Harry laughed, too. He said he'd known all the time what it was.

"Pour yourself a drink," Winster said. "Pays to let Harry have one first," he told us. "Good stuff from under the counter."

Matthews said he'd have beer. I said I could do with a pint if I could slip into the repair shop first.

"Three pints, Harry," Winster said. "What about you, Fred?"

"I don't drink with no ruddy Socialists," Fred said, and tipped me a wink.

"Give the old bastard a drink," Winster said. "Four pints, Harry, and make them like your own."

When I got back from the lavatory Winster and Matthews had chummed up and were deep in the last war. Matthews had been at Dunkirk and the landlord had had a boy there, too, so that made three. I collared my pint and sat alongside Fred. I'd taken him for a farmer, but he was a retired corn merchant. He asked if Winster was an old friend of mine, and I said he was.

"Known him all my life," he told me, "and his father before him. A rare one for a joke, Mr. Winster is. One o' the nicest gentlemen you'd ever wish to meet. Do anything for anyone, far as he can."

Something told me he was Suffolk and he was. We talked and talked and the others were hard at it and it was well after one o'clock when Winster was suddenly asking me what about another. I was full up, and Matthews refused another pint. Fred said he ought to have been home long ago, and I said I'd have to be going, too. Winster hollered for Harry.

"Couldn't you find these two gentlemen a spot of lunch, Harry?"

Harry said regretfully that it just couldn't be done. Now if we'd given him just half a day's notice . . .

I said we'd find a spot on the way home, and we shook hands all round. Winster said we weren't to be anywhere in the neighbourhood and not to drop in on him. I said I'd fix up a lunch at my club. Fred said I'd have to come and see him, too. Harry said Matthews would have to drop in when his boy was at home.

That was how we broke it up. Winster had ordered his meal in order to save the cold joint for the Monday. He came with us to our car. The walk home would do him good, he said, but usually he used all his basic to and from the pub.

He had one last private word with me just before I slid in alongside Matthews.

"Don't forget what I asked you about Ursula. Keep off Hather as much as you can. But, believe me, she didn't know a thing."

"Forget it," I said. "And thanks for everything. It's been a great morning. And remember to let me know about being in town."

He gave us a wave with his good hand as the car moved off, and when we'd circled round to our road he had gone.

"What'd you think of him?" I asked Matthews.

"A dam' nice gentleman," Matthews said. "How did you find him, sir?"

"He's quite a good chap, and I like him. Got a whole lot of useful stuff from him, too."

Once clear of the village, we stopped and changed seats. When we moved on I told him practically all that Winster and I had talked about.

"So the two things I've got," I said, "are information about Blange, and a confirmation of what I'd thought already: that Winster is covering up for Ursula Hather. He came out more into the open: didn't want her questioned too much."

"Then he's probably on the phone to her now," Matthews said gloomily, "and telling her to keep her mouth shut and act the innocent."

"We can't help that," I said. "If I were in his place I'd probably do the same thing. But what we will do is call on her as soon as we get to town."

I cut round and into the old Cambridge turnpike, then through the forest to where a couple of pubs were round a kind of open green. The first pub said they could give us cold lunch, and we had it, poor though it was, and we had to drink still more beer for the good of the house. Then we went by way of Waltham Cross and the arterial road and it was a quarter to four when we were in Whitehall. A minute or two later we were drawing up at South Mansions.

We went up the stairs and along the corridor and there was no sound of music as we neared the door. I rang. I rang again. Then I knocked.

"Looks as if she's out," Matthews said. "They might know something downstairs."

We went down and spoke to the girl at the desk in the entrance hall.

"Mrs. Hather's away," she said. "Went first thing this morning. She's gone on a short holiday."

"It's rather urgent," I said, "so may I have her address?"

"She wouldn't leave any address. She didn't want to be bothered."

"You're not forwarding letters?"

"Nothing was to be forwarded," she told me decisively.

"Well, that's cooked her goose," Matthews told me when we were outside. "She's done a bolt."

"And it wasn't Winster who gave her the tip," I said. "He couldn't conceivably have expected us this morning."

"Then Blange is in it up to the neck as well."

"Most probably," I said. "The devil of it is it's a Sunday. But you drop me at my place and then get back to the Yard. Get an enquiry going into taxis. Find out what railway station she went to. We might get a lead from there. I'll try to work out some means of getting into touch with Blange."

12

# BACK TO THE LAND

BERNICE HAD had tea, and while she was boiling the kettle for me I looked up Blange's firm in the telephone directory. Their offices, I learned, were in Whitemore Street at the back of Piccadilly, which meant a modest building which wouldn't need a night watchman, even if a night watchman could give me information about Blange's likely whereabouts. I'd seen Blange's Cranmer Square address and his telephone number which came just before that of the firm, but I was disinclined to speak to him direct. If Ursula Hather had really bolted, then he'd be the organiser. Far better let him think we were interested neither in him nor in her.

Then after tea I thought I might as well see if he were home, so I rang the Cranmer Square address and was ready to tell him in an assumed voice that I'd got the wrong number.

But nothing happened. His bell rang and rang but the house or flat seemed to be empty.

Just before six o'clock Wharton rang. He was apparently sick of the Yard and his own room and wanted to make something of a Sunday out of duty. I told him to drop in by all means. Bernice told him she was going to evensong at St. Martin's and she made him promise not to leave till she got back.

He arrived just after she'd gone and he was looking a bit tired. George, like most of us, isn't so young as he was, though it wouldn't do to hint as much.

"Where the carcass is," I told him as I took his overcoat.

"Carcass?" he said.

"Yes," I said. "The carcass of my forty-eight hours. Practically dead and gone. And you pop in like a vulture."

George said he thought it was the eagles that gathered together, not vultures. I brought in some beer and he didn't show any concern when I said my stomach was a bit out of order and I wasn't having any myself.

"I saw Matthews," he told me, "and we've got that taxi hunt started. Matthews thinks she wouldn't have taken a taxi. His idea is that this fellow Blange would have used his own car."

"Blange will have to be seen in any case," I said. "If he's at his office tomorrow we could see him there."

"No, no, no," George said. "Either he knows where she is or he doesn't. If he does, then he won't keep away. We'll put a couple of men on his office tomorrow morning if he turns up. If he doesn't, then we'll try another way."

Then he wanted me to give a really detailed account of what I'd done in my two days and just as if I'd never reported a thing, so I began with Maroulis, went on to Phyllis Parting and ended the morning with my fat friend Corbel and the strange affair of the actress. He made me go over that last part twice.

I went on to the afternoon and the birthday party at South Mansions, and I introduced him to Winster.

"Hather's wife," he said. "What's she like?"

"A brunette, petite, slinky, languid, modern. Bizarre sort of face. Looks a bit oriental. Utterly untrustworthy, I'd say."

He grunted. I went on with the afternoon and laid stress on Winster's efforts to cover up for Ursula Hather.

"You didn't happen to learn what nursing home she'd been in?"

I hadn't seen the point of asking. He didn't argue it, so I told him why I'd decided to look up Winster at Humbledown. I went into his alibi and how he must have left home remarkably early if he'd seen Hather on that Sunday morning. But he'd been miles away when Hather was shot and he'd been in the pub at five minutes past nine, so it couldn't have been he who made that London call to the Yard. And to end with I stressed again how anxious Winster had been that Ursula Hather shouldn't be harried.

He stirred in his chair, took a swig at his glass and sat bolt upright.

"Let's get one thing settled once and for all. You're thinking of Hather's wife and Blange for suspects for killing Hather. What further information have you got that Hather didn't commit suicide?"

"None," I said. "Except that a man dies, and his wife and her boyfriend begin acting in a most peculiar way."

"That could be accounted for in a dozen different ways," he told me. "So tell me this. Either you've got it worked out or you haven't, but how would you have done that killing so as to make it look like it did—like suicide?"

"To a certain extent it's easy. I call on Hather after I've made myself familiar with the lie of the land. I know there's no one in the rooms below, so I use a little gun that makes little noise, and I'm friendly or intimate enough with him to get close enough to him. I fire a second shot into a cushion or something, holding his hand on the gun. The hand absorbs the particles which are shown in the paraffin test. I place the body and the gun and that's that. I take the cushion and go out the back way."

"Leaving the door unlocked?"

"You can't think of everything. I just forget to slip the catch."

"Very nice so far," he told me. "You're using something I knew myself. I ought to. You and I handled a case the very spit of it just before the war. But tell me this. What about the last message? His prints, his writing, everything exact. How'd you fake that?"

"Don't know," I said frankly. "But you tell me something. Why wasn't that message signed?"

"You're chasing your own tail," he told me with a snort.

"Then tell me why Ursula Hather's bolted."

"I might do that."

The tone was curiously complacent. Then I saw him hesitate. He knew something, and he wasn't prepared to give it away. It was something big, perhaps, and he wanted a grand curtain.

"Well, tell me what you've been doing yourself," I said.

He was Atlas-Wharton, the world on his shoulders. He'd been up to the ears, he said—and then he paused.

"Before we leave it, just tell me something. Why should Ursula Hather want to kill her husband?"

"Winster said he gave her a hell of a time. I've told you all I know about Hather. He'd just delight in going on giving her hell, even if he wanted a divorce himself. He was a sadistic devil, and he'd make out he hadn't any intention of giving her a divorce. So she and Blange took the necessary steps. They thought he wasn't bluffing."

"Reasonable," he said and far too agreeably. Then he went on with his own troubles. He'd got hold of every group or circle with which Petriff had been connected and detailed enquiries had begun.

"Something you might like to know," he said, and hauled out his note-book. "This is what we have on her. First cropped up in 1934 when she was Louisa Patrick and married to a man named Walter Patrick who got five years for robbery with violence and died while serving sentence. She was suspected of acting as fence, but nothing could be proved. Then in 1938 she popped up at Worthing as Madame Yasmin and doing the crystal-gazing stunt. In 1939 the Great Yarmouth police had her for the same racket, only this time she was Madame Petrovina. Next she was heard of as tenant of a small lodging house which she was keeping in Waterloo Road. She was fined for an offence against the lighting regulations. Her identity card was for Lotte Petriff. And that's everything so far. A gap from then till she worked herself in with that Camberford circle in 1944, except that she sort of expanded her business. She left Camberford in 1947 and came to Hampstead as you know."

"What about Maroulis?"

"He's going to take a bit of time."

"The business in order?"

"As far as we've found out," he said. "It's an Import and Export affair. Just an agency, operating under, or hampered by, the Board of Trade. Acting for all sorts of Eastern Mediterranean firms—citrus fruits, wines, carobs, brandy, asbestos, and so on, and exporting what they can get hold of. We've had to be very guarded, mind you. No point in coming out into the open—yet."

Then Bernice came in. I was reproached for not ordering a meal for three, but we got something sent up. Over the meal and after it we were just three old friends, and it was George who got the reproachful look when he said he'd have to go. I walked with him to the lift and we stood for a minute or two on the pavement.

"What do I do tomorrow?" I asked him.

"Can't say yet," he said. "Just pop round about half-past eight."

I must have shaken a disconsolate head, for he was asking what was on my mind. I said I didn't seem to have done a great deal in my forty-eight hours.

"Like to have a bet?" he said.

I shot him a look. When you bet with George it's heads you lose and tails he wins. I've never known him pay. What he does is to badger you with hypotheses and saving clauses till you wash the whole thing out. George is close: he's closer than a photo-finish.

"Bet on what?" I said.

"How far off is Christmas?"

"You know that as well as I do," I told him testily. "A week today."

"Then I'll bet you a quid we have everything in the bag before Christmas Day. What about it?"

"What makes you so sure?"

"Sure?" he told me indignantly. "Who said I was sure? It's a bet, isn't it?"

"Maybe," I said. "But a bet with you is the same thing as a certainty. But give me a hint. What do you know?"

"Nothing you don't know yourself."

I tried to think that out.

"Look," he said. "I'll give you a chance. I think I know why Hather killed himself and why Petriff was killed. And how do I know it? *Because you told me tonight.* And now will you bet?"

I wanted all at once to get rid of him. I wanted to think and to think hard. And a quid wouldn't make me or break me.

"It's a bet," I said, and no sooner had I said it than he was off. A quick handshake and a "See you in the morning", and he'd gone.

I walked slowly upstairs and I didn't bother about the lift. That night in bed I didn't lull myself to sleep by going over that extraordinary plot that Hather had as good as stolen from Winster; I kept myself awake by trying to puzzle out just what it was that I'd told George to make him so certain. George hadn't made that bet for nothing, and to a man who'd resort to devious stratagems to avoid the bill for a couple of cups of tea or a round of drinks, a quid was something already in his pocket. And the more I thought, the more I was aware of one thing—that the Bright Boy of St. Martin's, as he'd once ironically dubbed me, had been very far from bright. And I knew he couldn't be bluffing. George wouldn't bluff and run the risk of losing a quid. What I did think at last was that he'd deliberately thrown cold water on my suggestion of Ursula Hather and Blange as priority suspects, and all the time he'd had the same idea himself. And that was all I could achieve. I thought and thought and maybe I thought myself into some kind of a stupor, for at last I fell asleep.

But during the night the old subconscious must have put in a considerable deal of overtime. I woke just before seven, and while I was giving my glasses a polish prior to hooking them on I found myself in a train of thought. Ursula Hather had not been at that séance at Ennison Square—that was the starting point. The thoughts moved without a break to that séance. They came to what followed as we had tea in the music-room, and then I remembered a forgotten factor, someone who was in danger of becoming a forgotten man.

Land! What about Land! Land the forlorn who'd just lost a wife. Land the jaunty, moustaches waxed and probably humming something about a beautiful morning, and that same Land, catching sight of me and nipping into the store. Land, catching me again, and dodging through the shoppers and bolting upstairs in a nicely timed lift. Land, terrified at meeting me. And why?

I went back to those few minutes I'd spent with him at that séance. It was he who'd made the approaches, for I'd had sufficient cool cheek and indifferent manners to refuse to budge from my place by the fire. Land—the look of him, his diffidences, his questions. Then as I hooked on my glasses I remembered what it was that he'd been so anxious to know. I remembered something else and I shot out of that bed as if the devil's hoof had propelled me. I reached down for my slippers—and then I stopped.

*I hadn't mentioned Land to Wharton the previous night.* And therefore, if Wharton had been telling the truth, Land wasn't a vital factor. But wait a minute, I said to myself. It is true I didn't mention Land, but mightn't I have said something that brought Land back to his mind? Mightn't he have connected things up?

I told myself that that was it. Land was our man, and not perhaps for what he had done as for what he knew. And there was a way of knowing just what that was, and Land himself could be dealt with later. So I put on the slippers, switched on the kettle and it was I who was humming as I went into the bathroom. I told myself that I mightn't be bright and I might be late in the uptake, but at least I could prove to George that I hadn't altogether wasted those twenty-four hours.

I was in his room that morning before him and I had a look for that red note-book, but it seemed to be nowhere about. Matthews came in, but he'd never heard of it. I asked him how the taxi enquiry was going and he said that so far there'd been no luck. Then George arrived and produced the red notebook. He'd taken it home the previous night for further study. I told him I'd like to put something up to him.

"It's in connection with that séance I attended. You've heard it all before, but I'd like to emphasise something. The medium—Madame Petriff—was supposed to be a sort of unconscious contact between the guide, Harebell, and those in the room, and we start at the time when things had begun to peter out. Then Adeline Doxon tried to keep the ball rolling by asking Harebell if there were any more messages from the spirits. I want you to note what Harebell was supposed to say. I've written it down as near as I can remember it:

> *There is also news for some who not with you today, but all of it is good. Pierre say tell you number twenty-nine very important. Number twenty-nine.*

"You'll note the repetition of the number. But the message conveyed nothing to me, so after the séance while we were having tea I spoke to Hather about it. He was pretty prompt and glib, though what he said was gibberish to me: that numbers had an occult significance and were related to the soul-path. He added a rider to the effect that the whole business would take a very long time to explain. That was to choke me off.

"But what he then did was to have a private word with Maroulis and I'm almost certain that he told him I'd been making enquiries about that message—poking my nose into what didn't concern me, in fact, and that was highly dangerous considering who I was. And hence all that melodramatic stuff that arose out of it, like my being followed by Corbel and so on.

"There's also another little thing. I mentioned a man who called himself Land who asked *me* what that message meant, and how I happened to catch sight of this Land later on in Victoria Street and how he was scared of meeting me. That's all tied up somehow with that message. So what I began to wonder was about those numbers in this book. Who exactly is number twenty-nine from the point of view of Petriff's register of members."

"We'll soon settle that," George said. "Number twenty-nine. Initials C. M-B. There's a tick against her and a cross, and the whole thing's been lined out. Look for yourself. A hyphenated name. One of three hyphenated names if I remember rightly."

"What group did she belong to?"

"We haven't got 'em all," George said, "but we might be lucky."

He took a file from the safe and said he'd be wanting it in any case. He grunted to himself as he ran a finger down the lists.

"Here we are," he said. "Haven't got the full name, but she's in the Camberford list."

"Who's the organiser or secretary of whatever they call it?"

He found that, too. A man named Kline. A bookseller—second-hand principally. A shop just past the town-hall.

There was his telephone number. I said I'd like to see him personally. A telephone gave what I call immunity of distance, and if he were mixed up in anything shady, then I'd rather have my eye on him while I talked. George asked what I had in mind.

"I think Petriff was conveying a message to Maroulis," I said. "It's only a theory, mind you, but I think she was telling him to do something about number twenty-nine."

"Yes," he said, and gave me one of his furtive looks. "But why couldn't she have telephoned Maroulis?"

"A score of reasons, and still pure theory. This business, whatever it was, may have cropped up at the last moment. She may have tried to get Maroulis and couldn't. Or Maroulis may have given orders that he wasn't to be telephoned."

George grunted. He gave me yet another curious look.

"Yes," he said. "There may be something in it. It might confirm a little idea of my own. Just an idea."

He waved an airy hand to indicate just how flimsy it was. I knew he didn't want me to ask any question.

"When are you going? Now?"

I said I'd like to go as soon as I could, and was Matthews available. He said he could be made available.

"Do you know," he told me, and his tone was what I call the unctuous-avuncular, "I'll be very interested to hear what comes out of all this. If anything emerges, you and I might pay a little call of our own this afternoon."

We went over Westminster Bridge and past the Oval. It was the rush-hour for heavy traffic, but we got to Camberford Town Hall in under twenty minutes. Then we nosed gently along till we found the shop.

It was no more dingy than most. Above its one tall window was the name—J. KLINE—and to the right of it—BOOKSELL-ER—and to the left—LIBRARIES PURCHASED. The black of the lettering had weathered to a dirty grey and the red background was cracked and chipped with age. Before the window on a trestle table were the usual trays, with books that ranged from threepence for the filthy dog-eared and antediluvian to a shilling for the reasonably clean and scarcely modern. The window itself had a far better selection. There were leather-bound sets of the classics, a *Seven Pillars of Wisdom*, an unexpurgated *Arabian Nights* for ten guineas, and a couple of French books opened to display the handsome illustrations. Behind the books were a few colour prints, and three or four definitely reproduction maps of English counties.

The door was open and we went in. There was an open space with tables on which stood more books. Even the floor was heaped with books. Behind and around and up to the ceiling were shelves with books. In the air was a faint mustiness blended with the odour of leather and furniture polish. A man of about forty, bald-headed and busy with a duster, came from the back towards us.

"Mr. Kline?"

"No," he said. "The guvnor's in the office."

"Scotland Yard," I said. "We'd like a word with him."

"Not more of you," he said, and clicked his tongue. But he moved off between the far shelves. We just heard his voice and then he was back. He beckoned.

"Along there. First to the right."

Kline was in what might once have been a small parlour. On the table was a pile of books and he was entering things in a ledger. His back was towards us and I didn't see him till he got to his feet and turned. And at once he reminded me of something, and as suddenly I knew what—*Christ Scourging the Money-Changers* in the National Gallery. He might have been el Greco's model, with his thin loose-limbed frame and the long, bony Byzantine head and the scanty brown beard.

"Mr. Kline?" I said, and gave him my warrant card.

He peered at it, switched on another light, and peered at it again. He gave it back. His voice was thin, like himself, and the tone more pathetic than querulous.

"I do hope there won't be any more unpleasant publicity."

I guessed that Wharton's minions had been giving him a harrying time.

"No publicity whatever," I told him. "Everything just between ourselves, Mr. Kline. I give you my word for that. All we want to know is the full name and address of one of your members, or late members."

He gave me a most uncomfortable look when he'd identified those initials.

"A Mrs. Merton-Beale of 5 The Ridgeway. She's no longer a member."

He looked hopefully as if that settled the matter. I wanted to know why she was no longer a member. He said he didn't quite know. He'd been told that she'd resigned.

He didn't seem to have had a very firm grasp of things. I kept on at him and badgered him into an admission—that he'd heard that her presence had been hostile to the medium. There were such cases, he assured me: people whose presence nullified all efforts to make contacts.

"We're much obliged to you," I said, and held out my hand. "I'm not saying we shan't have to see you again."

The hollow eyes screwed up in a brief misery, and that was the last I saw of him.

"A queer sort of fish?" Matthews said when we got into the car. "Looked like a poet or something. And where do we go now?"

I said we'd ease along out of sight of the shop and enquire about The Ridgeway. Five minutes later we were drawing into a pleasant residential avenue. The houses had decent gardens. Number 5 was a small detached villa in Edwardian Tudor. We went along a crazy-paving path and I rang the bell. At once we heard someone moving. A middle-aged woman came to the door.

"Mrs. Merton-Beale?"

She smiled.

"Mrs. Merton-Beale's away. I'm the housekeeper."

She was all of a fluster when she'd looked at my warrant card. I said there was nothing wrong and we wouldn't keep her five minutes.

We went into a smallish lounge and she switched on an electric fire. There were pipes in the room and a smell of tobacco.

"Mr. Merton-Beale isn't in?"

"He's at his office," she said, and looked rather helplessly at us till we'd all sat down. I said we were on a routine enquiry that really had little to do with Mrs. Merton-Beale. It was in connection with a recent happening—a sudden death, so to speak, and we were trying to interview everybody who'd known the dead person so as to know more about her.

"A person known as Madame Petriff," I said. "Have you ever heard of her?"

She'd heard. And she was more dithery than ever. I made a flank attack and it took me five minutes before I got her talking about herself and the Merton-Beales. In half an hour I'd heard all I wanted to know.

Her own name was Vender, and she'd been housekeeper for about five years. Her employers were very nice people to work for and she'd had no more than the usual difficulties in running the house, even when Mrs. Merton-Beale had had one of her nervous attacks. There had been an only son, it seemed, and he'd been killed—missing, believed dead—in a raid at the very end of the war, and Mrs. Merton-Beale had fretted herself almost frantic. Then she had joined the local spiritualistic society and had been very much better. She claimed to have got into touch with her son. But that was after her husband left for Malaya.

Merton-Beale, it seemed, was an important executive of Malayan Products Limited, and he'd gone to Malaya to investigate and assess the damage to the company's rubber holdings. He'd returned to England at the end of September after being away for well over a year. And he found his wife ill again. He'd had her sent to a nursing home in Hertfordshire, but Mrs. Vender had never gone there herself. The patient wasn't supposed to see anyone but her husband. But she was out of the nursing home now and was staying with her sister in Warwickshire.

"You ever go to a séance yourself?"

"Only once," she said. "She wanted me to."

"What'd you think of it?"

"I didn't like it. I wouldn't go any more. I said it'd given me a headache. I suffer from bad headaches. Not so bad as she did, of course."

"What'd you think of Madame Petriff?"

"Well, I didn't like her. I thought she was common. I didn't tell Mrs. Merton-Beale so."

"Very sensible of you," I said, and got to my feet. "I don't think we shall worry Mrs. Merton-Beale," I said, and gave a look at Matthews.

"Don't think it will be necessary," he told me.

"Then we'll forget the whole matter," I told Mrs. Vender. "Sorry to have been a nuisance to you."

She said it wasn't a nuisance. No one would be more glad than she when Mrs. Merton-Beale was back and the house was itself again. Not that she'd ever really be her old self. A mother couldn't ever really forget, as she knew herself.

I didn't mention the father. There was a telephone on the hall table and I didn't want her to ring and report the visit. All I said as I shook hands and thanked her again was that we'd probably have a good few wasted interviews.

"Where to now, sir?" Matthews wanted to know. "That Ma-

layan Products Company?"

I told him he'd got it first time.

## 13

# THE TREES AND THE WOOD

BLOCKS OF FLATS and blocks of office buildings. I was sick of the sight of them, and I told myself bitterly that I needn't worry about an occupation for my old age—I could write a volume about them. But this particular block was rather smaller than Raimond House, though the Malayan Products Company occupied its first and part of its second floors.

The ENQUIRIES said knock and enter, so we went in. Two girls were typing and one of them came to the guard-rail. I asked if Mr. Merton-Beale was in. She said she'd see, and what was my business. I asked for a sheet of paper and an envelope. I wrote a quick something and sealed the envelope.

She was back in a couple of minutes and said we wouldn't be kept very long. It was five minutes before the office buzzer went, then we were taken along a corridor and ushered into a room—a business-like room that smelt of new linoleum.

Merton-Beale was a man of about fifty: tallish, clean-shaven, thin-lipped and going bald. His eyes were cold and grey, and he was trying to conceal an uneasiness. He smiled after my opening, Whartonian gambits, but the thin lips clamped tight when I came to Madame Petriff.

"Afraid you gentlemen are wasting your time," he told us and got to his feet. "I never saw the woman in my life."

I told him to sit down. I said we hadn't even begun.

"I'm sorry, gentlemen, but there's nothing whatever I'm prepared to discuss."

"You're a busy man?"

"I am."

The lips had clamped together again. I looked at Matthews and tried some more of the Whartonian technique.

"Mr. Merton-Beale's a busy man," I said, "and yet he won't talk to us nice and comfortably and confidentially in this room. He'd rather lose best part of a day at an inquest and be asked questions in public which he'd have to answer."

That budged him a bit. He asked what we wanted to know. I said we wanted to know what had happened when he came back from Malaya. How he'd found his wife and so on. What she'd told him about that spiritualistic circle.

He sat with finger-tips together and the words came out as if reluctantly squeezed. He might have been Alfred Jingle in a tight corner.

"A damnable and dirty and dangerous fraud. You ought to do something about it. Not come to me. Worried my wife into a severe illness. Might have killed her if I hadn't got home when I did."

"What was the nature of the illness? A nervous breakdown?"

"Yes. I'd rather not go into it."

"I think I understand," I said. "And I sympathise. You got home to find your wife driven into a dangerous nervous condition because of her association with spiritualism, or whatever one calls it. And you've indicated what you did about it. I might tell you that we know that you had her immediately enter a nursing home."

I leaned forward.

"But didn't you do anything else? What about the people she'd been mixed up with? You've been telling us what *we* ought to do, but doesn't charity begin at home? What'd you do yourself?"

A moment or two and the thin lips unclamped. The frown was still there.

"I haven't quite told you the truth. Not a lie, but perhaps a deviation from the truth. I rang that Madame Petriff as she called herself and threatened her with what I'd do if she ever tried to communicate with my wife."

"When was that?"

He didn't remember, but it was early in October. I asked what time of the day it was, and he said it was one morning when he came in before lunch. I had to give Matthews a look. There was at least one confirmation of what I'd suggested to Wharton.

"That was excellent," I said. "Anything else did you do?"

The lips clamped again: there was the frown and the eyes across the room while he wondered what he should admit.

"What *was* there? I hoped I could make a case of some sort. I made enquiries—"

"And discovered that all these societies are perfectly legal?"

"Yes," he said. "Yes," and for some reason or other he looked relieved. It didn't pay me to tell him he was lying: that if he'd discovered that much, why had he accused us of negligence.

"And that was all?"

"Yes."

"And you never spoke to the Petriff woman again?"

"Never."

"And when you heard she'd been murdered, what did you think?"

"I wondered who'd done it," he said evenly. "If I'd known I'd have shaken him by the hand."

"But you didn't murder her?"

"No. I ought to have done, but I'm just not that kind."

I wasn't so sure. I asked him whether he could furnish an alibi for the relevant time, supposing we ever thought it necessary. He asked what the time was and said he doubted it. There'd been a rush of work and he'd rarely left that office much before six o'clock. But his secretary might know.

"I doubt if it'll be necessary," I told him, and thought it as well to relax. "You don't want my sympathy but you've been through a hell of a time. But I'd like your sympathy. I've got to do a highly unpleasant job."

I'd got to my feet and when I looked at him again he was somehow a different man. He told us he must have seemed damnably rude but was glad we understood. He asked if we'd have a drink. He brought out a cigarette box with gold-tipped cigarettes as long as pencils. He walked out with us to the lift, and thanked us effusively for at least the second time.

"Well, that's that, sir," Matthews told me indecisively when we got back to the car. "Couldn't make much out of him, could you?"

I said I didn't quite know.

"Wonder what he meant by making enquiries?" Matthews asked himself.

"That's it," I said. "You do the driving. Stop at Oxford Circus. I think I've got an idea."

I had to wait a few minutes at the Underground kiosks and then I rang Norris at the Agency. I said I wanted him to do an urgent job of work which shouldn't take him more than half an hour. When he was ready I told him just what I wanted.

"Ring up the reputable detective agencies, beginning with those who advertise, and ask in confidence if they've ever done any work for a man named Merton-Beale. If you can, do it without committing yourself, speak as if he wants to use the Agency and you'd like to be sure of his bona fides. I'll call you back in about half an hour."

He said he'd see what he could do. Matthews and I brought the car through Argyll Street and parked it in front of Liberty's, and went into Fuller's and had coffee and a cake. If Norris reported anything that had to be handled at once, and after it we had to get back to the Yard in time for Wharton, it might be as well to have some sort of stand-by instead of a meal.

We lingered out the time with a second coffee. When I got Norris again he had some news. A firm calling itself the Metropolitan Enquiries Limited had done a job for Merton-Beale in October.

"I talked to a man named Strout," Norris told me. "He was pretty cagey. Wouldn't even hint what the job was, but he did give the client an okay."

He said the firm had its offices in Natter Court, just at the back of Dover Street Station. It was then a quarter to twelve, which didn't give me too much time. But we made it before midday.

Natter Court was one of those little backwaters still undisturbed among the criss-cross of the traffic arteries. It had a remote, Dickensian look, and the outside of the firm's office had the dinginess of neglect. I had to dip my head at the doorway, and the ceilings looked low, and the whole place was like one of those old-time rabbit warrens where lawyers entombed themselves in documents and dust.

A thin-faced woman in the thirties slid aside a kind of hatch when I tapped on the frosted glass. I asked to see Mr. Strout and admitted I hadn't an appointment. I showed my warrant card and she didn't look impressed. She said if we'd wait a minute she'd make sure about Mr. Strout. She slid back the hatch, but we could just hear her on the office telephone.

"Bet it's not the first time they've had the coppers here," Matthews told me, and then back went the hatch again. We were to go straight along the corridor, through a door and it was the first on the right. It was a longish corridor with a couple of rooms to right and left. The door of one was slightly open and I could hear faint voices and there was the smell of tobacco.

We went on as directed. I rapped the door and a voice answered. We went in. Metropolitan Enquiries weren't wasting much on overheads, for the room had the essentials and no more. Strout, cigarette ash down the front of his dark waistcoat, looked hard-bitten behind the smile. His good morning was a bit too genial, and when he put out his hand I put my warrant card in it.

"Strictly business, is it?"

I said not necessarily. We were hoping he could give us some information.

"Sit down," he told us. "Might as well be comfortable. Have a cigarette."

I said we'd both been smoking too much, and I didn't want to keep him. But we'd been doing the rounds of the detective agencies and we'd like strictly confidential information about a possible client of his named Merton-Beale.

You could almost hear him think. He was wondering why Norris had rung him, and what we knew, and if it would pay to tell the truth.

"As a matter of fact I did have a client of that name," he said. "Did a job for him last October. Is anything wrong?"

"With him—no. Definitely no. But the job may tie up with something else. You realise that all this is in strict confidence?"

"Naturally. I wouldn't be in business if I didn't know that."

I caught the hint. Strout wasn't going to be easy to handle.

"It's tied up with a murder job," I said, "and you know what that means. What we'd like to know is the nature of the work you did for Mr. Merton-Beale and the nature of the information you handed him."

"Come now, come"—his smile was all pain and protest—"you know perfectly well I couldn't tell you that."

"Why not?" I told him brusquely. "You've no immunity in law. You're not a doctor or a priest—or are you?"

"Just your little joke," he said. "But it's the basis of my business. If a client couldn't rely on secrecy—well, there'd be no client."

"Maybe," I said. "That's why I want the three of us to talk confidentially. There's no necessity for the client ever to know. If you like I'll give you that in writing."

"Sorry. It just can't be done."

"Very well," I said. "Then we'll have to get what we want from the client himself. We'll have him in the box at the inquest. We might have you as well."

"Sorry," he said, "but that bluff won't work."

"What makes you think it's a bluff?"

"It stands to reason," he said, and spread his palms. "Suppose he was up to something illegal, which he wasn't. You put him on the stand. You put me on the stand. And what do we state? So much and no more. We just keep our noses clean. But this was a straight job. I didn't get the information he wanted. No one could have got it. After we'd spent time and money, he changed his mind and called us off."

"And what was it you didn't find?"

"That's nobody's business," he told me. "It doesn't exist."

"Suppose I tell you," I said, and pulled out my note-book for effect. But I didn't need the effect. I'd alarmed him. Just those words had made him bite his lip. And his eyes were watchful.

"Merton-Beale employed you when he returned from Malaya," I said. "He found his wife in a serious condition and he traced the causes to a spiritualistic society. He was furiously angry and wanted to bring in the law. But he couldn't do that without bringing what he thought was notoriety on himself, so he employed you to find evidence. You undertook the job. Your principal operative was a man who called himself Land. There's a whole lot more, but that will do to go on with. That make you change your mind?"

"Well"—he hesitated—"tell me what else you know and I'll be just as frank with you."

"Oh no," I said. "Bargain day's over. You tell me."

He called me instead. I'd thought I was pretty good at bluffing, but he'd outguessed me.

"Sony. It just can't be done. Let's leave it that we didn't get the evidence. He paid. We parted. That's all there is."

I had a last try.

"Admitted. But it boils down to this. You know as well as we do that such societies are within the law. What made him think this particular one wasn't? You couldn't have taken his money for nothing? He must have given you some indication of the lines along which he wanted you to work?"

"Sorry," he was telling me again, and this time he was getting to his feet. "We're just talking. We're getting nowhere."

Then he was trying something more suave.

"Why don't you people realise we want to help. Why should I get myself in bad with the Yard? I'd like to help, but I can't. No one could if he was asked things he didn't know."

"Well, so far so grateful," I told him, and didn't take the hand he held out. "All the same, you'll probably be asked to pay a call on the Yard."

He shrugged his shoulders.

"No use jumping hurdles till you come to them. You send an invitation and I'll be there. But not this afternoon, because I shall be out."

He saw us through the first door and he was still there when I closed the front door behind us. We got into the car and I drove through to Piccadilly and then drew the car up.

"You know, Matthews, I don't think I handled that any too well."

"I don't know, sir," he told me gallantly. "I don't see what else you could have done."

"He knows something," I said. "Something we've got to know. The something fishy that made Maroulis anxious about my being at that séance. And the devil of it is, I don't see how we can prise it out of him."

"Put him on the stand, like you said."

"Oh no. Didn't he hint that that wouldn't work? It's a pound to a penny he's now talking to Merton-Beale and telling him what to say and what not. They'll probably meet this afternoon and put the finishing touches. Strout'll collect another fee and we'll be just where we were before we went into his office."

"Yes," Matthews told me grudgingly. "But we've got to do something."

"I know," I said. "And we'll do it. We'll try the good old army system. Pass it to the Higher-ups. Why should you and I have all the headaches?"

It was almost one o'clock, but there's no rush hour for meals at a little place I knew in Soho. So we had lunch there, and it was still short of Wharton's two o'clock when we got to the Yard.

He'd had lunch in his room and he greeted me like a long-lost creditor. I wondered why.

"Well, what'd you get on to?"

I told him that Mrs. Merton-Beale had panned out well. I took him along with us to Kline and on to The Ridgeway and from there to Malayan Products and the distracted husband. When I came to Strout I did a discreet bit of editing. I didn't want George to tell me where I'd gone wrong.

"Strout knows something," I said. "Matthews and I haven't a doubt on that. Take my friend Land whom Strout didn't deny had been employed on the job. I see the sequence like this. Merton-Beale got an idea from his wife that something crooked was going on. He employed Strout to verify it. Strout found something that looked too dangerous to handle or else allowed himself to be nobbled. Probably by Maroulis. He may even have blackmailed Maroulis. Having seen him, I wouldn't put it past him. But Land was very definitely warned to keep his mouth shut. That's why he was so scared that morning when he caught sight of me."

"That's it," Wharton said, and didn't seem the least elated. "But we needn't worry about Strout or Land. What you've brought in is precisely what I want." He gave me a look like a drunken leer. "Remember a little financial transaction arranged last night?"

"What about it?"

"Pity I didn't make it a fiver," he told me, and added a shade too off-handedly that it didn't matter. But I'd know more about it before the day was out. Then he was looking at the clock and wondering where Anders had got to.

"What's on?" I said. "Some new timing or other?"

"Just taking him with us on a little trip," he said. "Almost the first time I've ever done such a thing. I wouldn't be surprised if you didn't find it interesting."

You see what I meant when I said George could be difficult? It's the Pooh-Bah in him. He likes to stage a play and act in it and be effects-man and write his own critique when he thinks it time to lower a curtain. Mind you, he'd given me a fair amount of scope. I'd been let loose for once instead of trailing at his heels, but whereas I'd come clean with what I'd found, he was holding back something that by his own admissions was mightily important. And I wondered again just how much truth there'd been in that self-satisfied assertion that all he knew was what I'd told him. And that what I'd told him only a few minutes ago had been an added confirmation.

He was telling Matthews about Blange. I was only half-listening, but I gathered that Blange had turned up at his office that morning and Matthews was being told to go there and see that nothing slipped up when he left. Then all at once I wasn't listening at all. Something had come to me; something that rose out of the morning's happenings; something that I'd missed.

Mrs. Merton-Beale had been ill and had gone to a nursing home. Protracted worry over a dead son and mental disturbance caused by deflated hopes, maybe, at the little she'd been told of that son in a life in a somewhere beyond had brought on some sort of breakdown. But Ursula Hather had also been in a nursing home, and she, too, might have had a nervous breakdown, but caused according to Winster by however it was that Hather had treated her. Yet it seemed more than a coincidence. And there was another coincidence of a less obvious kind. Ursula Hather had called Petriff a horrible woman. Merton-Beale had rung Petriff and warned her of the consequences if she dared as much as to communicate with his wife.

Matthews left and he and Anders had met at the door. Wharton grabbed overcoat and hat as if minutes were vital. When we got down, he had Anders in front with the driver. I guessed he didn't want my asking questions. Anders might have been the one who's seen the play before and spills the plot to all within earshot.

"Where're we bound for, George?" I asked him when we turned into Regent Street.

"No distance at all," he told me. "Be there in no time."

Then he began asking me to tell him more about Merton-Beale. He said it was a pity I hadn't got the name of the nursing home in which his wife had been. I said it didn't matter. We could get it any time.

"Why so anxious?" I said. "Think there's a chance it may have been the same one that Hather's wife went to?"

He shot me a look. But I was noticing something—that we were past the Marble Arch and going straight over into Bayswater Road. I didn't say anything till the car turned right.

"Calling on that actress, are we?" I said.

"That's right," he told me. "I thought you'd spot it at last."

I didn't give him a sign that I still had no idea what it was that I was supposed to have spotted. And the car was drawing up. Across the road there was another car. Wharton got out and went over to it. It was a police car, but his bulk hid the man to whom he was talking.

He came back. The other car hadn't moved. Ours went on to one of a series of small blocks of flats: self-contained by the look of them. Then the three of us piled out. Wharton had a quick look round and made for a door. We were close at his heels. Anders gave me a little nudge with his elbow. He looked so pleased with himself that I wondered if we were expected to find a corpse.

A woman came to the door, but she took some recognising as Minden Hope. I'd seen her in a fur coat and a smart hat: now she was wearing a one-piece frock that looked a bit rumpled, and her hair wasn't done. Her face was flushed a bit as if we'd roused her out of a nap.

"Miss Hope?" Wharton asked pleasantly.

"Yes," she said, and her eyes went past to us.

"I wonder if we might come in for a minute. We're police officers from New Scotland Yard and we'd like to ask you some questions."

She stared. Her hands stayed motionless. Wharton was stepping inside. The short passage was narrow and she had to move ahead of us. Wharton's voice was still pleasant.

"Hope we shan't keep you very long. In here? . . . Thank you. . . . No, you first, please."

We went into a small sitting-room. There was an upright piano at the far end and its top was crowded with photographs. There was a small settee and two easy chairs. There was a small desk under the window and a telephone and more photographs on the table top.

"Sit down, Miss Hope," Wharton was telling her.

She sat, and as if the cushion was a spiked board.

"But what's it all about?" Her hands fluttered in a stage gesture. "You're sure you're from Scotland Yard?"

Wharton handed over the warrant card with a flourish. It was at him that she looked first.

"Yes," she said, and gave the card back. "But you still haven't told me—"

"I'm telling you now," Wharton said. "We have reason to believe that you're in possession of dangerous drugs. I have a warrant to search this flat."

"No! . . . No!" Her face screwed up with a kind of horror. She cringed back. Then she went limp. The hands drooped. Anders caught her as she fell.

"Get her round." He snapped that at Anders. "What're her eyes like?"

Anders raised the lids and looked.

"Some dilation. She's had a shot today."

"Right," Wharton told him. I followed him out. At the front he was waving to that other car. It drew up and I recognised the two men who got out: Superintendent O'Hara and Detective-Sergeant Mole of the Central Office.

"Right," Wharton told them. "She's in there and she's all yours. You'd better have this. Let me know as soon as you can."

He handed over the warrant, watched them enter, gave a dour shake of the head and moved on to his car. We settled into our corners at the back and the car moved round.

"That's that then," he said, and let out a breath. "Took you a long time spotting it, didn't it?"

I reminded him tactfully that it was only the fools who never made mistakes. But he couldn't let it rest.

"It was under your nose," he had to tell me. "What'd she come bouncing into that man Corbel's for? Because she'd run short and had to have another consignment. What'd that slip mean that Corbel was putting in those magazines? That Maroulis had warned him to clear the stuff out of the place and let the customers know there was some sort of hold-up."

"Don't labour it, George," I told him. "I can put two and two together as well as most when you push it under my nose. What are you going to do now? Bring in Maroulis?"

"It's out of our hands. O'Hara'll handle that side from now on. Soon as we all get things worked out, then we'll move."


# 14

# MOST OF THE TRUTH

WE HAD TEA at the Yard while we waited for Matthews to report that Blange had left his office. I'd heard and was hearing quite a lot of things from Wharton.

I'd asked him what the drug was and he said he didn't know, though if Anders were right about that dilation of the pupils it might be cocaine. But what was found in that flat wasn't necessarily the whole story. If Maroulis knew his job, then he'd have a range of stuff—hashish, maybe, or opium or heroin or marijuana, or his own private mixture. It might be stuff to inject or sniff or smoke, according to the circumstances. But whatever it was, it was a good racket. A whole army of gullible, hysterical women as raw material. But there'd been a slip-up over Mrs. Merton-Beale. It stood to reason that Maroulis wouldn't have touched a married woman with a mile-long pole. Mrs. Merton-Beale, for some reasons of her own, must have led her circle to believe that she was a widow. Or somehow it had been taken for granted.

"But that wasn't why Petriff was killed," I said.

"No," he said. "But she might have been losing her touch. Outlived her usefulness. It may be a good racket—there must have been a regular gold-mine in it—but it's a devilish dangerous one. You can't afford to have subordinates that make mistakes."

He told me what he'd already picked up about Maroulis. It had come in only that morning from Egypt. Just after the war his name had vaguely cropped up in connection with a cargo of hashish that had been seized just across the border from Palestine. The crop had been raised in Syria and he had been behind the grower. The Egyptian authorities had delved back and thought they could identify him with an Andreos Paphilos who was still wanted for heroin smuggling just before the war.

I wanted to know how soon it'd be before the Dangerous Drugs people had enough on him to bring him in. He didn't know. What he did know was that they wouldn't jump too quickly. If drugs had been distributed from Raimond House or at meetings of circles, then the routine would have been changed.

"We couldn't make Corbel talk? Not if that actress incriminates him?"

"Bring in Corbel and you scare Maroulis," he told me. "Maroulis brings the dope in with his licensed import stuff. Either some consignment has to be intercepted and gone through at sea or else at port. Once we hold him for that, then we can rope in Corbel and everyone else and bring home a murder charge."

"What about Hather?"

"Hather," he said, and let out a breath. I've known him to be pretty unblushing, but I'd never thought him so barefaced as to say what he did.

"Hather," he began again. "I always did think there was something fishy about that Hather business. Everything was just a bit too pat."

I couldn't even gape. I daren't look at him.

"Mind you," he was going on, "I still think he did himself in. I reckon we shall find he was in it up to the neck. Maroulis might have been blackmailing him and he just couldn't stand the strain. But we'll know," he said. "With any luck we'll know a good bit before the night's out."

"You think you'll question Merton-Beale again?"

He didn't tell me. The buzzer went. He looked up at the clock before he took the call.

"Yes?" he said. "Fine! . . . Keep right on his tail."

"Matthews," he told me. "Blange has left for home in his car. At least he's heading that way."

He prowled restlessly about the room for a couple of minutes. I asked him again about Merton-Beale.

"No point in it," he told me. "Not yet. We ought to get the same, and better, from Hather's wife and Blange."

He began looking through that file he'd taken from the safe. I was thinking things out my own way, and it was the old stubborn way: the way of a man who's been convinced, as Butler's *Hudibras* has it, against his will and has his own opinion still. I wasn't so sure that Maroulis answered all the questions, I saw Merton-Beale, for instance, as a pretty good suspect for the killing of Petriff, and it wouldn't be hard for him to fake an alibi. His wife had almost certainly refused to give information, but he must have known the cause of her breakdown before he sent her to that nursing home or sanatorium. To avoid publicity he'd gone to Strout instead of the police. Strout had put Land on the job and then had decided that the whole thing was too dangerous, since what had happened was that Merton-Beale had given him as a basis for an enquiry things that ought at once to have been communicated to the police. That was reasonably clear and logical, but it didn't prove that Merton-Beale hadn't taken the law into his own hands when Strout had turned the job in. And take the question of Hather.

The buzzer went again. Wharton reached over.

"You don't say! . . . That's it. Let 'em get nicely settled, then carry on. Bring 'em both in. I'll see the Hather woman first."

"Where do you think she went to?" he asked me. "I was thinking we might have to go God knows where, and she's at the Red Anchor Hotel, just off St. James's. Blange must have taken her there that morning in his car. He took precautions, by the way, in case anyone was on his tail tonight. Made a quick cut through into Wardour Street and round the mulberry bush in Soho and along Piccadilly and into Jermyn Street."

He gave himself a nod and a pat on the back and settled to that file again. I went back to Hather.

If he'd been killed, I told myself, then Ursula Hather and Blange were priority suspects. As to the apparently insuperable thing—the writing on that last message—it seemed to me that Blange might have done a first-class job of faking. Somewhere in her possession Ursula Hather might have had a letter of his or some longhand manuscript that contained those words, referring, of course, to some other person, and Blange had reproduced the handwriting, of which Ursula must have had specimens enough. But they'd been in a hurry and neither had been able to get into the flat and take a sheet of Hather's own paper, so the job had had to be done on that pad, and the pad had been left in the back of the drawer as if it belonged. And if the copying had been done from a letter, then there wouldn't have been available a full signature. Hather would never have signed a letter to his wife with his full name. And so it had been thought best not to fake a signature as well.

I rather liked all that, even if there was still a lot that was unexplained. The fact, for instance, that Hather's sadistic and bluffing refusal of a divorce hardly seemed grounds enough for a murder. For why should a woman like Ursula Hather care about the proprieties? If she had Blange when she wanted a warm bed, why stick out for marriage lines? Or was it Blange who had had a moral streak?

George was saying something.

"Sorry," I said. "I happened to be wool-gathering."

"About that missing box from Petriff's flat," he told me. "You bet your life it was full of nice little packets of dope in case a customer called in. Maroulis took it after he'd done her in. He'd have to."

"Looks a certainty," I said.

"Wish to God I could lay my hands on it." He clicked his tongue. "That's the sort of short cut we'd never get. Tie him right up with the Petriff killing. Save the devil of a lot of time."

He grumbled away to himself for a bit. I went back to Ursula Hather. What I'd like, I was now telling myself, was a stronger motive for the killing of her husband. And then the buzzer went again.

A minute, and he was asking for the stenographer. Five minutes more and Matthews was bringing Ursula Hather in.

She shook off the arm that just touched her and glared angrily at Wharton. She was in full evening dress with a fur wrap across her shoulders and it slipped as she came furiously forward. Matthews caught it and she switched the glare to him as he replaced it.

"Keep your hands off me!"

She took a step nearer Wharton.

"What's the meaning of this? Why am I brought here as if I was a criminal or something?"

Wharton hooked on his antiquated spectacles and took his time about it. He peered at her over their tops.

"You're brought here for questioning," he told her mildly. "You're under suspicion of having been in possession of dangerous drugs."

"Oh!"

She said it blankly. There was a sudden limpness about her.

"Sit down, Mrs. Hather," Wharton told her. "Let's have a little friendly chat. You don't deny having been in possession of dangerous drugs?"

"I do. I most emphatically do."

I'd held the chair for her. She settled herself and primly adjusted the hem of her frock. But her eyes never left Wharton.

"You deny that you've ever been under the influence of such drugs?"

"Yes. . . . I deny it."

He grunted. He made play with the file. A finger ran down a page, and stopped. He leaned forward.

"Do you deny that you spent some time in a nursing home or sanatorium?"

"Why should I deny it?"

"It might be because you were admitted as suffering from the effects of dangerous drugs. Would you care to give me the name of the nursing home?"

She had to think hard. She shook her head.

"It wouldn't make any difference if I did. A doctor doesn't tell what a patient is suffering from, even if I had been ill as you say. . . . Which I wasn't."

"One can gather a shrewd idea from the look of the place itself," he told her. "Not that it matters. We can easily find out. Or perhaps some news we have for you might make you change your mind."

He told her guardedly about Mrs. Merton-Beale and Minden Hope. He said that at any moment he'd know what drugs they'd taken. And that's where I thought him wrong. That's where he should have lied. He should have said he knew. As it was he gave her a respite. It's my job to watch while he talks, and I saw it in her face.

"Why should other people concern me? I know nothing about any drugs."

"But you do know that it's an offence to be in possession of such drugs, except by a doctor's permission? That you can be arrested for being or having been in possession?"

She shrugged her shoulders.

"Ought one to know such things?"

"Just making the position clear," he told her suavely. "Explaining why it is that we shall have to hold you for a time."

"You mean I'm under arrest!"

"Oh no. Just held for further questioning. Unless you prefer to remain here and tell us all you know."

"I've already told you I know nothing."

"Very well, Mrs. Hather." He turned to Matthews. "Take Mrs. Hather out and then bring in Mr. Blange."

"But he knows nothing!"

Wharton had turned away. Now he turned quickly back. "Nothing about what?"

"About dangerous drugs as you called it."

"You never know," he said, and stepped away from the desk again. Ursula Hather gave an angry toss of the head. As the door closed on her she was demanding of Matthews where he was taking her.

"Well, that's made a start," Wharton told me grimly. "A bit of a spitfire, wasn't she?"

I said she'd probably be tamer before the evening had gone. That bit about bringing in Blange had shaken her.

"Yes," he said and pursed his lips. "We've got to go a bit more carefully with him. Wouldn't be surprised if we don't have to play battledore and shuttlecock half the night before we have 'em in together. But we'll see."

There was a tap at the door and in came Matthews with Julian Blange. Blange was wearing a black overcoat with a white wrap round his neck and he was carrying a black felt hat in his hand. He didn't make any fuss. He just looked at Wharton for a moment.

"Mind telling me what this is about? Why you've brought me along here?"

"Sit down, Mr. Blange," Wharton told him, and I indicated the chair. I got a nasty look for my pains.

"It's very easily explained," Wharton said. "You know, perhaps, that we've just seen Mrs. Hather. What she told us doesn't matter, but what we told her to begin with applies partly to you.

It's a serious offence to be or have been in possession of dangerous drugs or to have assisted in the procuring of such drugs."

Blange looked a bit blank. I thought he'd expected quite a different attack. He shrugged his shoulders.

"But how does that affect me? I didn't supply her with any drugs."

"But if you knew who did, then you were in possession of information which you withheld from the police."

"But I didn't. Not until—"

He broke off too late. He moistened his lips.

"What *is* all this? I want to see my lawyer."

"All in good time," Wharton told him. "But you surely wouldn't object to a full and honest statement of how you came to meet Mrs. Hather, and how you got on together, and so on?"

"There's nothing to tell. We met some months ago and we liked each other. People often do. Then her husband had no more use for her, and that was that."

"Just a moment," Wharton said. "Surely her husband had some use for her, as you put it. Otherwise why did he get her into a nursing home?"

"He didn't."

He stopped abruptly. He shook his head a bit ruefully. "Sorry, but I shouldn't have said that."

"It was you who sent her there?"

"Well, yes. No harm in admitting that. I got her to go there."

"I see. And so she virtually left her husband. You went to the nursing home to see her, of course."

"Yes, I did."

"And how long did it take her to throw off the effect of the drugs?"

"Well—"

He stopped again.

"Carry on," Wharton told him. "You'd be surprised, Mr. Blange, at the things we know."

"Sorry, I'm not saying anything. I'm not going to be trapped."

Wharton looked round with a pained bewilderment.

"Trapped? My dear Mr. Blange, no one's trapping you. You can refuse, if you like, to say a word." He shrugged his shoulders. "I was hoping to regard you as being here in her defence. But, as you say, you talk or you don't. It's entirely up to you."

Blange sat on in an uneasy silence. Wharton got to his feet and put away the spectacles.

"Take Mr. Blange out," he told Matthews.

"You mean I can go?"

"Oh no," Wharton said. "When you've told us the truth, and the whole truth, that's when you can go."

"Then will you do something? Let me have a word with . . . with Mrs. Hather?"

"Later—yes. Not at the moment. Take Mr. Blange out. If he or Mrs. Hather want tea or coffee or anything, let them have it. I'll let you know when I want Mrs. Hather again."

Blange went out with never a kick in him.

"Well, we're getting on," Wharton told me genially. "It was Blange, then, who made her go into that nursing home. That's something to confront her with."

He took his time before he had her in again, and this time he took pains to be most considerate. He placed the chair for her and apologised for the delay. He donned the spectacles again and the tone was quite paternal.

"We had to spend rather a long time with Mr. Blange," he told her. "He was telling us how he got you into the nursing home himself, even if it meant a complete break with your husband. He told us how he used to see you there. He didn't tell us, but he hinted you'd made a good recovery."

"He told you that?" she asked him evenly.

"Why not? He was doing his best to protect you."

She glanced across at him. She was motionless for quite a long minute, then she gave a sort of stir.

"All right. I'll tell you the truth. I did take drugs, but it wasn't my fault."

The lip curled in a childish sneer. She tried to be cynical and detached. At the back of her mind there was still the grievance: the indignity of having been brought to the Yard. Then something broke her down. It might have been a kindliness and an understanding on Wharton's face, and how he listened and nodded gently from time to time. But she cried. Then the story came out with the flood-gates ripped away. It was as if she wanted once and for all to rid herself of what had been pent up. There was a drive and a vehemence. There was a loathing that made her shake and her hands would tremble and the whole of her would seem to quiver with the hate she had of Hather and that flat in River View. I've heard some distressing confessions in my time, but this was the worst. It was not only the horror of what she had to tell, or how she told it, but the things she left unsaid and what the mind imagined.

Soon after that return to England, Hather had begun experimenting on himself with various drugs. Then he met Maroulis and it was after that that she was induced to experiment, too. She told us something of what used to happen in the draped room with the smell of incense, and how Maroulis would generally be there, and other people—never more than one or two—whom she never knew, except Madame Petriff who had been there perhaps no more than three or four times. But it was not till the last few months that she became an addict. She said Hather had come to hate her and he had tried to kill her or drive her insane. It was he who supplied her with the drugs, and, after a time, he virtually kept her in the South Mansions flat and if she did go out it was only with him, as if he was afraid to have her found there. Then one day in October—it must have been not long after I'd first seen her—she saw herself on the edge of insanity. Something told her to ring Winster and he came to the flat.

He was horrified. He saw Julian Blange and told him to get her away at once. Blange had been anxious, too, but had been told by Hather that she was in the country with friends, but inside twenty-four hours Blange had her in the nursing home. She said it was an even worse hell for the next few days, and then she slowly grew better. But there were still times when she was afraid: afraid even of sleep, and of herself. That was why she liked to drink. When you drank, you weren't afraid.

That was all. Wharton reached for a sheet of paper and began writing. She gave a queer, bewildered shake of the head and brought the wet handkerchief from her bag and began wiping her eyes again. Wharton handed me the paper and got to his feet.

"Thank you, Mrs. Hather. We're grateful to you, and we believe what you've been telling us. I don't intend to bring any charge against you. In fact, you may go. But I'd like Mr. Blange to take you home. I must see him first, so perhaps you'll wait. Will you come with me?"

He took her by the arm and they went out. That sheet of paper had various instructions. The stenographer was to get typewritten copies ready at once and a fresh man was to come up. I was to get hold of Winster and arrange for him to hire a car and come at once to the Yard.

Winster wasn't at the cottage, but I got him at the pub. I told him the Higher-Ups had seen Ursula Hather and she had spilled all the beans, and that we wanted his version of the affair. I said it would be largely formal and he wouldn't be kept long. The car could wait and his expenses would naturally be paid.

"What do you mean by all the beans?"

"The goings-on at River View," I said. "How Hather drugged her. How she thought of you. What you and Blange did."

"Right," he said. "I'll be along as soon as I can make it."

Wharton came in with Blange and I gathered they'd already had some talk downstairs. Wharton asked him to sit down and said he wouldn't keep him a minute.

"We heard a pretty horrible story, as you know," he told him. "You say she told us more than she ever told you."

"She told me more than enough," Blange said.

"Well, she's got to be watched," Wharton said. "She's still a sick woman. That drinking business ought to be cut out."

"She doesn't really drink," Blange said. "I mean, it isn't the amount she drinks. She's just in that state that a drink or two has effect."

"Well, it's up to you," Wharton said. "You're to take her home—not to that hotel—and you'll both be there tomorrow morning at, say, ten o'clock. I can rely on that?"

"Yes, sir," Blange told him soberly.

"An officer or officers of a special department will see you both and you'll give them all the information you can about that drug business. The job should have been done tonight, but she's not in a fit state. All that understood?"

"Yes, sir."

"Right," Wharton said. "No more reference to it. But there's something quite different. *Why* were you in Hather's flat on the night he killed himself?"

"W—w—why?"

"Yes, why? Come clean. You'll never have a better chance."

Blange looked away. He shuffled on his chair. His eyes blinked a bit.

"Well, it was nothing to do with him being killed."

"Well, tell us," Wharton said, and spread his palms.

He told us. There were some photographs in that flat: pornographic stuff in which Maroulis and Hather had dabbled once. Ursula Hather had posed for some. She hadn't actually told him so, but that was what he knew in his own mind or she wouldn't have been so desperately anxious about getting them back.

They knew Hather would be at Broadcasting House, so they went to the flat at just before nine o'clock. She waited while he went in with her key. He found Hather dead, but he also found the photographs. It was he who overruled her and rang the police.

"And the photographs?" Wharton said.

"Burnt. I burnt them as soon as we got back."

"That's something else you've got to remember," Wharton told him grimly. "I could hold her and I could hold you. But I'm not. But I'm warning you. Heaven help you if you don't come clean in the morning. O'Hara's like me. He can be a pretty hard nut to crack."

He gave a snort or two, then had another question.

"All that was why she bolted?"

"Yes," he said. "When she's had a drink she loses control. I was scared stiff she'd mention those photographs and things. And I didn't want the publicity. Mr. Travers will know what I mean, but we didn't think him quite genuine when he turned up that afternoon. But you can blame me for everything. She only did what she was told."

15

# BUSMAN'S HOLIDAY

WHARTON HAD gone out with Blange and I was left to my own devices. It was almost ten o'clock and so far we had been at it for well over four hours. And there'd be more to come when Winster arrived. And that couldn't be for another half an hour at the earliest.

Not that I worried. There was plenty to think about, though I didn't dwell too long on those revelations about Hather. The story had rung true, though it had been somewhat garbled, and it fitted in with the little I had known and the more I suspected. All I did know was that our job could sometimes be a dirty business. We had to find whoever it was that had caused a couple of deaths, and I didn't know how Wharton felt, but I was feeling like handing out a medal rather than getting ready the rope.

I said the story had rung true. We'd know more about that after Winster had given his version, but already, in the few minutes that had passed since I'd seen Ursula Hather in that room, I was being bothered by a faint mist of doubt. Before either she or Blange had set a foot in the room I'd been telling myself that I needed a stronger motive than I already had if I was to prove that Ursula Hather had killed her husband. *And now I had that motive.*

I told myself that if I'd been in her place I'd have killed Hather. I said that Hather ought to have been killed, and Maroulis with him, and Petriff, too. I could even gloss over the fact that if people had come forward with evidence, the law could have done the job for them. I couldn't, in fact, make myself so much of a hypocrite as to blame either Ursula Hather or Blange if they'd had a hand in the killings. And then I had to admit with some remnant of loyalty or common-sense—call it what you will—that we had to arrive at the truth. However much of a private citizen I might be in my thoughts, there was a job I was accepting pay to do. It was up to me to throw in my hand or carry on.

Then Wharton came in and for once he wasn't putting on an act. He said we'd heard some pretty horrible stuff. He added that Targe must have had a bandage over his eyes, or something.

"Targe is a bit of an old-timer," I said. "I thought of that in another context—that paraffin test."

"Oh?" he said. "What about it?"

"I'm like you," I said. "I try to keep up to the minute. Crime's not just a hobby. That paraffin test is out-of-date. It's recently been proved you can fire a gun and a good percentage of the times there's no reaction. The paraffin shows no nitrates."

"Yes, but in Hather's case it did show nitrates."

"I know," I said. "That may or may not prove he fired that gun. But suppose he was killed. Whoever killed him knew about the test, so he made the dead hand fire the gun. It was just luck that the test showed a positive reaction. If it hadn't, then even Targe must have wondered. I admit that that wouldn't have been conclusive. I'm merely trying to put myself into the mind of a possible killer."

"Far too vague," he told me.

"Maybe," I said doggedly. "But we've learnt other things to-night than what shows on the surface. Surely it must have struck you that Ursula Hather had the strongest possible motive for killing her husband. Or Blange for killing him for her. Especially when you add to it that divorce business."

"I know, I know," he told me impatiently. "He was killed or he wasn't killed. We're back where we always were."

"One other little thing," I said. "Did you notice that Blange used the word *killed*? He didn't talk of Hather's suicide. He used that word *killed*."

"You're splitting hairs. He *was* killed. He killed himself."

"Maybe," I said again. "But she had to be spirited away. And those photographs couldn't be produced. They'd been burnt. Conveniently burnt? Or did they ever exist?"

"Look," he said. "You're all hot and bothered. Winster won't be here yet. Go and get yourself something to eat. Get things out of your system. If Winster's here first, I'll hold him."

For once I didn't mind being treated like a child. I was mentally tired and I was hungry, and I thought that maybe he had something that I hadn't been told. Maybe Blange had convinced him that neither he nor Ursula Hather had had a hand in any killings. And if he hadn't, I just didn't care. I went out to a pub that would still be open and just had time for a couple of sandwiches and a double whisky. I felt a whole lot better when I got back, and I was just in time for Winster.

He came in rather uneasily. Most people do when they enter that room. But Wharton tried to put him at his ease. Then he gave him that typescript.

"I'd like you to skim through this, Mr. Winster. It's what Mrs. Hather told us tonight. I want to know if you substantially agree."

Winster read it, he didn't skim it. It took him best part of ten minutes.

"Yes," he said. "I think it's substantially correct."

"Right," Wharton said. "Perhaps you'd be so good as to tell us everything from your own point of view. How you saw things and what you did and why you did it."

"I think I'd like to," Winster said. "I hadn't seen her for several weeks. I didn't care too much for Hather, but I never suspected anything like what I've just read. Then I happened to be in when she telephoned me. She was almost incoherent, but I gathered she was in a pretty bad way, so I went along. My God, I was horrified! You never saw such a wreck! She was practically out on her feet. She cried on my neck and—" He gestured helplessly. "I can't really tell you. I thought I made out that Hather was killing her with drugs, but she still wasn't too coherent. I went out and got some brandy and gave her a shot. She was asleep when I left her and I went straight to Blange."

"You knew about her and Blange?"

"Of course." He looked surprised. "I'd known about it for quite a time. She'd told me about it once over the telephone.

She told me about him that night, as far as she could talk about anything, that is. I did what she says. I got Blange to take her away and be damned to Hather. Blange telephoned me about it and then I saw Hather; not at River View but outside. I told him what I knew and I warned him that if he ever had anything whatever to do with her again, I'd expose him publicly if it took every penny I had. Blange and I had agreed on that. We didn't want publicity for her sake and I thought I could handle him."

"And that's all?"

"That's all. . . . But no. There's something else."

"That you had to see Hather again during the week before he died?" I said.

"Yes," he said, and didn't look surprised. "I'd heard he was holding back on the divorce. I warned him that if he didn't clear out of the country altogether I'd blow the whole thing. I said I'd make his name stink. England would be too hot to hold him."

"What'd he say?"

"Well, you don't happen to have known him," he told Wharton. "He was a cocky devil. Eaten up with egotism. He couldn't believe such a thing could happen to *him*. And he said nobody would credit the ravings of a drug addict."

"And you never saw him again?"

"I never saw him again."

"There's just one other little thing," I said. "I wouldn't go so far as to call it a discrepancy, but I think we'd like your views. We naturally had to question Miss Parting—Hather's secretary."

"A very nice girl."

"She is," I said. "And how the devil she let herself be bowled over by Hather I don't know. But that's not the point. According to her your visit that day was perfectly friendly."

"Of course it was." He smiled. "That was an act for her sake. Hather was an oily, unctuous sort of devil. He had a hide like a pachyderm. You could kick him hard in the pants or you'd hear he'd been up to some dirty trick and when you saw him he'd act as if you were his dearest friend." He shook his head and his lip drooped. "Oh no, it wasn't hard to put on an act. Then we went out, ostensibly to have lunch together. That's when I told him how he stood."

"Clear enough," Wharton said. "But it's a pity you didn't come to us. Surely you know that we never reveal a confidence?"

Winster said nothing.

"But about something else," Wharton went on. "You knew about Maroulis?"

"Very little. I did hear more from Blange after Mrs. Hather left the nursing home."

"And the Petriff woman?"

"Yes," he said. "But not any details. I heard her name mentioned as being sort of connected."

Wharton grunted. He tried to look uneasy.

"Well, there's something I've got to ask—for your own sake. Everyone in any way connected has been asked it. Petriff was murdered. You know the date, and the time was half-past six. Where were you?"

He stared at Wharton and he looked round at me.

"Just routine," Wharton said blandly. "An alibi never scares an innocent man."

"Well"—he smiled just a bit ironically—"if that's the way it is, I haven't an alibi. Practically every night of my life I drop in at the local pub at about half-past seven. I must have done that night. I'm a regular sort of cove. Creature of habit, if you like." He shrugged his shoulders. "That's as far as I can go. The pub may know. I may have been a bit early or I may have been late. I can't say."

"Good enough for the records," Wharton told him genially. He went on to mention the morning's enquiry at South Mansions and said he'd like Winster to be there.

"And I'm warning you, as I've warned Mrs. Hather and Mr. Blange, that if a single word gets out about tonight, or anything even remotely connected with tonight, then I won't be responsible for what happens. I take back every promise I've made. I could hold you, Mr. Winster. Don't forget that. And see you're in time at South Mansions in the morning. I shall be there myself."

He got to his feet. The dour look went and he was smiling as he held out his hand.

"Good night, sir," Winster said. "And thank you for everything. You've been more than considerate."

He gave me a smile and a nod. Wharton went out with him.

Matthews came in. He said he'd been having a chat with Winster's driver. A nice chap. Wanted Matthews to run out and see him some time.

I said he might as well get home. I'd probably be going myself before very long. Then he was stooping and handing me something—a small button.

"It's not mine," I said.

"Put it in your pocket," he told me. "It always brings you luck."

"Fine!" I said. "That's just the commodity I could do with."

Then Wharton came in, and as soon as he saw us he was holding up a hand as if he was stopping the traffic.

"No more talk. I'm sick of the sound of talk. About time we called it a day."

I asked him about the morning.

"I'll have a pretty full day," he told me. "You're about due for a day off. Unless anything turns up I'll give you a ring some time in the evening."

That suited me. I said good night. Big Ben was striking midnight when I was leaving the Yard.

You may have gathered that I'm a restless sort of cove who thinks bed is a place to sleep in. Bernice wanted me to have breakfast there, but I had to be up and about. Bed in daylight reminds me too much of the few times I've been ill.

After breakfast and the newspapers I went along to Broad Street and tried to catch up with things. While I was there I knew I should have communicated with Phyllis Parting, so I rang her and she said she'd be in at midday. There'd been a frost in the night and it was a fine brisk morning, so I thought I'd walk back. There were two or three books I wanted to give Bernice for Christmas and there was a bookseller friend of mine in

the Strand, and that's what took me that way. And as I neared
Somerset House I happened to think, not unnaturally, of births,
deaths and marriages. A few yards on I found my fingers fum-
bling at my glasses.

So I went in. I asked for a copy of the birth certificate of an
Ursula Maze, and gave the approximate year and the probable
place of birth. I said I'd come back in a few minutes, so I went
on to the bookshop instead of waiting. When I got back the certificate was ready for me. It told me that Ursula Beatrice Maze,
daughter of Bertrand Frank and Helena Maud Maze, was born
at Cledfold, Essex, on July the 25th, 1918.

I walked on towards Charing Cross, but the pavement was
too crowded for thought, so I turned left to the Embankment
and found a garden seat. It seemed to me that I'd made a pretty
vital discovery. It hadn't been a birthday celebration that afternoon at South Mansions. And when one added this to that,
the mention of a birthday hadn't been merely the excuse for a
celebration. Winster wouldn't have been brought to town for a
simple celebration, and on a Sunday. And there was something
else—that remark of Winster's to Blange about the sleeping
Ursula. "Better get her to bed," was what he said, and it had
later prompted my remark to Winster that it was a queer sort
of ménage.

I walked along to the Underground and a telephone booth.
In two or three minutes I was talking to Wharton. He said dryly
that he'd thought I was on holiday. I told him what I'd just happened to find out. Marriage, probably, by special licence. One
day's clear notice and marriage on a Sunday with the consent of
the registrar.

"Oh, that," he said. "I rumbled that soon after you told me.
Blange admitted it just before I left him last night."

"Sorry you've been troubled," I told him, and he gave a
chuckle and hung up. I was feeling a bit indignant, and then
it seemed that it was something I ought to have known. And
I should have known it the previous night when Wharton had
arranged for Blange to take his wife home. But Winster hadn't
guessed that Wharton knew, for he had consistently alluded to

Ursula as Mrs. Hather. Maybe Wharton had mentioned it to him when they had gone out of that room.

And then, of course, I couldn't help think of something else. It had been a hurried affair so soon after Hather's death. Was it the old strategy of a husband's not being able to give evidence against his wife? Or vice versa? And was that something that Wharton for once had been so inordinately stupid as to miss? I couldn't believe it. And yet I didn't know. And I couldn't make up my mind whether or not I should mention the matter. Then I thought I'd say nothing. Twice already he must have thought I was losing my grip. I hadn't tumbled to the drug racket and now I'd missed the implications of that supposed birthday party. Three times was said to be lucky, but somehow I didn't feel like making a fool of myself three times in twenty-four hours.

Phyllis Parting looked much better than when I'd seen her last. We sat and chatted in that same room and she'd rung down for sherry. It was as cosy as before with a cheerful fire.

I'd said that nothing had happened to convince the authorities that we knew more than they. I was probably a man with an obsession, but I was still carrying on in a quiet sort of way and trying to prove that it hadn't been suicide. But the evidence I had so far had was anything but strong. It was based on things like hunches, surmises and probabilities: the probability, for instance, that one who knew Hather would have expected him to do certain things rather than others. I said you couldn't make a case out of things like that. What was needed was something more concrete.

"There *is* something," she said. "I didn't ring you about it because I thought I must have made a mistake. You won't laugh at me?"

"Heavens, no!" I told her.

"Well, it was about a rug. A small rug in Martin's room. He fell on it, so they said, when he . . . when he died. There was a little blood on it. I couldn't help seeing it when that man Targe was questioning me. There were some chalk marks on it and he warned me not to step on them. And—well, there was something funny about the rug. It didn't seem right, if you know what I mean."

"Just how didn't it seem right?"

"It's hard to explain," she said. "It was like it, but it didn't seem the same. Of course," she went on quickly, "I may have seen it differently. In a different light, or something. All the same, I haven't been able to get it out of my mind."

"It was the only queer thing you noticed about the room? Apart from the different atmosphere of the place and what had happened there?"

"Yes," she said. "Of course there was that pad which I didn't remember seeing before. That was the morning you were there. It was in the afternoon when I saw the rug."

"Yes," I said slowly. "I wonder if I could get my hands on it so that you could have a really close look. By the way, you didn't say anything to Targe?"

"I didn't. It wasn't till some time later that I began to re-member the rug and how it had seemed different. But you won't be able to get it. I went by the other day and everything looked empty."

I looked at my watch and I wondered if I might take a risk. I thought it worth it, and I needn't speak to Wharton. I could be asking if Matthews was there. As it happened, Wharton had just left. The enquiry had just been adjourned till the afternoon. The man at the telephone asked me to hold on. It wasn't more than a couple of minutes before I heard Matthews.

"Hallo, sir. Matthews speaking."

"Keep this strictly under your hat," I said. "But is there any chance of your having a word with the lady?"

"Don't see why not."

"Has she been through the hoop?"

"Finished with long ago," he told me. "And Winster. This af-ternoon they're doing Blange."

"And she won't be seen again?"

He didn't think so.

"Ask her this," I said. "What was done with the contents of her late husband's flat. Mention particularly a little rug." I cupped the receiver. Phyllis said it was a modern Turkish pattern rug about four by two. The usual red and blue. "A little red and blue Turkish rug. The one he fell on after he was shot. Make it cautious and ring me back."

He said I might as well hold on, so I stood there, receiver at my ear. I had to wait a good five minutes.

"Everything okay, sir. The good stuff's being sold by auction and the rest was sold to a second-hand furniture and junk dealer. The rag was burnt."

"Who burnt it?"

"I didn't press her. I guess that she or Blange did. It had some of Hather's blood on it."

So that was that. I think I made Phyllis Parting see there was nothing unnatural in burning that rug and she had to agree that she'd have done the same. But as I walked along to the bus stop, I wasn't so sure. The photographs had been burnt and the rug had been burnt. Maybe there hadn't been any photographs. That might have been an excuse to account for a return to the flat that night: an excuse to cover the fact that whoever had killed Hather had remembered something vital that had been left behind or might be a damning clue. As for the rug, Phyllis Parting might have been mistaken. But it was curious. And it's the curious for which one has always to look.

I had lunch at the club and while I was having a cigarette with my coffee I began thinking about Petriff. So far the day had been very much of a busman's holiday and I told myself amusedly that it might as well end the way it had begun. That was why—and because I hate loose ends—I went along to Malayan Products Limited. It was after half-past two when I got there, and Merton-Beale was in. I reminded the girl at ENQUIRIES that I was the one he'd seen before, and I had the entrée in double-quick time.

It wasn't quite the same Merton-Beale. I won't say he was hearty, but he had just enough geniality to be natural. I couldn't discern a tremor of uneasiness.

"You know what it is," I said. "Largely red-tape, but have you done anything about that alibi for the Petriff job?"

He was smirking as he dived into a drawer. There it was, all put down nice and business-like on a sheet of office paper. A Miss Dropworthy was prepared to certify that he had been in the office till just after six o'clock, dealing with an incorrect invoice. A Solly Mitzburg, owner of a newspaper pitch, was prepared to state that Merton-Beale had bought his usual Standard that night at ten minutes past six. As an appendix was a timing for both taxi and Underground from the newspaper pitch to Hampstead.

I folded it and put it in my wallet. I said we shouldn't have to trouble him again. I might have taken the satisfaction from that smug face of his if I'd told him what his wife's illness had been, but I didn't. Maybe he was getting his own kind of satisfaction out of having bamboozled the police, just as some people do over a railway ticket swindle, but I didn't see the point of telling him so. What I was wondering when I left him was how much his alibi was really worth. That facts-and-figures mind of his had revelled in drawing up that alibi statement. The alibi itself was cast-iron, and yet it wasn't worth a couple of dams. I didn't know the Dropworthy woman and the possible extent of her compliance, and Mitzburg read as if he'd remember anything at the sight of a ten-bob note.

But I didn't let it worry me. I rang Bernice and we finished the day with a cinema show. Wharton rang me rather late and said there was nothing for me at the moment. O'Hara had all the stuff he wanted and it looked as if he'd be the one for whom we'd have to wait. But one thing was clear about that red note-book. The drug customers had been marked with a tick. Those marked with a cross had been approached but found to be bad or risky prospects. Those crossed out had either died or left the neighbourhood of a particular circle.

Maroulis and Corbel were under surveillance night and day, he said, and watch was being kept on a warehouse at Tilbury. That was all he could tell me, except that I was having another free day at the tax-payers' expense. It wasn't altogether free since he mentioned keeping in touch. I said I'd be at the club from twelve to two and at home from then on, and that's how we left it. I wonder now what I'd have thought if I'd known where I'd be at that same time the following night.


# 16

# MAN WITH AN OBSESSION

THE CLUB was full of country members who'd come with their wives for shopping in town, and the lunch was going to be a kind of preview of Christmas. I was an old hand and had a strategic place near the dining-room when the gong went, even if I didn't get my favourite seat. But I had a first-class lunch, at least I had most of it, for just before my cheese and biscuits arrived I was called to the telephone. Wharton was on the line.

"Something's in the wind," he told me. "Two of O'Hara's men stopped a van at Tilbury. One of the men got away. That's all, but I gather they've got something."

I said I'd go back to my flat and wait there. The queue of members looked so hungry that I abandoned my cheese and went out to find a taxi. It was like looking for a cocktail shaker in a nunnery, so I hopped a bus and made it that way. Then I dug myself in before the fire while Bernice wrote Christmas letters and cards. I was sound asleep when the telephone bell woke me. I glanced at my watch as I shuffled across. It was just short of four o'clock.

"We're getting on the move," he told me. "O'Hara's men found enough dope down there to do half London in."

"You're bringing Maroulis in?"

"That's it," he said. "Hope to God that man who got away didn't warn him."

"I'll be right along," I said.

"Oh no. You stay there. Nothing you can do."

"Nothing be damned," I told him. "I'm coming along to the Yard."

"Look," he said. "We're bringing in Corbel first. You be outside Leicester Square Station at a quarter to five and Matthews can pick you up in the squad car."

"No monkey tricks?"

He gave an exasperated grunt and hung up. Bernice got a kettle going and I washed the sleep out of my system, and put my hat and heavy overcoat ready on a chair by the door. We had tea and then there was nothing to do but wait. Well before time I was on the pavement and on the look-out for that car. It was a bit late when it drew up. One man was with the driver and there was room for me with Matthews behind.

I was wanting to know what had happened.

"They'll have got Corbel by now," he told me. "Picking him up before the place closes down at five."

"What about Maroulis?"

"Last I heard," he said, "was that he was supposed to be in his flat. They'll pick him up as soon as he makes a move. If he isn't out by six, they'll get him if they have to break a door in."

"I think I'll get out," I said. "I'd rather be along at Maroulis's place."

He said I couldn't. The Old Man wanted us to go through Corbel's office with a small-toothed comb. I sat back again, but it was a dirty trick. I'm not bellicose. I'm just curious. I'd wanted to be there when they took Maroulis.

We drew in just short of Raimond House, and as we got out we saw Corbel being prodded into a police car ahead. Matthews moved on. He beckoned me from the car and we went up the stairs. He had Corbel's keys.

It was after five o'clock and the offices were emptying fast with a downward surge of people who hadn't waited for the lifts. Matthews opened the door and locked it behind us, and slipped the bolt as well. Corbel had put up a bit of a protest. A small table lay on its side and a chair with it and it looked as if a pile of books had been capsized.

We got to work on the room. There wasn't an article of furniture that we didn't tap and probe and test for a screwed-in fitment. We measured the drawers of desk, counter and table and looked for secret drawers and false backs and bottoms. By then it was nearly six o'clock. Outside on the tesselated landing there were few sounds of feet. We had a breather and a cigarette. It was cosy in there with the radiator going full blast.

We got to work on the books and shelving. Every book was opened and its pages flicked over. We'd done the far side when there was a tap at the door.

"Who's there?" Matthews said.

"Open up, Harry. It's me."

Matthews opened up. It was the man who sat in front of our car. Something had slipped up, he said, and word had just come through. They'd broken into Maroulis's flat and he wasn't there. Another car was coming along in case he turned up at Raimond House, and if we heard people moving about we'd know what was on.

Matthews locked and bolted the door again. He gave me a grin.

"I wouldn't like to be in somebody's boots. Whoever let him get out of that flat'll be for the high jump. The Old Man'll have the hide off him."

We finished the side along the window. I had a look out, but it was unlighted there and I couldn't see, and the cold night air was cutting in, so I shut the window again. Then we went through the far door to a tiny annexe with washbasin and lavatory. An old hat of Corbel's was hanging on a peg and I had a look at its greasy lining. We flushed the lavatory and had a look in the tank. Matthews stopped the in-flow and tested the ball. That was when we heard the quick steps outside.

Matthews tiptoed out and listened. I heard a voice calling something and there was a dull thud. Sounds were coming through the side of the lavatory and I put my ear against the wall. I could hear someone moving. I called softly to Matthews and he came back and listened, too. I was watching him, and that was when the queerest thing happened.

One of those sections of shelves on the side that we hadn't yet done began to move outward. It came full out and covered our open door. There were steps in the room. Then the books swung inwards again and a man was standing there. He pressed with his knee and there was a click as the shelf engaged again with its catch. Then he caught sight of us.

The three of us stood there: never a sound; breath held. Then Matthews made a move. Maroulis moved, too. His hand went to the overcoat pocket and he whipped out a gun. Matthews halted. Maroulis said never a word, but he slowly backed. He was half-way towards the door and Matthews moved out, too. I stepped out and we stood abreast as we cleared the door. Then Maroulis was at the locked door. With his right hand he kept the gun on us and he groped round with his left and tried to fit a key. It slipped in. He turned the knob, but he hadn't thought about the bolt.

We could hear shouts in the rooms to our right. Maroulis looked for the bolt. My hand went out and my fingers closed round a book. Matthews moved slightly forward and I slung that book at Maroulis. He ducked and it crashed against the frosted glass of the door and shattered it. Then he fired.

There was a roar in the room like some terrific explosion. Something hit me and I went backwards. I seemed to see Matthews hurtling forward and there was a tremendous pain at the back of my skull. And then I passed out.

When I opened my eyes again I was on my back and in a moving vehicle. They'd taken my glasses off and all I could see was a blur. I stirred and I felt a blanket round me. A pain like neuralgia shot through my skull.

"That's all right, sir," a voice said. "A couple of minutes and we'll be at the hospital."

I tried to speak. I croaked a bit. Then the words came.

"What's the matter? What happened?"

"Like a cigarette, sir?"

I said I would. Another blur bent over me and put a lighted cigarette in my mouth. I moved my right arm and there was another pain.

"You lie still, sir. A nice clean wound in the shoulder, that's what you've got. And you cracked your skull against a radiator."

The ambulance swerved left. The blur moved as the brake went on. The ambulance stopped and I heard the doors open. A couple of minutes and they had me on a stretcher. We went through into where there were lights and there were more moving blurs. One of them put an arm under my head and I winced with the pain. I was told to drink something. I lay back again and I was wondering if I'd been told the truth and if I was going to die. Then I began to feel sleepy.

It was about ten o'clock when I woke in a bed. As I stirred, a hand stroked my cheek and I caught a scent that could only be Bernice. She told me to lie still and she hooked my glasses on. It was quite a time before I knew I was in my own room.

She told me to lie quiet, but I couldn't be quiet. I had to know what had happened. She said I'd been X-rayed and the bullet taken out and I'd had an anti-tetanus injection and my head had been stitched. Two or three days, if my own doctor thought fit, and I might be up again. She said Matthews had rung her and she'd gone to the hospital—the one not three hundred yards from the flat, and on whose board I'd once been—and she'd had me brought home. I asked what had happened to Maroulis, but she said she didn't know. Then she was telling me to drink some more dope and taking my glasses off and tucking the clothes round me, and she was a blur that I just remembered moving as I fell asleep again.

I didn't wake till ten in the morning, and it was the doctor who woke me. He asked how I felt and I said I felt fine. A bit of a headache and a stiffness in the shoulder, but otherwise I was fine. He went through his repertoire and gave me some penicillin. Then he had a word with Bernice and not long afterwards she brought me some breakfast. She sat with me while I ate. One piece of toast and the bell went. When she came back it was with Wharton.

"Well, how are we?" George said, putting on a medical act.

I told him I was fine. In the same breath I was wanting to know about Maroulis.

"He got Matthews in the arm," he said, "and then he broke out. They had him on the landing. That's where he shot himself."

I was thinking back and I couldn't say a word. Then he was telling me how fit I'd be in less than no time. Old la Rochefoucauld will never be out of date while George can bear with such fortitude the misfortunes of others. I asked him if I was entitled to blood money. He found that a joke and quoted it to Bernice as a sign that I'd soon be on my feet. Then he said he'd drop in again as soon as he had a second to spare and tell me how everything had gone.

Later on Bernice brought in the papers. Before she gave them to me she said I ought to give up police work, and quoted the sooner or later. I reminded her that I'd been at it twenty years and hitherto no one had so much as spat on my beard. But she still had to shake her head.

The papers had quite a lot that I wanted to know. One even had banner headlines.

DRUG RING SMASHED IN LONDON
RINGLEADER COMMITS SUICIDE
POLICE-OFFICERS WOUNDED

My own name was there with a rather fanciful account: Matthews' wound was said to be superficial. Other arrests were said to be imminent. The murder of Madame Petriff was mentioned as closely connected. Hather wasn't mentioned at all.

I didn't hear the inside news till the following afternoon. The doctor had come in that morning and had looked pleased about me, even if he counselled another day in bed. But I'd like to die with at least my slippers on, so after lunch I managed to get a dressing-gown round me and made my way, to Bernice's consternation, to the living-room fire. I was there when George Wharton came in.

George—he stayed on and had tea with us—said it was all settled. Corbel had been remanded and was due for the Old Bailey. A couple of circle members had been roped in, and the manager of Maroulis's firm.

"Damned ingenious that moving shelf affair," he said. "Corbel's office was actually a part of Maroulis's own office. You just operated a catch masked by a big poster and in you went. That's how the dope could be slipped in when wanted."

I wanted to know why Hather's name had been kept out of the papers.

"No point in anything else," he told me. "He's dead, isn't he? Why rake up all that? You know what killed him?"

"A shot from a little Belgian automatic."

He made a gesture of disgust.

"Not that. It was Winster who virtually killed him. Soon as he warned him to leave the country, Hather's game was up. He may have put up a bluff with Winster, but he didn't bluff himself. He couldn't stand exposure and he didn't want to bolt. All that was left was suicide."

"And Petriff?"

"Almost certainly Maroulis," he told me. "Corbel says he didn't know a thing about it himself, but he admits Maroulis had got so that he didn't trust her. Ten pounds to a pinch of snuff Maroulis did her in. He shot you with a Webley, and didn't Anders say it was something like the stock of a Webley that hit her skull before she was strangled?"

"That's another case settled then," I said and hoisted myself up with my good arm. I took a pound note from my wallet in the desk drawer and gave it him.

"Here we are, George. With the compliments of the season from an old and occasionally lucrative friend."

He pretended not to want to take it. As he was stowing it away he said we'd have a lunch as soon as I could get out. I almost shuddered. I could see myself paying the bill.

"What about the Blanges?" I asked him.

He said they'd gone to Switzerland for as long as the money held out. Neither would be needed for the enquiry.

"Plenty of evidence without *them*," he said. "And more coming in."

"That bookseller Klint in the clear?"

Klint was in the clear, but his woman secretary wasn't. And that was about all I wanted to know. He did add that Matthews was about again and practically as fit as ever, and that he'd like to drop in and see me. Then Bernice was bringing in tea and we didn't talk shop again till just before he left and then it was only a hint that when I felt like it I might as well write my report.

I wrote that report on Christmas Day. Christmas is no time for a childless couple in a flat by themselves, even if I was practically myself again, and there was quite a bit of time on my hands. But I needed all that time. For the first time in my life I wasn't honest with myself or Wharton, for I drew up that report as Wharton would be wanting me to write it, and not as I should have written it myself.

And the things I felt then I went on feeling during the two days' holiday that came after the Sunday. Call me, if you like, a man with an obsession. Call me a myopic who, because he couldn't see himself, was refusing to credit the sight of others. Call me just an unreasoning and even a smug kind of fool. Call me what you like. You're not made like me and I'm not made like you. I can't help it when things keep nagging at me. It isn't that I'm all that conscientious and want to earn my money honestly. It's what I said. It's the way I'm made.

And get something else clear. I was ready to admit that George was right but not that I was wrong. He had a point of view and according to his lights he was right. Anyone not cursed with my mental make-up would have accepted his view as the only view. Another case had been finished, and finished successfully, and what the hell. Nor did I dream for a moment that George had twisted a point of view in order to pocket a poundnote. George has his own standards of integrity and maybe they're higher than my own.

I could count on the fingers of a hand the times I'd been out of action. I hate enforced inaction, and I hated it that holiday because it made too much time for thought. An unwary move in my chair and there'd be a twinge in the shoulder or the back of my skull, and that would set me thinking again. I'd read a book and find myself looking at words that were blurred. I went to a show with Bernice on the Tuesday afternoon, and my mind refused to concentrate on what was happening on the stage. I lay in bed and thought and I woke up thinking. And that was sheer stupidity, or was it?

But do some thinking yourself for a moment. Let me bore you just once more with my point of view about the death of Hather. Just the outlines, and categorically, with you to think back and fill in the details.

1. Why a pad and not the available paper?
2. Why no panache of a signature?
3. Why no will in favour of Phyllis Parting?
4. The night that should have been spent at the Anvil Court Hotel?

That's all. I omit the matter of the Turkey rug because Phyllis Parting might have been wrong. I saw no great significance in that rug and thought myself that she was wrong. But what you'll say to all the above may be this. Wharton added a something explanatory and vital when he said that Hather had committed suicide because he couldn't face the exposure with which Winster had threatened him unless he left the country. But did that explain? Was it so clinching?

Let's look at it for a moment. Hather was hand-in-glove with Maroulis and Maroulis was a man with no scruples. I learned later that he'd killed at least one man in an affair for which the Egyptian authorities wanted him. So Winster threatened Hather. What would Hather do? A million to one he'd have told Maroulis. And Maroulis would have ensured that Winster didn't talk. Winster would have been snuffed out as Petriff had been. Winster, in that comparatively lonely cottage, would have been a sitting bird. And Winster's death could have been quoted as a subtle warning to Blange and Ursula Hather in case they, too, were minded to talk.

I might hark back to one other thing. To me it still wasn't logical that Hather—a man resolved to commit suicide on the morrow—should have spent his last night at that Old Boys' Dinner. I quote that in order to be fair and to show the fallacy of relying on a point of view for it might easily be said that, with his end so immediately before him, Hather might have wished to spend his last hours in some sentimental past. But I couldn't see Hather as that kind of sentimentalist. I thought I knew him, and that dreadful story that Ursula Blange had told had merely confirmed what I knew. Wherever Hather went it was as an exhibitionist. Hather himself was being taken on show. He was a bantam-sized, latter-day Oscar Wilde. Whatever sentiment he had was for someone named Martin Hather.

But you can't go on thinking with that first pitch of intensity. Time dulls the edge of all things, and even a week made that mental nagging less of an irritation, or maybe I was becoming inured. The case, as far as I was concerned, was over, though at some time in the not distant future I might have to give evidence at the Old Bailey. The stitches had gone from my skull and only occasionally did I get a twinge in the shoulder. I was back at the old routine at Broad Street, and it was only when I lay waiting for sleep that things would insinuate themselves and I would have all the old doubts about the death of Hather. And there was something queer in the fact that I never gave a thought to Petriff. No questions about *her*. She was dead and I didn't care who'd killed her—even if after all it had been the facts-and-figures Merton-Beale.

The first week in January Bernice had an urgent request for a visit from an old friend. She didn't want to go, she said, and was making me an excuse. I overruled her. As I said, one would think I'd had a collision with an atomic bomb instead of stopping a nice clean bullet the nice clean way. So she went, if only to Oxford and for a long week-end.

On the Saturday I stood Matthews a lunch and over it we couldn't keep away from the case. Before we'd finished the meal we'd got ourselves into something. I'd felt a faint nostalgia for Humbledown and, as it was a day off, he thought he'd like to drop in on that garage proprietor who'd driven Winster that night to the Yard, so when the meal was over he rang his wife and Humbledown and reported that everything was set. We went along to the garage to get my car.

It wasn't the kind of day I'd have picked, for it was overcast with a threat of rain, though the forecast had said there'd be no rain till around midnight in the south-east. We took a slightly different route to make a change of scenery and came into Humbledown past the bungalows and wooden buildings and poultry farms to the green and the garage. I dropped Matthews there and we agreed to meet at opening time or thereabouts at the pub.

I switched on my side-lights before I moved the car on, and as I drove slowly along the lane I was thinking how much wiser I'd have been to ring Wistaria Cottage and ensure that Winster would be at home. Then as I came through the trees to more open country, I saw in the dusk that gardener of Winster's raking up some hedge dippings. I drew the car up.

"Jim, isn't it?" I said.

"Yes," he said, "and aren't you the gentleman who give me that half-crown?"

I said I was. I asked if Winster was at home.

"Reckon he is," he said. "He's busy doing his writing. But about that half-crown. Easiest money as ever I made."

"Lucky for you you saw him that Sunday morning," I said.

"It were and it weren't," he said. "There was something I had to do on the Monday—I only go to him two days a week—what I wasn't sure about, so I sort o' slipped along. He heard me come and after a bit he looked out o' the window. 'Ah, it's you, Jim,' he says, and then he tells me he'll see me at the back door. That's when I see his hand was bandaged. 'That old leg o' yours again,' I say and he reckoned it was. Sometimes he slip and hurt himself, like he'd done then."

"Pretty bad," I said, "having a hand like that. Good job it wasn't his sound one."

He stared. I could see the little wrinkles round his eyes in the gathering dusk.

"It *was* his good one what he sprained. Not that one he have to wear a glove on."

I don't know if I even said anything. It's possible I may have given a nod and moved the car on. I know that I was past Wistaria Cottage before I knew I was near it. But I drove on to the fork and there I turned the car. I drove back to the pub and asked at the back door if I could have some tea. The landlord remembered me and said it'd be no trouble at all. He showed me into a parlour and stirred the fire. I'd have to wait a few minutes, he said, but I didn't worry. All I wanted was to think.

In my very early schooldays I'd been none too good at mathematics: poor teaching, maybe, and certainly poor reception. Geometry was called Euclid in those far too distant days, and for three months I was taught Euclid without the least comprehension of what it was all about, and I became a regular recipient of impositions for homework badly done and even not done at all. Then one day my maths master went sick and another man instructed us, and that very first morning a miracle happened. Just what caused it I couldn't for the life of me say, but he did or said a something that transformed Euclid from meaningless diagrams and gibberish into a thing of meaning and purpose and even fascination. Suddenly I saw Euclid as a kind of puzzle which one had to solve, and if one thought back one had all the necessary clues. Even now I can recall the thrill when I first realised the sheer simplicity of that.

And that was just how it had been when Jim had told me about that good hand, and when I recalled that Sunday morning when I had first seen him and how Winster had tried to keep him from mentioning the hand at all. There was the thrill of first discerning a pattern, and finding obscurities becoming more and more clear, and knowing that questions had their answers. You remember the questions—the things I used to put to Wharton and the things I might have put. Why no signature on that message and why no will: why the writing pad and why no last message for Phyllis Parting. And other things began to emerge and make the pattern even more clear: why Hather, for instance, who'd always expected people to come to him, had suddenly gone to them. And there was even a meaning to that Turkey rug.

Probably you've seen the pattern, too, and, if so, you'll have thought of a line of action. And maybe you'd have expected me to make assurance trebly sure, but that wasn't how I felt. What I knew when the thinking was all over was that my own part was done, and there was no need for Wharton and the law to discuss and possibly confirm. The law wouldn't feel an urgency, but to me there seemed a danger in delay. Someone else should do the confirming, and at once. Or that was what I thought.

# 17

# THE SECOND SHOT

IT WAS five o'clock when I rang Wistaria Cottage.

"Hal-lo," Winster said. "Nice to hear your voice again. Where are you ringing from?"

"You'd be surprised," I said. "From the local pub. I've just had tea there."

"Good lord!" he said. "You're going to drop in?"

"For a few minutes, now I know you're at home. I just happened to be this way, so I thought I'd give you a ring."

"Fine," he said. "All alone, or anyone with you?"

"On my own," I said. "Be seeing you in a few minutes."

"Good. I'll be here. Sorry you've had tea."

Matthews was outside in the car. I apologised for breaking up his evening. He said it didn't matter. It had to be broken up some time. And he could come again.

"It's not what you think," I told him as I moved the car on. "You're not wanted anywhere. I want you myself."

I told him about it. He slid out of the slowly-moving car as we neared the cottage and I accelerated to the drive. I halted before I drove the car in. Winster was at the door before I could get out.

"Well, well, well," he said. "Come along in. There's a pretty good fire. And what about a short drink? Or is it too early?"

"Too early for me," I said as he took my hat and coat. "The fire's good, though."

"Never economise on a fire," he told me. He lowered himself carefully into his chair, then looked round with a smile. "And how're tricks?"

"Not taking too many. I'm on my own at the moment."

"Not working for the Yard?"

"That's right," I said. "Scraping a living together by honest means."

He chuckled.

"By the way, didn't I see you'd been winning medals and things?"

"First I've heard about it," I said. "A scar on my shoulder and another on my skull is all I've got to show."

"Maroulis, wasn't it?"

I said it certainly was. He nodded.

"A clever devil, that. I'm damned glad he had to do himself in. And I hope his pals get what's coming to them."

"They will," I said. "And by the way, have you heard anything about the Blanges? Are they back yet?"

He showed me a postcard and told me to read the back. It merely sent love and said they'd be back the following week.

"They owe a lot to you," I said. "A hell of a lot."

"I don't know." He shook his head at the fire. "In any case I don't want thanks."

There was a silence as if we were each busy with our thoughts. He spoke first.

"So everything's over and done with," he said. "The task accomplished and the long day done. You fellows made a good job of it, you know."

The opening had come. My heart began to beat a little too quickly. I had to force myself to be off-hand.

"Yes," I said. "We came out of it pretty well. And for that matter, so did you."

I could feel his sudden look, but my eyes were still on the fire.

"Me?"

"Yes," I said. "Wharton might have harried you a whole lot more than he did. After all, you were a perfect suspect."

"Nonsense," he said. "And what do you mean by suspect? Hather killed himself, everyone knows that, and someone did that hag of a Petriff in."

"Don't tell me," I said protestingly. "I know all about it. My thoughts happened to slip out."

I swivelled round to face him.

"Ever think of trying your hand at writing a detective novel?"

"No," he said slowly. "I can't say I have."

"Then you're the only author in England," I told him. "Most of them have had a crack at it and the rest think it's so easy they can do it any time. I've been a bit of an author myself, you know."

"Yes. I looked you up in *Who's Who*."

"Good," I said. "Every man his own biographer. And, like the others, I took care not to tell all the truth about myself. But I have written books. Crime analysis stuff mostly."

"And you're now thinking of writing a detective novel?"

"I might do," I said complacently. "This business has given me a whole lot of ideas."

"Really?" He raised his eyebrows.

"Yes," I said. "I've got it all worked out. Did it during my convalescence. And you're the one who does the dirty deeds."

"You don't tell me!"

"That's how it is," I said. "And I think it'll make a dam' good book—if only I can get it on paper."

"This is interesting," he told me. "Like to tell me about it?" I protested. A bald outline couldn't carry verisimilitude. You had to create an atmosphere and build up a background. Take your time over being plausible and persuasive.

"Damn all that," he told me. "You give me the outlines."

"You asked for it," I said, "so here goes. There'll have to be some disguising, of course, when I write the actual book, but we'll leave that out. We'll pretend it's the Maroulis Case. I think I shall call it *The Case of the Happy Medium*. Petriff, you know. A neighbour of hers told me she was always merry and bright. Quite the ray of sunshine."

"*The Case of the Happy Medium*. Dam' good."

"Not too bad," I said. "But we don't start with her. We start with Ursula Maze and you. Brought up as children together and virtually engaged to each other when the war broke out. Of course it won't be quite like that in the book. I shall have to twist things round. Change the names and everything. May change the place from London to, say, Birmingham. Where was I, by the way?"

"I was just engaged to Ursula Maze."

"Of course. And then we introduce the villain—Hather. The false friend and all that. Chap who picks people's brains. I'll have to draw him as like the real Hather as possible, of course, even physically. You'll follow that later. But then comes the war. You march away, having kissed your sweetheart a fond farewell. Comes Dunkirk. You get badly knocked about. You're captured and spend the rest of the war in an Oflag. There you learn two things: that your precious friend Hather has not only stolen and married your girl but he's also bolted to America to save his skin. That doesn't make you feel so good. In fact it makes you feel pretty bad. That snivelling little Hather is sitting pretty and will probably sneak back home after the war as if there'd never been a war. But there's been a war for you. No more fun and games for you—at least not with a ball. You're going to be a cripple for life. Mind you," I said quickly, "I shall have to pile that on. Not that it matters. No one's ever going to spot you as the prototype."

"I hope to God not," he told me, and tried to make it genial.

"Trust me," I said. "But then we get something else happening. You find Hather's become a celebrity, thanks to using some of your own ideas. That makes you feel a whole lot worse. I may bring in there about your writing to him and getting no satisfaction. I don't know yet, but we'll skip it and come to when you get home after the war. When you confront Hather.

"Again I don't think I'll make you accept his two hundred pounds. I'll let him out-smart you somehow. I'll let his wheedling voice get round you. But when you get away from him, you think to yourself what a pleasure it would be to do him in. You think that still more as time goes on. Then the inevitable happens. You really make up your mind to kill him."

"Good," he said. "It'll be fine to hear about me killing Hather."

"Ah, but something else happens," I said. "We get Ursula, calling you up—you know, what really did happen that day she was frantic and you went to see her. After what she has to tell you, you're dead certain that Hather's got to be killed. Not because you want her in any way for yourself. You've got over that—or haven't you? She hasn't turned out quite as she might have done, perhaps that'll be it. You don't mind her being in love with Blange. In fact you're rather glad."

"Altruistic sort of devil, aren't I?"

"As I see you in this book—yes. But about what you do, and this is the really interesting part. I thought it rather clever myself. You're not planning a murder, by the way; you're merely an instrument of justice. Hather doesn't deserve to live. He's a menace to society, but it's no use appealing to society to kill him because he'd have to add murder to his other offences before it'd do that. Besides, when one goes to the police there has to be publicity. I'm not boring you, am I?"

"Quite the opposite, my dear fellow. I'm profoundly interested. It isn't every day one gets a chance to hear oneself manhandled—so to speak."

"Good," I said. "We'll get on to the method. You've been studying Hather for months past when the idea of murder was far more vague. You've kept on good terms with him and you've told him ideas. Later on, after Ursula's disclosures, you have to tell Blange that you've seen Hather and warned him. Still later you'll tell the police that you presented an ultimatum to Hather not long before he died. But that's all bunkum, of course. The last thing you wanted to do was antagonise Hather.

"But, as I said, you've been studying him. You make a final reconnaissance during the week before he died. Ostensibly you're the best of friends—at least good enough to convince his secretary. You'd like to get a sheet of his paper, but you just can't manage it, not without creasing it or leaving your prints on it. But you take note of a Turkey rug. It's of conventional pattern and, after you leave him you buy one as near to it as you can. You also get from him his probable movements during the week-end, and are interested to know he's going to an Old Boys' Dinner and sleeping on the Saturday night at River View.

"Now you're all set except for one thing. You've got to get Hather to come to you, and that's not easy. He always has people come to *him*. But you think you see a way. You might do it by playing on one of his own weaknesses. Hoisting him with his own petard. You go, in fact, to Madame Petriff."

"Petriff?" he said. "Why to Petriff? Surely I don't even know the woman."

"You've heard of her from Ursula," I reminded him. "She mentioned her when you saw her that horrible day and you've learned a whole lot more since from Blange. So you go to her. You tell her you've got her where you want her. You blackmail her, in fact, but in a highly subtle way. Her only chance, you say, is that she should ring Hather early on the Sunday morning and tell him that all night she's had the most vivid dreams about him and how he's going to get a message of some sort that he simply must obey. It's going to change the whole of his life for the infinitely better. If he doesn't obey it there may be disaster.

"I know that sounds pretty footling, but I make it very plausible in the book and it happens to work. You ring Hather just a bit later that Sunday morning. 'Hather, I've got the most marvellous idea. Better than *Man With Two Souls*! It's stupendous.' 'Well, what about it?' Hather says, and you say you're taking it along in the morning to some famous writer for the screen who'll jump at it. 'Why not let *me* see it?' Hather wants to know. And that lets you make your own terms. He's to come to your place at once. You suggest by train and you'll meet him at some intermediate station. He says he can't: he's got an engagement for lunch. You say you'll drive him wherever he wants to go. In any case he has to agree, if only for the sake of the book I'm writing."

I stole a look at him. He was sitting there motionless, eyes on the fire. His shoulders were hunched and his good hand held the other tightly.

"So you meet him," I went on. "You drive him here, say, in your car. You come in from the south and it's way out from the village and at once you let him in and garage your car. Then you fake a fall. You've sprained your wrist and it hurts like hell. You tell him where to get a bandage and he binds it up for you. You say that after he's gone you'll get a doctor to look at it, and you'll hire a car to take him wherever he wants to go. But it's the very devil, you say. There was something you had to get away to your publisher in the morning.

"And this is the tricky part. I don't quite know yet how I'll write it, but I imagine your saying something like this, 'Do something for me. See that pad? Got a pen on you? Good. I've got to write a letter in a bloke's own handwriting and it'll be reproduced exactly in the book. I was going to fake it, but your writing will be even better. It's about a chap who's going to pretend to kill himself but doesn't. Here's what he writes as I drew it up this morning.' So Hather writes. You're looking over his shoulder, and no sooner does he write the last word than he gets a bullet. The little gun makes hardly a pop and you lower him down with his head on that Turkey rug you bought. Then comes a dramatic moment. I think it's one of the best parts in the book. It's like the knocking on the gate in *Macbeth*.

"There is a knock at the door. For a moment you're paralysed with fright. But whoever it is mustn't come in. You go quickly to the window and look out. It's only your man, Jim. You let out a breath and tell him to go round to the back. You lock the front door and go to the back and see him. You get rid of him and you watch him down the road. But you haven't had time or have forgotten to remove the bandage. He notices it and you tell him you've just had a fall and hurt it.

"Then you go back to Hather and you draw the curtains. You wipe the gun clean, put on a glove and force the gun into Hather's hand and fire it into a cushion or something. That'll take care of the paraffin test. Then you lay him and the rug in the back of your car. Then you go to the pub, and you probably walk over the fields by the church so as not to see Jim again. Then as soon as it's dark that evening—a cold night with patches of fog, the forecast has said—you take Hather and rug and gun and confession to River View. You back your car in and it's a Sunday night and no one about, and it's misty as well. You unlock the back doors with Hather's keys and you take him up and fake the suicide." I let out a breath.

"Well, what do you think of it so far?"

"Good God!" he said. "Don't tell me there's more?"

"There has to be," I said. "What about Petriff? She'll read about Hather's suicide and she'll do a hell of a lot of wondering. Will she tell Maroulis? Will there be counter-blackmail? You don't know, but you aren't going to risk it. You ring her and warn her. You make an appointment for the Friday night because you don't want her death to be so near to the time of Hather's as to draw any attention to it. So you keep the appointment, hit her on the head with a gun and strangle her. Doing it that way makes no noise. You think you can't possibly be connected with her but you get back here quickly all the same and get to the pub at your usual time. I shall prove, by the way, that you've made yourself that creature of habit for some months past. Ever since, in fact, you had in mind that it might be a good thing to kill Hather."

You could feel the silence heavy in the room. He nodded to himself. He forced a smile as he stirred.

"And that's the lot?"

"That's the lot," I said. "What do you think of it?"

"Well," he told me judicially, "I think you're wrong on fundamentals. They say truth is stranger than fiction. Let's look at it another way. Isn't fiction—this kind of fiction—too strange to read as truth?"

"All a question of creating atmosphere," I told him airily. "You just have to put these things across."

"I'd say it's too far-fetched."

"I still think I can do it," I told him doggedly. "I think I can write that book the way I've said and find myself a publisher."

"Good luck to you," he said, and he couldn't help the droop of the lip. And then he was turning towards me. "But the book isn't finished yet. There's no ending. How can this chap get found out."

"I think I've got a way," I said, and just a bit dubiously. "And by the way, aren't you wearing the same jacket you wore that night when Wharton asked you to come to the Yard?"

"I am," he said. "But what's that got to do with it?"

"Nothing at all. But isn't it the jacket you were wearing on that Sunday Hather committed suicide?"

"Maybe. Almost certainly is. Why do you ask?"

"Look at the sleeve," I said. "Isn't there a button missing?"

He looked, and he stared.

"My God, there is!"

I put my fingers in my waistcoat pocket. I held something up. "And this is it?"

He stared again.

"Know where I found it?"

His eyes narrowed.

"Where *did* you find it?"

"In Hather's flat, the morning after."

He was very, very still. He had to clear his throat before the words came.

"Tell anybody about it?"

"Not yet," I said, and put the button back.

He made a little grunting noise. Then he slowly hoisted himself to his feet.

"Excuse me just a minute."

He went behind me, and past. The hairs felt cold on my neck, but he went on. I turned my head and I heard the click as he locked the front door. I hoped to God Matthews had heard it, too. I hoped Matthews had had his ear against that window and had heard every word that'd been said. I hoped it even more when Winster went to a table by the window and took something out of a drawer and slipped it into his pocket. But I got to my feet and was standing with my back to the fire when he came back.

"Sorry about all that," he said, and lowered himself into the chair again. "But I wonder if you'd mind giving me that button?"

"Afraid not," I said. "I might like to show it to—well, my publisher."

"Let's stop fooling," he said, and out came the gun. It was a Colt or a Webley and it looked as big as a cannon. "Throw me that button."

"And what then?"

"I don't know," he said. "Maybe you'll disappear. Maybe your car will be found somewhere in town and you not in it. I don't know."

I was straining my ears for Matthews and hoping to God he'd give some sign. But there wasn't a sound.

"You'd be stupid to do that," I said, and wondered how to make time.

"Why?"

"Just listen a moment," I told him. "You're a creature of habit. You go regularly to the pub. This house is empty. Very well, then I didn't come here by chance. See that picture just above the sideboard? See anything like a slight discolouration? Know what's been fixed there? A tiny microphone. Every word that's been said in this room has been overheard. I've only got to raise my voice as a signal and a couple of men will break in."

His eyes shifted a moment. They had to. It was then that I kicked. I was taller than he and I'm still pretty agile. My foot caught his wrist and the gun flew out of his hand. But I over-balanced. As I fell I caught the side of my head against that easy chair and my glasses came off. I fell—but I fell on the gun.

A second, perhaps, and no more since I had let fly with my foot, I could see as good as nothing, but I knew I was in the open space beyond the chair, and I had the gun in my right hand and with my left I was frantically feeling about for my glasses. Then I saw him move, like something in a fog. The blur of him heightened. He was on his feet.

"Give me that gun."

There was something deadly in the quietness of his voice.

"Stay where you are," I told him. "Make another move and I'll shoot."

"Give me that gun!"

He was nearer. The moving thing was almost on me, and I fired. I fired just above his head. Matthews, and I must have thought that as I squeezed the trigger, couldn't help but hear. Then the roar of the shot echoed about the room and suddenly the blur that had been Winster was gone and nothing was left but the fog. And there had been a noise like a thud. And then I heard Matthews trying furiously to open the door. Then there was the crash of glass. More crashing. I heard Matthews grunt as he ripped the curtains aside and came through the window.

"You hurt, sir?"

"Find my glasses," I told him.

"Here they are, sir. Right by your hand."

I hooked them on. I was in a real world again, of solidity and colour and shadow. Beyond me Matthews was bending over Winster. He lay with his feet towards me, and he lay very still.

"Good God, sir! You got him clean in the head!"

He sounded awestruck. I got up from the floor and walked slowly across and I looked down at Winster. Explanations didn't seem to matter. Then suddenly I was in a furious rage.

"What was the matter? Why the devil didn't you come in!"

"Didn't know a word, sir. I had my ear against that window like you said, but I couldn't hear a thing. Just sort of voices. I hadn't the faintest notion what was going on or I'd have been in. You bet I'd have been in. No one would have stopped me."

Nothing seemed to matter again. I said I was sorry. I told him to forget it.

"He tried to kill you, sir?"

"Maybe," I said. "But I didn't mean to kill him."

"Makes you go hot and cold," he said, "when you think of it."

"Then don't," I said. "Get into the car and run down to the village and see if you can locate a doctor. He may be dead, but I'd like him looked at. And remember just how you found me when you broke in."

I heard the car back out and then accelerate as Matthews shot it off, and then there was a silence that pressed on me like a weight. I was shaken and there was a numbness about my head. I felt for my pipe and lighted it, and I sat there looking into what was left of the fire. The heat had mostly gone and there was a queer play of white ash and red glow, and I might have made pictures out of it if I hadn't had to think.

"I didn't mean to kill him, but I did."

I said that aloud and didn't know I'd said it. Then I told myself that it was just one of those things. And so he was dead. And Wharton would have wanted him alive. Or would he? Would he have wanted him at all? I just didn't know, but it was still somehow as if he'd won and I'd lost. And what I'd lost I didn't know. All I knew was that I was alive in a room that was as still as death. I think I smiled to myself at that. It *was* as still as death.

The pipe had gone out and I lighted it again. I puffed out the smoke and began to feel better. I began to wonder what I should say to Wharton. Tell him I had just dropped in for a friendly chat and out of this talk and that the truth had emerged? Tell him about the bluff of that button, or keep it to myself? And how explain Matthews with his ear to that window? Once more I didn't know. All I could see was that I'd better keep to the truth. And I thought I knew what Wharton might think when he heard the whole truth: that I'd staged a curtain for myself; that the Bright Boy of St. Martin's had kept things back; that he'd done things his own way and cut himself a slice of publicity.

I got to my feet. Maybe I could show him it hadn't been like that. Maybe I could prove it had been just one of those things and that I couldn't have stopped it happening, and because I was made that way. And at least I could convince him that I didn't want my name as much as mentioned. I didn't want publicity. All I'd done was to follow a hunch.

Then something else struck me. If I told him the whole truth, mightn't he regard my version of things as high-flown or even hysterical nonsense.

"Where's your actual proof he did all you say he did?"

That was what he'd say. And I could instance the gun and how he'd been prepared to kill me to get back that button. Then I could add something else.

"When you know the big things are right, George, you don't worry about the small ones, and that's how Winster was. He knew the bulk of what I told him was true. And I knew it, and for this reason: because when I told him where I had found that button, he didn't laugh and say he must have dropped it there when earlier in the week he went to Hather's flat."

The pipe was out again and I put it in my pocket and walked back to Winster. I'd expected a sneer on his face, but it was as peaceful as if he were asleep. I stooped to the limp, out-flung hand and gently moved off the glove, and I winced as I put it back over the mutilated stump. There was something symbolic that I felt and couldn't put into words, and I was shaking my head as I straightened myself.

I let out a breath and I went across to the telephone. I put out a finger to dial. I looked at it. Maybe I'd expected it to be shaking, and it was—but not too much. I read the instruction chart and I dialled Exchange. I waited till I heard the voice and I asked for Whitehall one-two-one-two.

THE END